HIDDEN EXISTENCE

Tori and Alex

Hidden Existence

ISBN: 979-8-218-96981-3

This book is for anyone who has ever felt
invisible to the world and alone in their pain.

Prologue

The summer adventures would lead to quiet desperation.

The track runs along the edge of the field. I can hear the whir of the train in the distance.

"Get ready!" an older kid yells. The noise of the train whistle starts. "It's almost here. Start running. Run, and get the flag. Go, go, go!"

I watch the kids race to see who will be lucky enough to grab the flag—if the conductor decides to throw it and join in the children's game.

Screams of laughter and joy roll through the field. The train rounds the corner. The conductor waves the flag out the window, finally throwing it to the children just before he rounds a corner. The white flag of surrender is all I can think of.

"I got it!" one calls out.

All the children gather around and examine the newfound treasure. Discussion ensues: the opinions of how they are unsure whether the conductor will throw it again; the bickering of who pushed, who was faster, and how unfair things were, because the ones who wanted the prize didn't get it.

On some summer days, the train stops on the tracks. These are the funnest days. My friend, Rose, and I make sure no one from the old farmhouse is watching us. Then, we hop onto the train, clinging to the ladders.

I yell to Rose, "It's going to start anytime! Are you ready?"

She replies with a nod of the head. I wonder if she is just too cool to respond or if she is so afraid of what we are doing that she can't even think about looking over to give me an answer. Either way, I am ready. The noise of the train starting to move is both startling and exciting.

I yell, "Here we go!" and the train slowly but surely speeds up as we head through the woods.

Faster and faster and faster. I can feel the wind blowing my hair. I look down at the ground moving faster and faster and faster, and I think to myself, **Just hold on, and never let go. Hold on, and let it take you to wherever its next destination is. It will be better there— safer, less painful.** *Thoughts roll through my mind, faster and faster and faster, as if they are keeping time with the train itself.* **Just run away on this train, and you will be okay.**

Then, just as quickly as those thoughts went through my mind, something jolts me back to the reality of the current situation. I gather my senses and yell, "It's time to jump! Jump now, Rose. Jump!"

We leap off and roll into the ditch. The train never really ended up going that fast, but for Rose and me, it felt like we were flying. It could have been a train to freedom. If only I was brave enough to just hold on.

Part I:

Fragments of a Life

The feelings of deep-seeded fears.
The pain of correction with endless tears.
The joy of unknown sorrow, love, and masked gain.
The lie of the heart leads only to drain.

Faces of the past flow quickly through my mind,
The terror of their laughter.
So cruel, so unkind.

Covering up all of these realities, only to embrace.
Building a foundation—later to be our fate.

The groans of our souls,
Heard only in our ears.
The screams of terror getting louder through the years.

The wandering wonder of endless pursuit.

The race never to be won.

The question of freedom . . .
Persistence. It's done.

Slipping toward Oblivion

I wasn't living.

When you think about your life, what do you think of? Family and friends? The past and present? Your choices and why you made them? Are there chapters of your life that you've erased? Pieces of yourself that you've let go?

For Tori, it was the what-ifs of her life that echoed in her mind.

What if she and Rose had stayed on one of those many trains they rode when they were young? What if she had been just a little braver? A little stronger? Where would they be now?

Surely, things would be better. Maybe they would be living in houses next door to one another, somewhere safe and beautiful. Maybe they would have families of their own and warm beds to sleep in. Maybe they would be happy.

You see, every part of Tori's life had been cracked, broken, and glued back together in a hodgepodge mosaic by the time she was 14 years old. She often wondered what it would look like if it had remained whole—if she had remained whole.

Tori dreamt of the day she would be better. She wanted to be kinder, more responsible. She longed to sit at a dining room table, surrounded by loved ones, instead of sitting alone in a grimy tourist trap in California. But she hadn't been able to do those things. She hadn't been able to make a life for herself in that place. She had only been able to run.

....

Outlines of bodies swirl around me—splotches of red, orange, pink. The dirty windows of the too-small space are cracked open, allowing outside air to mingle with the weekend bar smell, cutting its foul odor just slightly. Bon Jovi's latest hit plays on the radio.

It takes half a water bottle of vodka to even get me through the door because of that smell—the smell of sweat and cheap perfume. Fake, desperate, lonely people. If it hadn't been three days since my last meal, I would just go home. But you know what they say about desperate times.

I push my discomfort down, burying it under a heavy layer of brash arrogance. With my hands thrust deep into the pockets of my too-big, leather jacket, I make my way through the congested room and slide into place at the bar as if it is my work desk. In a way, I guess it is.

"What're you drinking?" the bartender asks. Her red hair is styled in a pixie cut. She isn't rude, but is hardened in a way that says, "don't fuck with me."

"Vodka. On the rocks."

I take a minute to look around. I had already scanned most of the people on my way into J's Corner Bar, but now I am granted an unimpeded view of the place. I like watching other people live their lives around me. Ever since I was young, I have learned to observe. I notice things that most people would never care to know—things that if someone else had noticed them in me, maybe I wouldn't be in this bar right now.

I have always been just slightly invisible to the world. People take notice of me for one reason or another but eventually discard me once I have served my purpose. I am always on the verge of being nothing. So now I make sure to get something out of the deal before I disappear completely—to use others as much as they use me.

My drink being set in front of me interrupts my digressing thoughts.

FOCUS, a voice whispers to me from somewhere deep within.

As I turn my attention back to the room, I notice that most people are either coupled up at tables or standing in small groups, while a few slightly drunker, slightly dirtier ones sit near me at the bar rail, scattered and alone. The tourists, blissfully buzzed from a day of drinking on the beaches, float somewhere in the middle. It is nearing the start of the holiday season, and they almost outnumber the locals in the bar—flocking to California to escape brutal winters.

Lighting a cigarette, I turn my attention to the door. Open, close, open, close—couples, singles, fellow beggars, more tourists. The door reveals two snapshots—what I see and what the world sees—of people entering the bar before the crowd swallows them. A girl walks in alone, her purse slouched loosely over her shoulder, her hair stringy with seawater. She is sad and alone, looking for something or someone to make her feel better. A man walks in with a group of people, his gait confident, his face dark from a day on the ocean. He is brewing, angry, looking for someone to hurt.

I watch, entertained, as a woman elbows through a cluster of perky blondes, making her way toward the nearest bartender. Despite her age, she wears only a skimpy swimsuit top and jean skirt, exposing parts of her untanned skin as the thin fabric shifts around her chest. I can't blame her. ***It is hot as hell in here.***

Extinguishing my cigarette and sipping my now watery drink, I smile faintly and wish Rose were here to laugh at it all with me. She would shake her head at my people-watching, nudge me gently in the ribs, and say, "We should just mind our business, Tori." But then she would see the woman who was inadvertently showing half her breast to the bar, and with a quiet laugh, Rose would give in to my game. "See her? I bet she's here with her family. Bet you that she waited until her husband and children fell asleep, and then snuck away from their hotel room for the night. A vacation from her vacation."

As I play the imaginary scenario in my mind, I can almost feel Rose next to me. I pour the rest of my drink down my throat.

"Another one?" The bartender asks.

"Why not?"

"Coming right up." She scoops up the glass, fills it to the brim with fresh ice, and pours clear liquid over it. Making small talk with another customer while she works, the bartender only turns her attention back to me once the glass is mostly full. I can tell that, like me, she is also paying close attention to the people in the bar—doling out smiles and light-hearted conversation to those who look like they have the thickest wallets, while barely glancing at the sloppy regulars. A kindred spirit—we are both seasoned in the game of working others for survival.

The dense smell of grease lingers momentarily in the air as one man walks past me carrying a burger. I sigh. There are a variety of souls entering the space, but no one who can provide what I want. Accepting defeat, I begin to come to terms with the fact that the sporadic clusters of drunken men at the other end of the rail might be my only options for the night. I prepare myself to turn on the charm—a stroke of ego in exchange for a meal, that's all this is. One deep breath and a large gulp of vodka later, I begin to stand—just as a new voice hits my eardrums.

"Now tell me, what's a beautiful woman like you doing alone at a bar like this on a Saturday night?" The owner of the voice comes into my peripheral view as he leans against the bar space next to me.

He is going for a laid-back, I've-been-here-before approach, but when I turn to face him, I can immediately tell he doesn't belong in this bar. He is blonde, thin, and pretty. He wears a shirt that probably cost more than my entire wardrobe put together. He can't be much older than me, probably about 22, leading me to guess that he is likely attending college on his parents' dime. A frat boy looking for some local excitement—a story to tell his buddies over beer—before he goes home for Thanksgiving in a week. Lucky for him, I am looking for someone with enough money for a meal. **Maybe we can use each other.**

"Okay then, sorry for bothering you, I guess." He turns to go, and I realize I have just been staring at him without offering any sort of signal that I heard what he said.

"It's a long story," I spit out before he can leave.

"What?"

"Why I'm here tonight. It's a long story."

"Oh." He grabs an empty stool and sits down. "I like long stories."

"Nobody likes long stories. They're boring." I have his attention again.

GOOD.

He laughs. "Okay, fair enough."

I smile and lean in slightly. Keep him on the stool long enough to get what I need—that is the goal. "What's your name?"

"John. Well, Jonathan if you wanna get technical about it, but everyone calls me John."

Even his name is expensive, a different voice taunts.

"Well, John, are you gonna buy me a drink or what?" I make a point to finish what is in my glass while I speak.

"Um, sure. I mean, yeah." He waves down the bartender, who takes one glance at the sparkling watch on his wrist and comes right over.

"Can I get ya something?"

"Yeah, another drink for her and a beer for me."

"And some wings." I try to add the food like it is an afterthought, like I don't feel as though my stomach is shrinking into my spine. John goes with it.

"Yeah, and throw some fries in there too." He winks at me. I try not to roll my eyes.

While we wait for the food, my mind begins to bicker with itself.

REALLY? CHICKEN WINGS? FOR HOW BORING THIS GUY IS, WE SHOULD'VE ASKED FOR A BURGER.

A burger? Yeah, because that would make being a slut better.

Better. Better. Better. We should be better.

The booze is not doing its job very well.

"Be right back," I whisper the words in John's ear as I stand, brushing my hand across his knee.

THAT WILL KEEP HIM THERE UNTIL WE GET BACK.

Once alone outside, I reach into the inside pocket of my jacket, take out a pill, and pop it into my mouth.

JUST A LITTLE BOOST.

Chasing the pill with the sweet buzz of another cigarette, I lean against the side of the building. Lingering heat from the day reverberates off the metal siding, making me sweat even though the sun is long gone.

The air outside is a stark contrast to the bar's gut-churning smell, although I would never call it fresh. To me, it seems as though the polluted air in California waits until sunset to show its true state, like a woman waits until she is alone at home before wiping away her makeup.

I can feel the liquor and nicotine starting to take effect. Soon I am filled with silence.

....

Once my stomach is full and my head is buzzing, I don't care what happens next. John can pay the tab and leave me alone at the bar, or he can fuck me in the men's bathroom. It doesn't matter. I have gotten what I wanted, what I needed, and now it is his turn.

We eventually end up in the back of his car, sharing a joint in silence. Then, his tongue down my throat. His hands on my body. Escape. I open the car door.

"Nice meeting ya."

Only when I am driving back to my worn-down apartment later that night do I realize that he didn't even ask for my name. **Oh well. I will forget his by morning.**

I shower as soon as I walk through the door— washing the smell of John's cologne off of me, scrubbing until my skin is red, trying to remember the last time I was touched by a man I actually wanted. Flashes of a brief high school love come to mind.

A paintbrush.

Paint, paint, painting me with bright colors.

Erased.

I think of my last long-term boyfriend.

Fire.

Burn, burn, burning me.

From ember to ash.

Finally, as I lie on my makeshift bed of blankets, I drift back to **what if. What if I hadn't been ruined?**

....

"When I get married, I'm going to wear a crown," Rose laughs while she speaks, like she knows her words are utterly ridiculous. Although, I'm not sure if it's the idea of affording a crown or the idea of a future that seems more out of reach to her. "What about you, Tori? What do you want to wear on your wedding day?"

We're sitting in a clearing near the old farmhouse, picking daisies, and I begin working the stems of some of the biggest ones together while I think of an answer.

"Black."

"Black?! Are you nuts?"

"No," I grin. "I'm joking. I don't think I ever wanna have a wedding."

"No wedding? Why?"

I place the finished makeshift crown on her head, and she giggles.

"Just not my thing, I guess."

"Don't you want to wear a white dress and eat cake and stuff?"

"Nah, I'll eat enough cake at yours to last me a lifetime." I wink at her and lay down on my back to look at the sky. Rose laughs and lies down next to me, pointing out clouds that remind her of wedding cakes.

I don't have the heart to tell her we are too dirty to ever wear white and too broken to ever be married.

The Price We Pay

My life didn't matter.

"What do you want to be when you grow up?" That's the question. The question that children answer differently each time you ask. The question that teenagers battle as they try to determine their future. The question that adults repeatedly ask younger generations while praying that the answer is a good one, a thoughtful one— one that will give them hope for tomorrow. The question that always seemed ridiculous to Tori.

If she were completely honest, Tori would tell you that she never expected to live past age 10, let alone age 16, let alone age 18. She never expected to have a future, and eventually, she stopped wanting one.

....

Sitting in my car before work, I wonder how Rose is spending her Sunday. Surely, she isn't still going to the morning church service—God knows we both lost faith a long time ago. I wonder if she is working, or maybe she is passed out on a stranger's dirty couch somewhere with a needle in her arm.

A NEEDLE IN THE ARM SOUNDS NICE RIGHT NOW.

NO, NO, NO NEEDLES. WE HATE NEEDLES. THE HIGH IS WORTH THE PAIN.

"Shut up!" I scream the words loudly into the sound chamber of my car before opening the center console and taking out a container that used to hold mints. However, it now serves as my clever little drug stash. Opening the tin, I take out one of the small, white pills, note that I only have two left, and swallow it dry. That's the nice thing about speed—if you get it in the right form, taking it can be as easy as popping in a breath mint.

Closing my eyes, I lean back against the headrest and feel the mid-morning sun hitting my face. The last notes of a song by The Doobie Brothers rolls over my nerves, and I open my eyes in time to see a patrol car pulling into the parking lot. Two officers eye my vehicle as they come to a stop in front of the gas pump nearest my parking space. ***Can't have one goddamn moment of peace.***

Haphazardly pinning my nametag on, I get out of my car and throw them a sarcastic wave as I walk around the building to the back door.

The break room is empty when I get inside. My hands shake slightly as I punch my timecard, and I almost immediately regret not bringing any booze. ***Maybe I'll kill myself tonight.***

"Tori," the mousey voice of my coworker, Miles, makes me almost jump out of my skin. He must have snuck into the break room while I was clocking in.

Miles walks so softly that sometimes I convince myself he is a ghost. I mean, he certainly has the complexion of one, despite the fact that we live in southern California. He is harmless, but a little unnerving nonetheless. Also, kind of annoying. Then again, everyone annoys me.

"Steve wants to see you out front," he continues, ignoring my blank expression of someone who does not care. "Something about some missing candy? I dunno. Anyway, I'm leaving. Been here all night."

I nod. **Good for you. Gold star for Miles.**

As we walk past each other, he turns slightly. "Your name tag is crooked."

Without missing a beat, I respond with a curt middle finger. Before he has a chance to retaliate, I push through the doors leading from the break room to the front of the gas station. Out on the floor, my manager, Steve, is waiting alongside my other coworker, Lisa. He begins speaking before I even reach them.

"Tori, I'm gonna need you to restock the candy before you leave," he says between sips of what smells like burnt coffee mixed with a little whiskey. "Damned kids wiped us out of Skittles and Smarties yesterday—stole a shitload of 'em while Lisa was in the bathroom." Without further comment, he turns and strides away. I note that the back of his mullet is a little frizzier than usual—meaning he probably spent the night in his office. "Little punks, damn thieves, spoiled brats . . . " He continues muttering vague insults at imaginary children until the door to his office closes, and we can no longer hear him.

I turn to Lisa with my eyebrow raised. She just smirks. Lisa loves candy, especially Skittles and Smarties, and we recently discovered a few blind spots on the cheap gas station surveillance camera—one of which was in the candy aisle. Fifty bucks says there is no gang of candy-hungry thieves. Just one high and munchy Lisa.

"So, you got held up by a few kids, huh?" I half-whisper to Lisa while we walk from the candy aisle to the cash register.

"Yep. Those damned kids." She winks at me from behind her curtain of black hair and pops a handful of Skittles from her back pocket into her mouth. "I'm gonna go for a smoke."

With that, she is gone, and I am left to stare at the empty store while static-filled music drones on the speaker. *Miserable place.*

Out of boredom, I begin to count the cash in the register, turning all the bills to face the same way. The fact that this shitty place has any money in the register is nothing short of a miracle. The job hardly pays enough for rent, let alone food and other such luxuries. I don't blame Lisa for stealing the candy. In fact, I am kind of happy for her. In a way, we deserve whatever goods we manage to swipe. On more than one occasion, I have thought about just tossing my cheap nametag on the floor and driving away. It would be so easy. **Maybe tomorrow.**

I finish counting the cash, then turn to the wall of cigarettes behind me and begin sorting: turn all the labels out, move the boxes to the front of the shelf, put the most expensive brands in the direct eyeline of the customer.

The smell of cigarette smoke spills out from underneath Steve's office door while I work. Unlike the rest of us, he doesn't bother going outside. Perks of being the boss, I guess. You get to do whatever you want while everyone else follows your rules.

....

"Barb, I know this is a difficult time for you and your family, but you have to remember that the Lord will never give us more than we can handle." Mrs. Archer leans on the countertop while she speaks into the landline. The smell of cigarettes wafts through the small kitchen, despite her best efforts to blow the smoke out the open window. "If we just simply ran from our problems, what kind of Christians would we be?" Her voice drops an octave as she struggles to hide the smoke in her lungs. "This is a test of your marriage, of your faith. Embrace it. We all pay a price in this life." She pauses. **Barb must be talking now,** *I think to myself.*

I had come out of the room where Rose and I were playing to use the toilet. The kitchen was in between the bathroom door and me, and I couldn't help overhearing as I made my way. Now, without realizing it, I've stopped in the middle of the hall to listen.

I know Barb. She lives in the center of town with her husband and their two children. She always brings the best dessert to church potlucks. The treats are only supposed to be for the adults, but Rose and I always sneak a piece when Mrs. Archer isn't looking.

"Listen, some of the ladies are coming by the house later for coffee and to talk about the clothing drive," Mrs. Archer continues. "Why don't you swing by? Then, we can chat more after they leave. I think a proper prayer session might be in order."

More silence.

"Oh, yes. I think they would love some lemon bars. That sounds lovely. Okay, see you then."

The click of the receiver brings me back to my senses, and my bladder reminds me that I have yet to go to the bathroom. As quietly as I can, I continue moving. Keeping my head down, I slowly cross in front of the doorway to the kitchen. I can hear the clattering of pans while Mrs. Archer starts to cook dinner. She always cooks on nights when she is expecting company.

"Tori, is that you?"

"Yes, ma'am."

"Oh, come be a dear and help me for a moment, will you?"

"Um, I really gotta use the bathroom."

"Now, Tori, let's not be selfish. This will only take a moment, and you had time to eavesdrop on my conversation, didn't you? So, certainly you have time to be helpful."

"Yes, ma'am."

"Good. Then, when Mr. Archer gets home, you can go help him with chores outside until this is done cooking."

My stomach drops.

"Please, no. Please, don't make me, Mrs. Archer. I promise I won't eavesdrop no more."

"It's 'anymore,' dear, and don't argue. You will do as you're told. That's that. Now peel these potatoes," she says, handing me a bowl of potatoes and the peeler.

I swallow my fear and, with shaking hands, begin to work the peeler across the rough skin of the vegetable. I guess this is my price to pay in life.

....

The ding of the bell above the gas station door brings me back to reality. I look up to see a somewhat familiar figure walking into the space. His routine consists of filling up his obnoxiously large truck, then coming in to pay and see Lisa.

He is good-looking, in a terrifying sort of way. His hair is close-shaven, forming a dark fuzz around his perfectly sculpted skull. Faded, indecipherable tattoos snake along his arms. He has at least six inches of height on me, and as he approaches the register, he rests his elbows on the counter, bending to meet my eyes. His entire persona screams bad news, but I don't allow anyone to intimidate me anymore.

WE CAN HANDLE HIM.

"Can I help you?" I keep my tone even as I speak, asking the question even though I know what he is going to say.

"Lisa here?"

"She's on br—" I don't get a chance to finish before Lisa saunters up next to me.

"I got this one, Tori," she says casually—as if we don't go through this every couple of weeks or so.

I pick up one of the magazines from the small rack on the counter. "Be my guest."

I watch out of the corner of my eye as she rings up his gas, and he slips a small baggie of pills between the bills. She drops the baggie into her bra and gives him his change, which consists of more money than he paid in the first place. It is hard not to scoff at the routine as I think of how much better I'd be as a drug dealer than this guy. *I mean, who does regular meetups at their customer's*

place of work? Not to mention at the one place in the building that is practically guaranteed to have security cameras? Seems dumb to me.

"Something funny?"

Shit. I look up from the magazine I have been pretending to read and see that the man is staring at me, his green eyes turning almost gray. I guess I laughed at his stupidity out loud, not just in my head.

TELL HIM HIS FACE LOOKS FUNNY.

FLIRT.

Walk away.

Scenarios tumble through my head, jostling around like loose cubes of Jell-O.

We're so much smarter than him. Just say anything. He'll buy it.

"Have you read this week's dating advice column?" I hold the magazine out toward him. "It's comically bad."

He doesn't respond—just counts his cash and turns his attention back to Lisa.

"You're short, babe."

"Damn. Really? Okay, meet me in the back. I'll make up the difference." Lisa says the words without flinching, like this is just another part of her regular workday. The man nods and walks out to the parking lot.

"See you in 20," I say as Lisa walks to the back door.

"I'll have it done in 10," she replies smugly.

Sure enough, Lisa is only gone for about 10 minutes before she returns, slipping a piece of gum from a pack on the shelf into her mouth.

"You know, I used to want to be a dancer," she says between snaps of her gum. "Not like a stripper. More like one of those fancy ballerina types. When I was a girl, my mom put me in all sorts of dance classes."

"So, why didn't you become a dancer?"

"Blew out my knee in a middle school competition. That was the end of that." She shrugs and hoists herself to sit on the counter. "What can ya do? At least I got some killer pain meds out of the deal."

"The price we pay," I mutter under my breath as I try to think back to my childhood hopes and dreams.

"What?" Lisa's question brings me back to the present. My face must betray me, though, because she is staring at me like I might combust—explode into a million emotional pieces.

"Nothing." I search my mind for a new topic. "Hey, I'm actually looking for a new hookup. Does your guy always accept alternative payments like that?"

"Who? Dane? Oh, yeah. I pay with my body more than I pay with paper." She chuckles. "If you're a broke woman in need of a sale, Dane's your guy. I can give you an intro next time if you want. Otherwise, he usually hangs out at that bar on Broadway. Just flirt a little, and he's sure to offer you something."

"Cool, I'll handle it. Thanks."

A Deal with the Devil

That's how I survived—I sold my soul to the highest bidder.

By Monday morning, Tori's old mint tin was empty—leaving her head way too full. Thoughts pummeled her brain during the day, and terrors beat her nerves senseless at night.

By Tuesday, her weed and booze stash had been depleted—leaving her without any armor in her battle against painful thoughts. Death beckoned to her in the form of a peaceful surrender.

By Wednesday, she found herself in a bar—looking for the drug dealer who would accept company as payment. Drugs were her last defense in the fight to live long enough to make it home for Christmas.

....

I notice Dane as soon as he walks through the door of the bar—the small crowd of Wednesday night drinkers seems to part down the middle as people go out of their way to avoid his path. Clearly, my initial synopsis of him being bad news isn't too far from the truth.

SO WHAT IF HE'S BAD NEWS? WE'RE WORSE.

I wait until I am in his line of vision and draw inspiration from the con artist inside of me. Smoothly, I turn my stool in his direction, holding up my empty cup as if to say, "Come here and fix this." Within seconds, he is seated next to me, waving down the bartender.

TOO EASY.

"What're you drinking?"

"Vodka."

I watch as Dane signals to the bartender. "Another vodka for her, and a beer for me." Turning to me, he taunts, "A drink for a name."

"Tori," I respond with a straight face. Even though it is part of the game, I don't like being told what to do.

"Damn! Okay, Tori. Nice to meet ya. I'm Dane." He doesn't hold out his hand. Instead, he hands me one of the drinks that the bartender just passed our way. Clinking his glass annoyingly against mine, he takes a long swig, beer spilling from the rim, down the stubble on his chin. Watching him, I recognize the fact that he is likely much older than I originally thought—probably double my age— but I have made my bed. I realize he is watching me too, and something shifts as recognition registers on his face.

"Hey, wait—you're that bitch from the gas station, aren't you? The one with the magazine."

"Again, my name is Tori." I make myself smile, not letting the anger that is edging into his voice rattle me.

"Well, you're lucky you're hot, Tori." He laughs arrogantly, as if he is doing me some huge favor by not shooting me on the spot.

"And you're lucky that you have something I want, Dane."

"Oh, I do now, do I?"

Just as I am trying to decide whether or not drugs are worth dealing with this asshole, one of the more intoxicated patrons stumbles past us to the jukebox. Putting money in, he flips through the records for a few seconds before landing on "Faithfully" by Journey. I smile a little in spite of the lingering bitterness. I love music.

"Dance with me?" Dane holds out his hand, slamming his empty glass on the bar. I realize with shock that I haven't touched my drink.

"Sure," I say, downing the vodka in a single swig, pushing past his hand into a clear space in the center of the room. "On one condition: I lead."

"So, where are you from?" he asks as we move in rhythm with the beat.

"Here," I lie.

"Bullshit. No way is that accent from here."

I roll my eyes. "Where are you from?"

"Here," he says, and I know this is also a lie.

We dance until the jukebox sputters out the final notes of the song, and I mention to Dane that I want another drink. Making my way back to the bar, I order a burger to share and another vodka, praying to God that he will pay when the tab comes.

Sure enough, when last call is announced, and our bill is set in front of us, he scoops it up and places a neat stack of bills on top.

SUCH A GENTLEMAN.

Beef and beer on his breath, he leans across the bar and kisses me forcefully. "Let's get out of here," he says. With a smooth flick of his wrist, he shows me a glimpse of a clear, plastic bag of little, white pills in his jacket pocket.

HEAVEN.

I don't remember saying yes; I don't remember sliding off my stool; I don't remember going out the door. But I must have done all those things, because, all of a sudden, we are walking down the street.

I keep Dane in my peripheral vision as we make our way, the sparse streetlights sporadically illuminating his dark features. His gait is confident, even as he leans slightly off-kilter in order to drape one arm over my shoulder—claiming his prize. The more we walk, the more the animal instinct inside of me screams, *run*, while the addict inside of me whispers, *STAY.*

....

The drug-laced sugar dissolves slowly on my tongue. I close my eyes and imagine I'm at the corner gas station with my siblings, spending change we scrounged from the street, greedily reaching into the bucket of assorted sweets. I can almost feel my sister's arm linked through my own when the bitter aftertaste brings me back.

I open my eyes to see the world is distorted. A mix of straw and dust greets me as I fall to my knees in the center of the barn stall. I think I might be sick. The stuffy stench of the animal home intrudes on my nose, making it hard to breathe.

I surrender myself fully to the dirt floor, the straw pricking at my skin as I lay on my back. Gunny sacks and ropes hang from the rafters above me. A horse complains from the other side of the barn. Tendrils of warmth spread through me, dulling the sensation of calloused hands picking me up, moving me to a wooden table in the center of the stall—lessening the pain of what comes next.

Ten Seconds of Bliss

Safety was fleeting.

Tori spent two days with Dane, only realizing how long it had been when a page from Miles jolted her awake. The past 48 hours had been a blur of drugs, alcohol, and sex, with sporadic deep sleep in between.

When she told Dane she had to leave for work, he took her in his arms and kissed her as if he loved her. Maybe it was the drugs, but at that moment, Tori felt like she had won the game—so much so that she told him she would return that night after her shift. He agreed, promising a hot dinner and expensive wine.

....

A sort of euphoria that only comes from days of drugs and newfound power rushes through my veins that day at work. When I clock out for the night, I practically run to the bus stop—my mouth and mind salivating with the thought of food and drugs. My car is still at the bar where Dane and I officially met. I figure it will be fine for another 24 hours.

The 20-minute bus ride feels like an hour as I tick off the things I wanted to get from Dane before I leave the next day: another dose, another meal, maybe a sweatshirt or jacket if I can manage.

Standing in a hallway that reeks of weed, I knock on Dane's door once. Then again. And again. By the time the hinges finally creak, I am on the verge of kicking at the cheap paneling. Irritated, I start to walk forward as the door gradually opens, but stop short when I see it is not Dane who stands in front of me. Instead, a shirtless woman—her pink bra glowing obnoxiously in the dim lighting of the hallway—offers nothing except an indifferent stare and an exhale of a cigarette.

"Nice," I say the word in a sort of whisper, pushing past the woman and into the apartment. "Dane?" I call into the darkness of the interior. Over the last couple of days I had become familiar with the layout of the place, so I know where to find the sole light switch. With the apartment now slightly illuminated, I stride toward a half-conscious, half-naked Dane lying on an air mattress in the center of what is supposed to be the living room. I suspect nobody has ever done much living here.

Awareness spreads across Dane's face, his eyes scanning my body. The smell of his stale breath makes me want to gag as I squat to meet his eye level. "Oh, hey babe." He grins cunningly as he speaks, clearly proud of his ability to remain active while I was away.

Disgust replaces what little attraction I have for him. Glancing in the other woman's direction, I see she is struggling to get dressed. She is high as a kite.

"Babe, babe, babe." Dane is groggily reaching out his arms, trying to pull me to bed. I stand and make my way into the kitchen.

"Dane, did you happen to get any food?"

"Food?"

"Yes, food."

"Oh, you know, I got so busy that I didn't have much time to go out. There are some leftovers in the fridge."

By this time, the woman is slipping on her heels. "See ya, Dane. Thanks for the fun," she says as she closes the door behind her. My anger unexpectedly boils over.

"You're an asshole," I say while I move to the fridge—cursing Dane loudly as I rummage through the half-moldy cartons of take-out.

"Tori, why don't you just take a seat?" Dane is sitting up on the edge of the mattress now, motioning to a chair next to the table. I don't sit.

"No, Dane. I won't sit. I won't sit until I find something to eat and something to drink and until the smell of your hooker leaves that general area." I motion to where the woman had dressed near the table. I can hear Dane walking toward me as I continue to go through the fridge, opening containers and tossing them into the trash one after another. Only when he grabs my wrist mid-throw do I stop.

"Here's the thing," he says through gritted teeth. "The thing is, you're being kind of a bitch. I mean, come on, do you really think you're any different from her? You just gotta relax a little."

He begins to fumble with his pockets. "Speaking of," he trails off as he finds what he is looking for, carefully dumping white powder from a small bag into a thin line next to a pile of pills on the table. He opens a dusty bottle of wine that sits atop the fridge and motions again for me to sit. I do this time, the thick plastic chair hard and uninviting.

Watching Dane pour cheap wine into cheaper glasses, I silently weigh my options: leave him and go home for the night, or stay and get high for free. The drugs from last night have faded, and reality is beginning to close in. I won't have any cash until next week, and I am not sure I am ready to be sober. So, I let my rage simmer, snort the powder, pop some pills, drink some wine, and kiss him on the cheek when he sits down with one of the takeout containers I haven't tossed. It is only when I make a snide comment about him not being able to perform sexually twice in one day that he hits me, his open hand knocking me to the floor.

....

My small head connects with a hard surface, sending stars shooting around behind my eyes.

"You are bad."

"I am bad."

The room twists around me, reminding me of the funhouse my siblings and I had run through at the carnival last week. The distorted figure of a man stands at the center of the twisting.

He bends, retrieving something from the floor by my feet. He places the something in my hands. I don't want it. It's bad. I'm bad.

"You belong to the dark now."

"I belong to the dark." My meek voice cracks slightly as the words push their way out.

Survive.

"Now do what you're told," he says.

The stars still linger behind my eyes, reminding me of what happens if I disobey. My stomach and heart harden. I retreat into myself.

A Lover's Retreat

I should have died.

When people hear about perilous situations that others find themselves in, they sometimes think about what they would do better—how well they would handle things. If their partner abused them, they would leave. If they found themselves in need of help, they would ask. If they were in danger, they would evade. Thinking these things helps to distance them from the possibility that one wrong choice could launch anyone into a downward spiral. However, the truth is, that until you feel the sting of the hand you used to hold hit you, until you wake up one day with no escape from a hell you created, until you watch those you should trust turn into monsters—until that happens to you, you don't know what you would do.

Tori's survival instincts had served her well for many years—keeping her body alive when all her heart wanted was to die. But now, her instincts were tired, and she was tired, and neither of them cared very much about seeing tomorrow's sunrise.

....

I rest my head against the dirty truck window, my skull thunking rhythmically against the glass as we make our way along the bumpy road. It reminds me of when Rose and I used to sneak into the back of my father's pickup truck, giggling as we bounced along the gravel road.

I don't remember agreeing to a road trip with Dane, or even getting in the truck. Nevertheless, here I am. We drive for roughly three hours. As we wind up the narrow mountain roads, civilization seems out of reach.

I smoke a joint while we make our way, chasing the skunky taste with gulps of vodka. Soon the substances all seem to be taking their toll at once, and I can't keep my eyes open.

....

When I wake up next, Dane is parking the truck, shifting between gears and cranking the wheel sharply, rocking us back and forth. He is trying to back into a somewhat clear space, but the terrain is rough, and the wheels of the truck keep getting stuck: hitting ruts, roots, and rocks. Dane swears in frustration. Just when I think I might vomit out the window, we finally get into a satisfactory position, and he shifts into park—the truck resting in front of a dilapidated cabin. The roof of the cabin sags from decades of weather, the wooden siding splintering out at odd angles. Some of the windows have been replaced with boards. The sight makes me grow wary of what is to come.

As I open my door and angle my legs toward the ground, I wonder if this place is an old family heirloom of

Dane's or if he is just planning on breaking into some random house in the mountains. The latter seems to be the more likely scenario. Either way, I don't care.

I hop to the ground, slamming the truck door behind me. Looking around, I can't see anything except the outline of dense forest in the moonlight. Insects hum in the stillness, and I can hear a stream trickling nearby. The smell of pine trees washes over me. In a normal situation, this place could've been considered beautiful, peaceful even. At this moment, however, with Dane stoically standing by my side, it is anything but serene.

Dane only remains next to me for a moment. Moving closer to the cabin, he crouches down and begins lifting stones from the ground, one by one. There are a lot of different rocks lying around, and I assume he is looking for the biggest one—one that will knock a sizable hole into one of the few remaining windows. But, to my surprise, he smiles as he turns over a medium-sized white stone and lifts a key from the dirt underneath it. Sliding the key into the lock, he opens the door and signals for me to follow him inside.

Once inside, it is so dark that I can't even see my hand in front of my face. Without a word, Dane takes his lighter from his front pocket, flicks it to life, and instinctively goes to one of the cupboards. He brings out several candles and lamps, lighting them one by one until I can make out the room. Heads of dead animals decorate the walls—the fear frozen in their eyes—and a small fireplace serves as the central focus of the room. It appears the structure only has one level, with a living room, dining room, kitchen, and bedroom. Random furniture, blanketed with dust and dirt, sits sparsely throughout the space. An old stove sinks into the rotting tile floor of the kitchen. There is a back door situated on the wall opposite from where I stand, and I guess that it might lead to an outhouse.

"It's nice." I smile warily in Dane's direction. "How did you know about this place?"

"That's none of your business," he replies quietly as he plants a quick kiss on my forehead.

"I'm going to have a smoke," I say. Trying not to show my nerves, I dare to turn my back to Dane and walk out onto the porch.

As I look at the stars, I can hear the faint sounds of him moving around the kitchen. We had stopped at a convenience store before leaving the city, but I hadn't bothered to go inside with him—or to look at what he brought out. I wonder what he is making.

I stay outside for as long as I can without risking Dane's rage. Once back within the walls of the cabin, I gradually approach the kitchen where Dane is hunched over the stove. I am shocked the thing even works.

"Dinner?" I ask hesitantly, not knowing what else to say.

"Yeah, let's eat," he responds, as he turns to me with a look that makes me feel like one of the animals on the wall.

....

The plate of food that Dane slams down in front of me a few minutes later shocks me. Apparently, he has not taken kindly to me leaving him to do the cooking. Chunks of unknown meat swim in a thick, brown broth, and I take small, shallow breaths to avoid gagging from the stench. I look across the table to where Dane sits, a steaming slab of steak bleeding across his plate.

"What is this?" I don't try to hide the disdain in my voice. **He is truly insane if he expects me to quietly eat this slop while he dines like a king.**

"Your dinner. Now eat." His stare is cold and callous as he looks at me, waiting.

"Dane, there's no way I'm eating this garbage. No fucking way."

He doesn't respond, just continues his glacial stare.

Throw the plate at him.

DISTRACT HIM WITH SEX.

Just do as he says.

"Can't we just split your steak or something?" My voice is childlike as I plead. "Why do I have to eat this?"

With that, Dane rises quickly to his feet. His hand forms a fist, and he slams it onto the table, shaking the contents of my bowl. "Tori, shut the fuck up, and eat the goddamn food! You think it's garbage? Well, I think you're garbage. Now eat it before I come over there and shove it down your throat!"

The harsh words rattle a familiar feeling loose inside of me. My brain goes blank, my mouth goes dry, and I instruct my senses to shut down. **We are going to have to do this. I am going to have to eat it.**

"Okay," I say, trying to keep my voice level. "Okay." I lift the bowl to my mouth and hurriedly swallow, not bothering to chew the chunks as they wash down my throat.

....

A metallic taste coats my tongue. I can feel eyes on me, and I will myself not to cry.

"Keep eating," a heartless voice instructs. I obey.

Looking down at my plate, I see broken shards of who I was before this moment swimming in the bloody meat. They scrape my mouth raw as I try to guess how many bites I'll have to take before the plate is empty.

Ten. Ten more bites. I can do this, *I tell myself.* ***I have to do this.***

··········

"Slower," Dane's voice cuts through my haze, and I almost choke.

"What?"

"Eat slower. Take your time. No need to rush. Really chew the food. Enjoy it."

I force myself to chew, holding my breath in increments as I make my way through the remaining contents of the bowl.

After we are done eating, Dane stands up and clears our dishes, dumping them carelessly into the sink while wiping steak remnants from his chin. As a reward for my dining table etiquette, he hands me a paper cup of booze and a handful of pills. I swallow two, chasing them with the drink, and put the rest into my pocket, saving them for later.

I go to pour more drinks, and Dane heads outside to get firewood. I figure it is close to two in the morning, and the temperature has dropped dramatically since our initial arrival. I shiver in my tank top and jean shorts as I splash booze from the bottle into the cups.

Walking into the living room, I am just in time to see Dane walk through the back door, a pile of wood in his hands. Murmuring to himself, he drops the pieces on the floor near the fireplace. The crash makes me jump slightly, and he chuckles.

"Something scare ya, babe?"

I don't answer. Instead, I hold out one of the two drinks in my hands. He takes the cup, but places it immediately on the floor. I feel his hand on my arm as he pulls me closer to him, kissing me hard, biting my lip until it bleeds. I know if I push him away, it will only make things worse, so I let it happen. When he is done with me, he zips up his pants matter-of-factly and goes back to work at the fire, while I go back to finishing the drink that is still in my hand—the alcohol stinging my split lip.

As I watch Dane trying and failing to stack the firewood, I quickly realize that he is no Boy Scout. It is pathetic to watch.

We are going to freeze if he's the one in charge of that fire.

"I can take care of that. Why don't you just drink and relax," I say calmly as I walk to where he sits hunched over the haphazard pile. A servant wanting to help.

"Thanks, babe."

I have a blaze started in no time, and soon we are staring into the warm glow of fire.

"Dammit, Tori, it's hot as balls in here now," Dane says, and he begins to remove his shirt.

As he strips, I notice something I had not before: white, thick scars speckled across his back. I count three total.

"What're those?"

"What're what?"

"The marks on your back. The scars. What're they from?"

"Oh, those. Bullets."

"Bullets from what?" I struggle to keep my voice level.

"Just some business gone wrong."

I nod as if this is a normal explanation. "I'm gonna turn in," I say, placing my cup on the table. "Night."

Dane responds with silence.

Fine by me.

Not wanting to offend him, I leave the door to the bedroom open. As I lie on the bare mattress, I can see slightly into the living room. I watch Dane as he watches the fire. My eyes feel heavy. I want nothing more than to sleep, but I know better. Resting is not an option with this much danger so close by. So, when Dane crawls into bed beside me sometime later, I feign sleep and wonder how much longer I can do this.

....

Lying in bed, I listen to the sound of tree branches tapping on the house. My head is spinning, and my body aches. I can hear my father bustling around in the other room, getting ready for a day of work. My mother will be in soon to wake my siblings and I for school. I know I will have to go—even though I didn't sleep. I wonder if I'll be able to make it to the end of our driveway to wait for the school bus, or if I'll just simply crumble from exhaustion. As the first rays of light begin to come through the window, I contemplate how much time I'm likely to have left on this Earth and ask God if he will shorten it.

....

The sun peeks through a small crack in the upper corner of the wall as Dane snores in bed beside me, his arm draped across my stomach. Careful not to wake him, I move his arm and slide out of bed.

The outhouse is as disgusting as one would expect, and as I pee, I close my eyes and imagine I am in a hotel. A clean hotel, with a white, spotless bathroom. My mind mocks the fantasy.

UM, HELLO? EARTH TO TORI. THOSE THINGS ARE FOR PEOPLE THAT MATTER, AND WE WILL NEVER MATTER.

Instead of going right back inside after leaving the outhouse, I wander to the front of the cabin and stare at the scenery in front of me. Forest stretches for miles, covering the sides of the mountains around me. A stream flows smoothly along a ridge that runs parallel to the cabin.

My legs ache. I need to move; I need to walk. So, I decide to follow the stream, telling myself that I won't go far—just far enough to stop my body from combusting.

As I make my way, I think about the night before. I wonder what I will have to eat tonight and what Dane will do if I refuse. I think about the bullet marks on his back and wonder what happened to the people who had held the guns that shot him. It is only when a headache starts to blind me that I realize how far I have gone. I quickly turn and start back in the direction of the cabin.

While the trees offer some shade, the sun has grown warm, and I can feel toxins leaving my body via sweat. What started as an even mix of post-party high and hangover soon becomes just a hangover. My head starts to spin—the cabin coming into view just as I think I might pass out.

Dane stands waiting for me in the doorframe, his arms firmly crossed over his wide, hairy chest. The smell of alcohol grows stronger the closer I get.

"Morning," I say as I trudge past him.

I make my way to the kitchen where, to my delight, I find a working faucet. Water rushes out to greet me as I splash it over my face and hands, chugging the cool, clear liquid straight from the tap. I turn off the faucet and look out the kitchen window, popping the pills from the night before into my mouth.

"Where were you?" I feel Dane's gaze burning a hole in the back of my head from the doorway, but I keep looking forward.

"Went for a walk."

"And you didn't think to wake me up?"

"Why would I? You were out cold. Figured you'd want to sleep."

"How do you know what I want?"

I hear the thud of Dane's boots as he walks into the kitchen, and spin around just in time to greet his fist with my face. He knocks me sideways. I feel my head hit the side of the counter as I grip the edge of the sink, trying not to fall to the floor.

"You bitch. You were trying to leave me."

"No, Dane. I swear, I wasn't. It was just a walk." This is different from the other times we have fought. The timid side of me is speaking now, any anger scared away. I feel small. Blood drips into the sink as I speak, and I can feel my face swelling. I don't yell, don't turn to face him, don't run. I just stand over the sink, clutching the fake marble counter, trying not to collapse. We aren't going to fight back. **Why bother?**

"'Just a walk,' my ass."

His fingers grab at my hair, pulling hard enough to jerk my face back from the sink. The tops of my eyes meet his, and all I can see are his pupils. He is gone, and I know it. The smallest urge to fight back arises from deep within me.

I twist and turn, grabbing at his thick arms as he pulls me by my hair into the living room, where he throws me toward one of the random chairs. My body is moving too fast, and my feet tangle over themselves, the side of my face hitting the arm of the chair as I fall to the floor. The room is spinning around me, and I can't tell what is floor and what is ceiling. **No use in fighting this time. This is it. Time to go.**

I try to take a breath but don't get to finish before I feel his boots connect with my ribs. Black spots cloud my vision.

"Shut your fucking mouth."

I wasn't talking.

"Why would I want you? You're nothing but a dirty whore. I had to get drunk to even be able to look at you today." As he speaks, he grabs the nearly empty bottle of vodka from the table, dripping the remnants onto my head. "See?"

Once the dripping stops, he brings the bottle down, hard, onto the floor next to me. I instinctively turn away as much as I can manage, shielding my face with my hands as glass shards launch into the air. Crazed laughter leaches from Dane's mouth into the room as he paces around the small space for what feels like an eternity.

Seemingly satisfied that I have been punished for my betrayal, he takes one last glance at me, spits the word "pathetic" in my general direction, and storms out, slamming the front door.

I wait and wait for some sort of inclination as to what he is doing, but I don't hear his footsteps on the rocks or the start of the truck. Then, the smell of a cigarette drifts into the room, and I know he is just outside the door.

Turning my head slowly, I look at the glass shard nearest me.

Beautifully sharp.

Reaching out, I press the soft flesh of my thumb against its clear edge, pushing down until a bubble of red appears.

....

Rose's hand quivers slightly as she hovers the sewing scissors over her palm. "Tori, how bad does it hurt?"

"Oh, it's nothing. I promise. Kind of like a mosquito bite." I say with mock confidence as I hold my left palm facing the summer sky, a small pile of blood forming in its center.

Swiping the scissors from Mrs. Archer's sewing kit, we had hurriedly walked to the railroad tracks with them in the waistline of my shorts, smiling with triumph as soon as we cleared the yard. I had gone first, calmly pushing the cold steel into my hand, pretending it didn't hurt. Now it was Rose's turn.

"See mine? It's not even that bloody." I hold my palm out to show her. "You can do it, Rose. I'm right here. And if it hurts too bad, we'll just forget about the whole thing."

"Okay, okay." Rose timidly pushes the tip of the scissors into her hand, wincing as the skin breaks open.

"See? Piece of cake. You ready?"

"Ready."

Gently, we join hands, squishing our cuts together until I can no longer tell what blood is mine and what is hers.

"Connected for life," I say with a smile.

"Now we will always be together, no matter what," Rose whispers.

Escape

I didn't stop running.

Ever since she was a young girl, Tori had been on the run—so much so that her family had given her the nickname "gypsy." She didn't know why, but she was always aching for change. A change of scenery, a change of herself. She would only feel at peace in a new place for a few months before the need to run would ignite in her gut like the spark of a match. But the more she ran, the higher the flames would rise, until finally, they engulfed her—burning her alive.

....

I don't remember leaving Dane. I lost roughly 24 hours from when I lay on the cabin floor to when I woke up in my apartment, blood crusted on my face. I don't know what happened, and I don't care.

What I do care about is the fact that I hate California. I feel trapped. I need to go somewhere, anywhere. I will die if I stay.

It takes less than a day for me to decide what to do: I will drive until I find a place I like, until I feel oxygen come back into my body. Soon my bags are packed—well, my bag—and I am out of here without even so much as a call to anyone.

When I get into my car, the driver's side setup seems all wrong: The seat is too far back, the radio is turned to a station I never listen to, and my sunglasses are nowhere to be found. With a note of irritation, I adjust my seat and the radio dial, then send the strangeness of the situation into the recesses of my mind.

Driving out of California, I think about what I am leaving behind and realize it is nothing. I am not leaving family or friends or even a job that I like. It feels like the only thing I am leaving behind is misery.

I don't have a job lined up anywhere or any savings, so a hotel room or an apartment is out of the question. Instead, I just drive. I drive and drive and drive until I find a place I love: The smell of rain, the sporadic buildings, the rocky beaches—it feels right. So, I park my car, cover up with as many layers as I can, and fall asleep.

....

Adrenaline jerks me awake the next day as the sounds of a man's voice and aggressive banging fill the small space of my car. Immediately, I sit up, throwing the clothing I used as a blanket onto the floor of the car. The windows are thick with condensation, but I can make out the hazy figure of a man trying to open the driver's side door. Over and over he pulls, the handle thumping rhythmically with each failed attempt.

Telling him to leave, I match the volume of my voice to his. I honk the horn over and over as I grapple for the keys. I had put them inside of the center console when I parked so that I wouldn't lose them. At the time, I thought it had been the smartest move. Now I curse myself while my half-numb fingers search through the clumps of napkins for the feel of a car key.

After what seems like a lifetime, I find the key and jam it into the ignition. The car sputters to life, and the man takes a startled jump back. It is dusk and barely light out, but as my windshield wipers work to clear the windshield, I can see his features slowly come into view—a white beard tinted brown with tobacco, a scrawny frame made bulky by the heavy coat that he wears, a shopping cart full of trash keeping him company.

"It's cold out here. Let me in, and we can keep each other warm," he says, a new tone in his voice as he sees my face.

"Oh, hell no," I say as I shift the gears into drive and hit the gas pedal.

"You fucking bi—"

I don't allow him to finish. As I drive away, I roll down my windows and turn up the radio, deafening his crude calls. The air flowing through the window is chilly and damp, but I don't mind. When you've felt trapped all your life, a breath of freedom is worth some rain.

A Forced Safety

For me, winter wasn't about Santa Claus or playing in the snow.

The month of December often means different things to different people. For some, it's the most stressful time of the year. For others, it's a quiet time of reflection and peace. Oftentimes, people don't even notice it passing by until red donation buckets don the shop doors and traditional hymns overtake the radio airwaves. Not Tori, though. Tori spent 11 months of the year waiting for December. For Tori, December was a time of relief.

As a child, she didn't count the days until she could open presents. She counted the days until she could be safe. The final week of December brought Christmas. With Christmas came traditions—meaning her family's constant presence surrounded her like a force field, and her mother's watchful eye ensured there was no trouble. Anyone who wanted to harm Tori would have to wait until after December 25th.

Even when she was an adult, living in her car on the coast, she made plans to return home for Christmas. She began saving any money she could find to pay for gas, only spending the bare minimum on 5-cent packs of Ramen and cheap drugs.

....

The rain pelts my leather jacket, drowning out all other sounds as I make my way on the poorly lit street. Water drips into my pale blue eyes, smearing the dark liner that runs along my eyelids. Protectively, I clutch the plastic bag tighter in my fist, stuffing my hands deeper into my jacket pockets.

I had decided to make the trip to my dealer on foot that day to save some money—a decision I now regret. Washington's winter air is cool on my face, and the rain seems to be soaking into my pores. The water on the streets rushes into the soles of my worn-down boots, and my feet are going numb. Yet I am still moving. **How is that possible?**

December 25th is in less than a week, and I quietly hum one of my favorite Christmas songs as I make my way around the corner. Bright lights decorate the windows of stores, illuminating my path, reminding me of holidays from my childhood.

....

Laughing so hard we can't breathe, my sisters and I scramble toward the small foam basketball. We don't have a lot of money, and Christmas isn't much this year. A small hotel in a rundown city has become our temporary home and holiday headquarters. I can see a factory out of one dirty window and a line of bars out the other—all illuminated by the city's sad attempt at Christmas decorations in the streets. But I don't mind the disheartening scenery. I'm with my family.

The room we are in is essentially a small box. It has brown curtains and dull, flowered wallpaper with two queen-sized beds. My siblings and I will inevitably end up fighting over who will sleep on the floor tonight, which consists of soot gray carpet and unknown stains.

When I first looked around the room, I imagined that, at one time, it was made up of white carpet, fresh wallpaper, and plush furniture. My favorite part of the room—the only part that required no reinvention—was the west wall, which was made up completely of mirror.

My older sister, a basketball player through and through, had gotten a plastic basketball hoop from a friend: the kind that children put on their doors when they decide to transform their rooms into a homemade basketball court. My siblings and I had stuck it to the mirrored wall upon our arrival in the room. Now a viciously competitive game ensues between my parents, my three siblings, and me.

I brush my ragged bangs out of my eyes just in time to see my mother jumping from one hotel bed to the next, basketball in hand. Her strong legs are launching her petite figure through the air as she bounces, dodging my older brother and my father.

The salt of sweat mixes with the salt of tears streaming down my face as I try to contain my laughter.

Finally, my mother jumps from the bed nearest the hoop and slams the ball into the circle. I can't hold back the laughter anymore, and it bursts from my siblings and me in an uproar that I'm sure shakes the whole city.

....

A break in the stream of traffic grants me entry onto the street. As I go, I count the white squares of the crosswalk. ***One, two, three, four***—that is as far as I get.

A noise like nothing I have ever heard before resonates throughout my body, knocking me into the air—rattling my core in its entirety.

The music notes I had been humming surround me; the sound waves drift through me. I feel nothing. Nothing beneath me. Nothing above me. Nothing inside of me. ***Am I flying?*** My body is definitely no longer on the ground.

I try to look around, but it hurts to open my eyes, so I keep them closed. I wonder if this is what it is like to feel truly free, but then pain starts licking at my skin, and voices begin to penetrate my senses—bringing reality somewhat into focus.

"Call 911."

"Oh my God. Is she dead? Is she breathing?"

"For fuck's sake, someone call 911!"

Have you ever closed your eyes and pushed down on the surfaces of your eyelids, rubbing them until you almost start to hallucinate? Brown, green, and gray swirls.

It feels like you're floating through another galaxy. That's all I see, except with added explosions of red as the voices get closer and closer. Hands lift my head gently. Cold fingers touch my neck.

"She has a pulse!"

"Where's the damn ambulance?"

"Did anyone see the car? Where did they go? Does anyone have a description of the driver? A license plate?"

What car? What driver? I wasn't driving.

The sharp sound of an approaching siren.

Oh shit—the police.

I try to get up, try to run, but my legs won't work.

Maybe I am paralyzed. Serves me right.

Something wraps around me, and I am moving forward now—no longer floating. Someone is groaning. It is a nasty kind of gurgling noise, and I wonder who could be making those kinds of noises. Then, I realize they are coming from my throat. The pain is growing to be almost unbearable. I wonder if I am dying. ***Please, God, let me die.***

Beeping, more alarmed voices, more hands on my body. I think of my family and Rose. I remember the smell of my father's pipe and how it feels when my mother hugs me. I remember a young Rose, running with me into the woods back home, our clothes stained with dirt. A twinge of sadness pricks at my heart as I recall how I haven't seen any of them in so long. Then, the music comes back in full force, and I am swept away into the utter darkness.

....

When I wake up a second time, the air is warm and dry. Unfamiliar clothes hang loosely on my body. The cold hands and panicked voices are gone.

I try once more to open my eyes and, this time, it works. A blurry picture comes into focus: egg-colored walls, thin bed sheets, beeping monitors, a tube in my arm. My clothes sit in a half-open plastic bag on a chair in the corner. Pictures of sunny days and fields of yellow flowers hang on the walls.

I can hear people talking quietly outside of the room. I try to move my head to look into the hallway, but a sharp pain shoots from my neck into my skull, and my vision goes dark yet again.

The next time I wake up, the voices are no longer in the hallway. A woman speaks directly over me now, while a deeper male voice comes in from the doorway. The scratch of a pen registers in my brain, and I feel the coolness of metal against my chest. Suddenly, I realize where I am: a hospital. The woman is checking my vitals.

"She's stable," the woman says with a breath of relief, and I can hear the man's footsteps retreat down the hall. Pressure begins building, and my head feels like it is going to explode. The beeping of the machines increases as the pain gets more and more intense.

"It's okay, just hold on. I'm almost done," the woman coos.

Soft hands and fresh cotton press against my forehead. *That means my head is bleeding enough to need bandages. Oh, God. What the hell?*

I remember my bag, the drugs. The damn machines keep beeping rapidly as I force my eyes open, an hourglass figure coming into my vision. Her brown eyes squint in concern as she circles my bed, trying to figure out why my heart rate has risen, trying to figure out where the pain is coming from. Concern turns to shock as she notices I am watching her.

"Oh goodness, you're awake. One moment. I'll grab the doctor. He will explain everything."

Just like that, I am alone again. Looking down at my hands, I note a pale blue and white hospital bracelet informing everyone of my name: Tori Becker. Careful not to move my head too much, I take in the room once more: no police, no social workers, no goddam plastic bag—just me.

Run, run, run.

A short, balding man who I guess is the doctor enters just as I am about to pull the IV out of my arm. Pretending I hadn't been ready to flee the hospital, I drop my hands to my sides and begin guessing how much trouble I am in. From the looks of it, I am not under arrest, but I am severely injured—or at least have a bad head injury. I can see bruises on my arms. I can move my toes, though, so that is good. The man doesn't look up from his clipboard as he begins speaking, his nostrils wheezing incessantly.

"Well, Ms. Becker," wheeze, "you must have one hell of a guardian angel. You were hit by a car while crossing the street. Do you remember that?" He looks at me now.

I try to think back. I remember the rain, the bag, the music, counting the squares. I remember floating through the air. I remember the pain. I don't remember a car. I nod my head slowly as if to say, "I remember a little." I'm not sure if the message translates.

"Okay, good." Wheeze. He turns his attention back to the clipboard. "You suffered a severe concussion, a serious back injury, and several sprains." Wheeze. "You'll need to undergo physical therapy, and we would like to keep you for observation at least one more night. We need to run some more tests, just to double-check things, but we are optimistic that you will be able to make a full physical recovery." Wheeze. He pauses, checking to see if I understand. I understand I am alive. I am lucky to not be a vegetable. I am also screwed.

"We checked your personal belongings, but we didn't find any information besides what's on your ID. It looks like you're pretty far from home." Wheeze. "Is there an emergency contact you'd like us to call? Do you have anyone in the area?"

I decide to try and speak. My voice comes out hoarse, unrecognizable.

"They don't live here, but you can call my sister." **Mom is going to have a heart attack.**

"Okay, very good. Can you give me her number?"

"Um, yes. It's um . . . " It hurts my head to try and think of the numbers. The only number I can remember is my mom's.

"I can't remember. You can call my mom, though." I give him the number.

"Okay, I'm going to go notify your family. A nurse will come by to check on you in a few minutes."

He adjusts the pouch of liquid flowing into my arm before making his exit. All I can think is, *I ruined Christmas.*

A Model Drug Addict

My system started to crumble.

It was a random act of cruelty. It was fate. It was a terrible accident. It was a coincidence. It was a crime.

Whatever you want to call it, the car hitting Tori that night was an event that would alter the rest of her life. Besides cursing her with long-term physical pain, that accident also forced Tori into a drug treatment program.

While conducting tests, the hospital staff had found drugs in Tori's bloodwork. The wheezing doctor had recommended treatment in exchange for painkillers and not reporting the hospital's discovery to the police. Tori had responded curtly with a "fuck you."

Unfortunately for Tori, the doctor knew a lot of cops in the area, and he also knew of a "wonderful" treatment program. He admitted to Tori that he had struggled with cocaine addiction in his pre-med school years. What were the odds of that? For once, Tori was given help from a stranger—although she didn't see it as help at the time.

Tori considered herself an expert drug user. She knew what she liked. She knew where to get it. She knew how to pay for it. She wasn't afraid of the drugs; she felt numb and invincible with them. She did not want to try sobriety just because a doctor suggested it.

However, in the end, some part of Tori made the deal, and the doctor sent in a referral—and told the treatment program when to expect her. He gave her instructions and said he would be calling to check with the program on the day she was supposed to start. A few days later, Tori got off a bus in front of Brighter Days Treatment Center.

....

The building looks like a shithole, and I feel like a pile of shit. The outside walls are flaking brown paint, and half-dead vines cling to the structure. There are at least 20 steps leading to the front door, and by the time I get to check-in, I am sweating profusely—despite the coolness of the early January morning.

It has been a week since I last used—not counting the painkillers from the hospital, of which they put me on an obnoxiously small dosage. My jeans feel rough against my legs, and it seems as though fire ants are burrowing in my skin. Strangely, in all its horridness, the feeling is vaguely familiar.

....

My brain is groggy as I try my best to swallow the oatmeal my mother made for breakfast. My stomach churns. My head aches. I am sweating. The sunshine streaming through the window makes me feel as though I might combust at any moment—burst into flames right there at the table. Unfortunately, as is customary for the Midwest, the sun does not mean warm weather, and I need a coat to walk down the long driveway and wait for the bus.

Normally, I love days when I can show off my coat, indulge in my obsession with the thing. Poofy, fur-lined, and pink—it usually makes me feel like I can win over the world with just one look.

Right now, however, it is my biggest foe—the most dreadful piece of clothing to ever be invented. It suffocates me as I prepare to walk out the door—trapping in the heat and cutting off my air supply. Buttoning it across my body, I feel like I am sealing my coffin.

Once outside, the driveway stretches for what seems like miles. My siblings walk beside me, but I hardly notice them—hardly hear my brother's teasing and my sisters' giggles. Later that day at school, the teacher sends me to the nurse with what she deems to be "a bad stomach bug."

....

Shaking my head to clear the memories, I resist the urge to scratch as I somewhat walk, mostly hobble, my way to the desk. A plump, middle-aged woman looks up at me as I approach. Her blonde hair is pulled back into a loose bun, and her bright red lipstick cracks a little as she smiles at me.

"Well, hello there! Are you here for check-in?"

"Um, I'm just here for the day group session?" I say it like a question, because I honestly have no idea what is going on. The doctor had vaguely explained the process to me as he scrawled an address and directions on a piece of scrap paper. He said it would be free and told me to just go for the day sessions—for 30 damn days in a row. He didn't recommend I stay overnight. He thought a more casual approach would be best. He thought it would introduce a "small but radical" change to my life.

I just want a fix.

"Oh, perfect! You must be Dr. Miller's referral?"

"Um, yeah, he said to just come here, and you would take care of the rest?"

"That I will. Just give me one moment here."

She turns and opens a filing cabinet behind her, the drawers screeching in protest as she pulls them open one at a time, until she finds what she is looking for. Wetting her fingers with her tongue, she separates several pages of paper and lays one of them in front of me.

"Here you go. Just fill this out, and we'll get you checked in. The first group session starts in 15 minutes, so your timing is perfect. Just give us your name and age. Then, we will take you back for a UA. Don't worry if you're not totally clean—most people aren't on their first day, but it's nice to know what we're working with."

Slowly, I fill in the squares on the form and wonder if it is too late to run. ***What in the hell have I gotten myself into?***

....

I feel like a zoo animal on display as I crouch over the toilet, plastic cup in my hand, and try to will the urine out of my body. An aide stands on the opposite side of the room, watching me intently over the bridge of her pointy nose. Her swamp-green uniform blends into the hideous walls, and I try to imagine she isn't there at all.

After what seems like hours, I finally feel the release of liquid leaving my body. I make an effort not to noticeably cringe as my piss goes both in the cup and on my hand. A blurry memory of the time I had drunkenly puked on someone else's floor comes to mind. ***Karma is a bitch.***

The aide takes the cup from me, tightening the lid so that there is no chance of an accidental spill. She stays in the room while I wash my hands.

"You're out of paper towels," I say coldly as I wipe my wet hands on my jeans and brush past her.

Once we are in the hallway, I take a moment to look around. Paintings of sandy beaches and blue water hang on the white walls of the corridor. I scan them, my stomach flipping when I land on the last one in the row: It depicts a large ship, sailing on open water. If I squint, I can see small figures aboard the red vessel. I want nothing more than to be as far away from that photo as possible.

"Where to next?" I turn away from the image to face the aide, internally cringing at the urine cup still in her hands.

"I'll turn this in while you head to group. It's the first door on the left further down this hall. I think they're scheduled to start soon, so you should get going." With that, she pivots. The clacking of her shoes against the tile echoes as she leaves me alone with the paintings.

Moving in the direction of the room, I ready myself for whatever waits inside. As I stand outside the door, I picture a well-dressed shrink calmly asking me about my sobriety as the rest of the group quietly wipes their tears with soft tissues.

"What're you waiting for? Easter?" A gruff voice interrupts my thoughts as someone tries to make their way into the room.

I turn, almost hitting my nose on the chest of a surprisingly large man attempting to squeeze past me. He wears a red, flannel shirt and dirty jeans. He is bald, and it is hard to tell where his body ends and his head begins. I step aside and try to count the rolls on the back of his neck.

He opens the door as wide as it will go upon entering, and I realize I am fully exposed—visible to everyone. People sit, looking at me as I stand in the door.

"Welcome. You must be Tori." A voice that sounds as if it is coated in honey seeps toward me.

"That's me." I will myself to not trip on the freshly polished hardwood floor as I begrudgingly walk into the room.

Bodies shift with my movement as the others continue to size me up, some more subtly than others. The man that pushed me into this situation sits awkwardly half-on, half-off one of the chairs, staring unabashedly as I carefully sit down on the opposite side of the circle.

I notice a girl next to me. A large bruise covers some of the freckles on her face, and I wonder what happened to bring her here. ***What happened to bring me here?***

I think of my family back home and my mother's worried voice on the phone last week. I know she wants me back within the same four walls as her, but I just can't bear the thought of my hometown. Even the idea of driving through the place makes me feel sick: the scraggly dirt roads, the brick school, the smell of farms. I think of Rose. I think of the Archers' farm—the idea of that place makes me cringe in a way almost equivocal to fear.

"Everyone, please help me welcome Tori into our group. She's new to the program." The honey voice interrupts my thoughts. "Tori, my name is Annalise, and I'm your group leader. It's great to have you here with us."

A white smile breaks through Annalise's copper skin as tentative clapping reverberates off the walls of the room. I dig my nails into the skin of my palms, praying for the noise to stop and the attention to be off me.

"Now, Tori, we won't make you go first, but if you would like to share your journey at some point today, we would love to know more about you."

I nod in acknowledgment and silently swear that I will get through the next 30 days saying as little as possible.

"Carl, why don't you go first?" Annalise turns to the fat man from the doorway with a smile. He does not smile back.

"Name's Carl, but everyone except the new girl knows that. I'm still sober and hating every second of it. I miss the coke the most, I suppose—" A guttural cough interrupts Carl as the woman next to him seems to choke on her body fluids. Sweat plasters her dark brown hair to her forehead, and the color has drained from her face. Shakily, she lifts a bottle of water to her cracked lips and holds up one hand apologetically. Carl pauses and shows something dangerously close to concern. He waits for the woman to stop coughing.

"Sorry. Sorry. Go on," she says between ragged breaths.

Carl continues with, "Anyways, coke was the fucking shit, and I miss it more than I miss my hooker."

More hesitant claps.

"Very good, Carl. Thanks for sharing," Annalise quips, unphased by his brashness.

The girl next to me shifts slightly, and I can hear her trying to stifle a laugh. I don't blame her. *If you think about it, the whole situation is pretty hysterical. We are like a druggie circus show.* I look down at the floor as a small grin dances across my face.

Slowly, but surely, Annalise makes her way through the majority of the group before giving us a quick break to use the bathroom, smoke, and fill up on coffee. I follow suit as everyone stands from the chairs, stretching and cracking their backs. While most of the group forms clusters around the room, I find myself standing alone in the corner, sipping burnt coffee from a Styrofoam cup. I see the woman who had interrupted Carl with her near-death experience making her way toward me. I stand up straighter and brace for impact.

"Tori, right? I'm Patty. Nice to meet ya. Sorry if I grossed ya out with that little display earlier. Smoke?" She extends a cigarette in replacement of a handshake. I gratefully accept.

Patty's teeth are mostly missing, and the ones that she does have are stained brown. She shakes a little as she puffs her cigarette and sips her cup of coffee. The stench of booze seems to leak from her pores.

"Inpatient or outpatient?" she asks.

"Out. You?"

"Lucky asshole. In. Definitely in. Got no self-control when it comes to this addiction nonsense. Been here less than a week, and I already feel like hell. Managed to get my hands on some booze last night, but that didn't do much good. Now I'm hungover and coming down, but what can ya do? A woman's gotta have something to lessen the blow of reality or else I'd off myself, ya know?"

I do know. I hold up my coffee cup in a "cheers" motion and toss my cigarette butt into a metal pail near my feet. Annalise makes a motion for us to come sit. My heart rate increases as I realize it is highly likely that I will have to talk next. I take my time coming back to the group circle, summoning the bold me to come do her thing.

"Tori?" Annalise says as we take our seats. "Think you have the hang of it?"

"Yep. I can go."

I clear my throat and sit up a little straighter. The metal chair is cold through my thin sweatshirt, and I feel goosebumps make their way up my arms.

"My name is Tori. I'm here because, as it turns out, some assholes are not very good drivers."

Some slightly forced chuckles emerge from the group. **Nobody cares. Get to the point.**

"Anyways, I got in an accident, went to the hospital, my doctor found out I was on drugs, and now here I am—earning my pain meds." I say the words in a single breath and slump slightly as I finish, being careful not to make eye contact with Annalise. Unfortunately, my obvious anxiety doesn't stop her from asking a follow-up question.

"Thank you for your honesty, Tori. I think you'll find that many people here can relate to your experiences. Can you tell us about the first time you used drugs?"

I think about what to say. I could easily make something up—tell them your typical, tragic story about the first time I fell into the devil's grip—but I feel like I need to be honest with these people. It is kind of like a druggie's version of going to confession.

"Honestly, I guess I don't know," I say. The truth of this statement hits me harder than I expect. I have never stopped to think about my first time using—the drugs have just always been a factor. I can't even remember where or how I first learned about them. I shift my weight forward, putting my elbows on my knees, before continuing. "I mean, maybe the drugs have affected my memory or something, but I really couldn't tell you about the first time I popped a pill. Drugs have just always been in my life. I've always known how to use them and what I like. They've been a part of who I am for so long that sometimes I'm not sure where drugged-up me stops and sober me begins." Heat rises to my cheeks, and I feel ashamed. This is the first real thing I have said, and even though we are all admittedly a mess, it feels like I am somehow messier.

"Thank you for sharing, Tori."

....

After group, Annalise walks with me to the cafeteria. She explains that we all rotate lunch duty, and today is my lucky day.

I work in silence, scooping mashed potatoes onto plastic trays and washing dishes alongside an array of people from an array of lives. We eat after everyone else, but I don't mind. I am just grateful for food. While we eat, some of the others try to make conversation, but I just stay quiet until they leave me alone. I am all talked out.

After lunch comes time outdoors, then one-on-one therapy. By the time I am finished for the day, I am exhausted. I had hated almost every minute of it, but, somehow, I feel a little better. I still have cold sweats and am shaking, but it seems like I am less alone—like other people are living through this hell with me.

Sober Pink Elephants

That was the beginning of the end.

As Tori progressed through treatment, one of the counselors discovered she was living in her car, and Annalise began asking her social worker friends if anyone knew of a place for Tori to stay.

Annalise also started bringing Tori job applications for places where she knew the owners. Sometimes Tori saw the efforts as charity and was disgusted by it. Other times, however, she found herself immensely grateful.

Although comradery was a major benefit of treatment, the program also came with detriments for Tori—such as sobriety. No drugs, sex, or alcohol—those were the rules, and they rendered Tori without any form of escape. Sleep evaded her, and when she did manage to catch a couple of hours, sober sleep was not peaceful sleep. Nightmares plagued her, and she would often wake up hyperventilating, sweat drenching her clothes.

When she was in the nightmares, Tori would usually be floating above a young girl's body, watching as if observing a movie. She would see the girl endure something terrible and think, **That poor child. Someone should help her.** Then, she would wake up, haunted by the idea that that child was her.

Sometimes, though, the nightmares got much worse than being a silent observer. Sometimes, she was in the girl's body and could feel cold surfaces against her bare skin. She could hear footsteps, twigs snapping. She could smell blood and sex. But she couldn't see. It was as if she were blind. She wanted to run, but she couldn't move.

Those were the worst. Those were the nightmares that would jolt her awake. Those were the nightmares that were becoming more frequent, more real. Those were the nightmares that would lead her to the edge, staring down into a life-altering abyss.

....

Unresolved trauma, unresolved trauma, unresolved trauma. The words of my therapist replay in my mind as I stride along the path that loops through the woods surrounding the Brighter Days building.

WHO THE FUCK DOES SHE THINK SHE IS? SHE DOESN'T KNOW US. WE DON'T HAVE UNRESOLVED TRAUMA. YOU WANNA TALK ABOUT TRAUMA? BEING THIS SOBER IS TRAUMATIC.

The internal dialogue has been getting louder and louder lately, and now it is hard to hear anything else.

The shrink knows nothing. Nothing! She wants to hurt us.

Dr. Crane is her name—my therapist. I told her in our one-on-one this morning about my trouble sleeping. Avoiding the gritty details, I mostly described the nightmares as "unpleasant," which was a major minimization. Nonetheless, Dr. Crane credited them to unresolved trauma, and I left her office without saying another word. Now I am rage-walking through the forest.

Just goes to show you what good therapy does.

The wind cuts through the trees and echoes in my ears. I put my hands over them to block it out, hoping it will also dull the angry voices in my head. There is no such luck.

SCREW THE WIND.

At this moment, the clouds shift, blocking out the sun, and the forest grows still. No wind, no birds—even I stop muttering to myself. Nobody else is visible on the trail. We are supposed to walk in pairs, but I hadn't been in the mood for company—a decision I now regret.

The air around me seems to grow heavy as anxiety trickles into my veins. Something isn't right. I am in danger. I can feel it in my gut. Scanning my surroundings, I slowly spin in a circle. Trees, trees, more trees. The forest seems exceedingly peaceful, despite the turmoil rising within me.

THE FOREST SCARES US. WE DON'T LIKE IT HERE.

Suddenly, I see it: A cloaked figure stands roughly 10 feet from the path, watching me from the shadow of a large oak tree. My breath catches in my throat, my feet freeze in place. I can no longer feel my body. It is as if I have entered one of my nightmares—full of adrenaline, but unable to move. I feel small, like a lost child. A scream rises in my throat but becomes caught amidst my shock. Then, just as quickly as the figure appears, it is gone.

Oxygen rushes back into my body as I frantically search the tree line. Nothing, nothing, nothing. ***Am I going crazy?***

The figure disappearing does not bring me peace. Fear—so powerful that it makes me feel nauseous—continues to course through my body, winding my gears up, up, up like a jack-in-the-box. Pop—I am gone.

As the forest turns gray with the night,
The fear of the unknown arises as evening befalls us.
The forest comes alive with the trouble
And unforgettable stares of evil.
The ugly memories of the crooked, gnarled faces and broken hands,
Once embracing our lonely souls.

The eyes that we feared can see through our beings.
The endless stares of darkened memories.
Terror and revenge their names now become.

The mystery of the sun rising over the meadow,
Casting its light over the terror of evil.
Where does it flee as we sit and remember
What was so real not seconds ago.

The warmth of a new day casts confusion on us all,
As we embrace and try to erase
The dirty emptiness that the night just held.

Wondering when
Our new hope would disappear
Into the taunting of each
New creation.

One Step Forward, Two Steps Back
Reality was terrifying.

It's easy to judge a drug addict—easy to think they're weak, they're lowlifes, they're pathetic. But what's not easy is to ask questions about addiction: questions like, what happened in an addict's life to make them so desperate for escape? How did the addiction start? Did they even stand a chance?

Oftentimes, there is much more going on beneath the surface of what looks like a simple life choice. For Tori, addiction was survival—numbing her mind just enough to enable her to function, and without it? Well, without it, life was seemingly undoable.

After her experience in the woods, Tori woke up a few hours later in her car, unable to say where she had been or what she had been doing. Scared out of her mind, she looked down to see her mint tin had been replenished and an empty bottle of vodka was on her front seat. Overcome by dread and shame, she realized the gravity of the situation.

The next day she felt like a complete and utter failure when her drug test came back positive. She was convinced she was going straight to jail. But, to her surprise, it only resulted in her being forced into a very long conversation with Annalise after group.

"Can you tell me why you chose to use?"

"I don't know. I don't remember. I guess, maybe I just needed to feel, just for a minute, something other than miserable."

Annalise said she understood, even though she probably didn't—not really. Two days later, Tori emptied her mint tin into a gas station toilet. Three days after that, she started work at a clothing store. Eventually, near the end of her 30 days, Annalise found her a home to stay in— to which Tori reluctantly agreed.

Annalise called her progress a "bounding success" and said she should be "tremendously proud." All Tori felt was an ever-growing gap where the drugs used to be and an ever-growing awareness of the voices.

....

"My name is Patty, but most of you know that. I've been stone-cold sober for 30 days now. The cravings suck, and all I want is a fix, but I'm still doing the damn thing, and I'm proud. My daughter said I can see my grandkids if I'm still clean in a month. I can't wait."

I clap enthusiastically, along with the rest of the group, as Patty wipes tears from her eyes. Her hands only shake a little as she rubs the mascara from her slightly rosy cheeks. It is impressive how much healthier she looks than the coughing, pale mess she was the first time I met her.

We shared many nature walks, cigarettes, and coffee talks over the last month or so, and I have grown to adore Patty. She is funny. I also feel bad for her—but I will never dare tell her that. After her husband died in a botched gas station robbery last year, she fell apart: lost her job, lost her house, and started spending all she had on drugs. It was her adult children who suggested she come to the program, and she had done it for them—them and her grandchildren. Listening to her share now, I feel proud of her.

"Tori, would you like to go next?"

"Sure. I'm Tori. I've been sober for about the same amount of time as Patty. Um, one slip-up, but I'm totally clean now. Sleeping still isn't very easy." I take a deep breath, debate how much to say. "I think, um, I think I might be hallucinating, maybe? But I'm sure that will all get better as time goes on." I look at Annalise to see her response. She nods calmly, urging me to continue. Her poker face is unbeatable.

"My new job keeps me busy, so that's nice, I guess. I'm getting really fucking good at folding clothes. I just hope this new family I'm bunking with can handle my bright and cheery personality." Genuine laughter. "In all seriousness, though, it's my last day in the program, and I feel better than I have in a long time. I'm happy that I got to know all of you, even Carl." More laughter, joined this time with zealous clapping. I smile slightly and lock eyes with Patty. She is smiling too, rotten teeth and all.

After group, we split into pairs to go for a walk on the property. Patty and I share a cigarette as we make our way to the wooden swing just out of sight of the rest of the group. There is no way we are walking a mile.

"Hey, can I ask you something?" Patty says as she passes the cigarette in my direction. Our movements cause the swing to creak in the damp early February air. It reminds me of when Rose and I used to play on the school swing set after a rainstorm, our small bodies flying over what then seemed like massive puddles.

"Of course," I say through a puff of smoke.

"When you said you've started hallucinating, what did you mean exactly?"

"Oh, I don't know. Just the usual detox stuff, I guess."

She looks at me, confused, which only prompts me to try and make her understand.

"It's just, my thoughts seem to be taking over my life, you know? Like sometimes I'll be doing something, and I'll get this sudden rush of adrenaline, kind of like I'm in danger or something, and then I can't function for a minute. And this one time, I thought I saw something in the woods . . . "

The shadow of concern on Patty's face makes me trail off. She is a little more still than usual and her lips are in a straight line. She puts her hand on mine.

"Honey, have you told Dr. Crane about this?"

"Um, no. Do you think I should? Do you tell her about your thoughts like that?"

"Tori . . . I don't have thoughts like that."

....

I go to my one-on-one therapy session later that day. Keeping it surface-level, I fail to mention my possessive thoughts and darkening reality. It is my last day, and I figure that will open up a whole other can of worms that I do not want to see.

Patty still has some time to go before she is completely done with her program, so we say goodbye later that evening. As I hug her and the rest of the group, I think about how much has happened in the last 30 days—how I have spoken more about my feelings in the last month than throughout my life. But I still feel incomplete, as if dealing with my drug problem is only one checkpoint in what is likely to be a very long journey.

After leaving treatment, I try my best to ignore the thoughts, voices, and visions—tell myself they will go away with time. I push them down, down, down until they are mostly muffled noise. Sometimes, though, I can't ignore them. The thoughts completely take me over, paralyzing my body. I smell a certain smell or hear a certain noise, and in an instant, I am not walking down the street anymore—I am in a dark place, terrified and hurting. Sometimes it gets to be so much that I can't remember who I am.

Part II:

The Search for Internal Truth

The Smile has left the face of this child.
Only fear and sadness remain.
You can see in her eyes the emptiness and sorrow.
The rolling tears on her cheeks show her pain.
The smile has left the face of this child.
One can only wonder, will her heart save its place?
The smile has left the face of this child.
She's too small to carry the shame.

What Happened Last Night?

My life was a blur.

Blackout. Within this word is an array of definitions and experiences, depending on whom you ask. At the mention of it, you might hear things like, "Blackouts are terrible for business! There was once a blackout at my work, and we had to shut down for the entire day," or, "It's the whiskey that makes me blackout every time. Drank four shots of it last weekend, and I have no idea what the hell happened." Pretty typical definitions, typical examples.

But if you asked Tori about her idea of a blackout, you might hear something a little unique, a little puzzling. She might say something like, "I lost five hours and woke up in clothes I didn't recognize," or, "I came to in the middle of having sex with someone, and I had no idea how I got there." If, when searching for an explanation, you ask if she was drunk, she would almost always say no. Although, alcohol certainly helped her to cope after one of these experiences.

The toll that these kinds of blackouts have on someone and their life is incomprehensible. Imagine feeling like something, or someone, else is controlling aspects of your existence, and you have no way of knowing what is truly going on. Imagine feeling like no matter what you do, your life will never belong to you. That definition of blackout is its own special kind of hell.

....

Blake:

Tori is not good at relaxing. Never has been. Every time that we want to have fun, I come out and take over the body. I have to. Tori is too vigilant, too on guard, and ever since treatment, it's only gotten worse. I mean, without the pills, the girl is an absolute freak show. We can hardly function, let alone go out and have a good time. So, whenever sex or partying enter the equation, so do I.

A slap to the ass—that's all it takes for Tori to shut down this time. A dirty man, wanting to get some. Pretty typical, expected even. Tori used to be able to handle stuff like that, but not lately.

Before all this no-more-drugs nonsense, I was reserved for special occasions: that Dane asshole, Tori's birthday, the ships, the darkest forest nights—real high-pressure situations. But with sobriety comes nerves, I suppose.

After downing our drink and tossing the butt of our cigarette into the nasty ass-hitter's beverage, I saunter over to the ladies' room. Looking at our reflection, I am disappointed in Tori's lack of inspiration. The girl has never been one to wear much makeup, but would it kill her to try just a little?

"Excuse me?" I turn to the woman gazing into the mirror next to me as she carefully runs a tube of red lipstick over her lips. "Can I borrow that?"

"Sure, sweetie," she replies.

I want to slap the woman for calling me "sweetie," but I don't. Instead, I take the lipstick from her outstretched hand and manage a smile. "Thanks."

Tracing the body's lips with a well-practiced touch, I think back to all the different mirrors I've done this in front of: mirrors at parties, mirrors at bars, mirrors at strange men's homes. If only Tori didn't wipe it off when I leave; if only she saw how much it brought to the body's appearance. But she never will. I know this. Just like I know when Tori needs me. We're connected. Although, I think I'm more aware of her than she is of me. I sigh, hesitantly handing back the lipstick. Tori will never appreciate me, not really.

Back in the bar, I do not sit on a stool. Instead, I hoist myself onto the actual bar itself. This immediately draws the attention of the bartender, and every other man in the room, which is my intention, of course. Donna feeds us pretty well, so we no longer need men for food, but having all eyes on me is the second-best high I can get at the moment. The bartender is pissed. *Good.*

"You better get your ass off my bar and onto a chair, little lady," he says.

"Aw, com'n. Have some fun." I wink at him. "I'm just allowing someone else to have a seat at the bar. Real smart for your business, actually. You should consider bartop and barstool seating from now on."

The bartender doesn't say anything else. He just shakes his head and walks away. *What a jackass.*

"I'm drinking vodka!" I call at his back as I light another cigarette. It is going to be a fun night.

....

"Shit." I wake up swearing as horns honking on the overpass shake me from my hazy sleep. "Dammit, dammit, dammit."

I sit up and look in the rearview mirror at myself. I have always hated my reflection, and my mind fills with thoughts of self-loathing as I push my light brown hair out of my eyes and wipe mascara stains from my cheeks. My lips are an odd shade of red, even though I don't remember putting lipstick on. Confused, I quickly rub away the color with a loose napkin and take a swig from the bottle of vodka in the console next to me. The warm liquid offers little comfort as it goes from my mouth, down my throat, and into my empty stomach.

I don't remember going out, but that doesn't mean that I didn't. Desperately, I try to remember how I got here, where I went, what I saw. Nothing—no matter how hard I try, I don't have a single memory of what I did last night.

"Shit."

It is the second time since leaving treatment that I have woken up in my car with no recollection of how I got there. These blackouts were never cause for alarm when I had been on drugs, but now I feel some uneasiness creeping in with each instance.

Oh, God, what day is it? Turning the keys that rest in the ignition, I scan the radio channels until I find a news station.

"Well, it's looking like another sunny Sunday in Washington," a clear voice comes through the static.

I hurriedly check the watch on my wrist, squinting to see the hands of the clock through the glass cover. It is almost nine in the morning. I am going to be late for church.

....

I'm sure I look like an absolute lunatic as I try to quietly close the church doors behind me and slip, unnoticed, into an empty pew. My clothes are dirt-stained and wrinkled from my overnight stay in the car. My hair hasn't been washed in days, and although I tied it back on the drive over, it doesn't seem to be doing much for my appearance. Even the pastor seems to judge as he pauses to take note of me while the front-pewers turn to cast condemning looks my way.

I have always thought it is ironic that the cruelest people sit closest to the front of the church, as if that alone is enough to cleanse them of their sins. Mrs. Archer used to always sit in the front.

Snake in the grass.

After the service, I rush back toward the safety of my car, but I am not quite fast enough. A cold hand grabs my arm as a warm voice asks, "Tori, what happened to you last night? We were worried sick."

It is the woman I am staying with: Donna. I have been crashing with her and her family since I left the treatment program almost two months ago. When people ask how long I am staying, Donna likes to say that I am with them until I "get back on my feet." They are decent, Christian people, who feel as though I am their newfound purpose in life, their responsibility. To my dismay, the only rules of the house are that you don't miss church and that you don't eat if you aren't present at the dinner table. Donna's overbearingness can be a titch overwhelming. Otherwise, living with them is probably the least terrible situation I have found myself in in a while. It is a roof over my head, three meals a day.

"Oh, nothing. I just stayed at a friend's house." I try helplessly to squirm out of her icy grip while I sell the lie with a pretend smile.

"Dear, you really shouldn't stay out all night," Donna says with a knowing look. She was the one to find me sleeping in my car, only a block away from her house, after my prior escapade. I'm sure she knows where I actually woke up this morning, but I am not about to admit it.

Luckily, Donna isn't granted enough time to press me further. Her two young children promptly swoop in and save me from the confrontation as they pull her in different directions—one demanding an ice cream cone, while the other insists on playing at the church playground.

"Mommy is having a conversation," she says sharply, but the children don't notice her tone, and I am halfway to my car before she turns back to say something else to me.

"I'll see you for dinner tonight," I call as I wave my hand and slide into the driver's side door. Once inside, I take my first deep breath of the morning and turn the keys.

While I drive, I try to remember anything from the night before. I am so focused on finding my memory that I don't notice the gas gauge going past the "E" until my car sputters and comes to a stop.

"Of, fucking, course," I curse under my breath as I slouch back in my seat, gazing longingly at the empty mint tin sitting on my dash. ***This is shaping up to be a beautiful day.***

The door to my car matches my internal groans as I hoist myself out of the vehicle. Luckily, I know where I am and remember that there is a gas station about two miles up the road. Unluckily, my body is still recovering from whatever adventure we went on last night and is running low on energy.

As I make my way, my black, leather jacket seems to absorb the heat of the abnormally warm spring day. Eventually, I give up on wearing it and tie it loosely around my waist. Soon afterward, my feet begin to ache and burn. ***These shoes belong in hell.***

SO DO WE.

I bend over to pull my thick-heeled boots away from my feet. Angry at myself and the world, I stuff my socks into the heels of the boots and fumble with the laces, stringing them together. Swinging the boots over my shoulder, I feel the sizzle of hot pavement on my feet and move to the gravel section of the road in search of relief. Ignoring the pain of rocks in my heels, I light a cigarette and continue walking.

Roughly 10 minutes later, I pass a bar and decide it is fate. Hastily, I drop my cigarette butt and pull the boots back over my feet. Stuffing my sweaty arms into my jacket, I make my way into the building. The smell of the previous night's booze washes over me. With it, comes small details.

I remember sitting on a hard stool. I am drinking, but I am not drunk. I remember laughing. I remember leaning over to the nearest hand with a lighter and puffing on a cigarette. I remember the stench of a trucker-type man as he walked past me. Then . . . blank.

I swat away the panic poking at me and sit at the bar. The surface is sticky, and my legs cling to the stool. It reminds me of the bars in California.

"Back for more?" The bartender's gravelly voice is rough against my ears as he saunters over, a bottle of vodka in his hand. I must show my confusion, because he quickly realizes that I have no idea who he is. "Girl, you were wild," he explains as he reaches for a glass. "I served you not more than two drinks, but damn if you weren't on something else." He laughs as he pours.

"'Something else?'" I accept the drink and welcome the familiar burn as it sizzles over my nerves. "What was I doing? Who was I with?"

"Woah, woah. Slow down with the questions. My brain ain't that fast. You were just actin' a little crazy is all, carrying on as if I had served you 10 drinks instead of two. You weren't with nobody from what I could tell, but everyone was trying to be the one to leave with you—now that's for damn sure." He shakes his head. "I would've kicked you out for causing such a raucous, but then what would that make me?"

I shrug.

"Not a gentleman. That's for sure. My pops would've rung my neck to see me kick a pretty lady to the curb on a Saturday night."

Suddenly, I don't want to know anymore. I am not interested in what this creep thinks of me, or whatever version of me he previously met. All I care about is getting back to Donna's and into a cold shower.

"Thanks for the drink," I say and place a few bills under my empty glass.

The man tips his baseball cap. I try to not run out the door.

We Need to Talk

It was like things started clicking into place.

Nobody can dispute the fact that humans are flawed—sometimes fatally so. But what makes a character trait into a flaw? What makes it fatal?

Tori spent a lot of time alone in her life. Because of this, very few people even took the time to notice her character traits, let alone to decide whether or not they qualified as flaws. They noticed her long enough to use and discard her—not long enough to truly see her. Even those who hung around for more than a few days very rarely cared, and those who cared had their own time-consuming problems. Living with Donna was the first time since living with her family that Tori shared a space with people who seemed affected by the way she acted.

Why did they care? That's up for debate. But one thing is for certain: Living with that family brought forward ideas about Tori's behavior that she had never stopped to consider before, which brought forward questions that she had hoped never to have to answer.

....

The television buzzes as the children sit in front of it, staring at a rerun of the same cartoon from last week. I watch them as I pick apart the green bean casserole that had been placed in front of me 20 minutes ago. I am not hungry, but I know Donna will be unimpressed, and a little hurt, if I don't present a clean plate at the end of the evening.

I had waved Donna off when I got back to the house after finally getting gas in my car. I ignored her many questions, explaining away my absence with the all-encompassing excuse of errands. I don't care if she knows I am full of shit. I have other things on my mind—like wondering what happened last night and why I keep missing chunks of time. Staring down at the food I should be eating, I think back to years before, to one of the first times I visited my hometown as an adult after having left the moment I graduated high school.

....

The dinging of cash registers bounces around the wide-open space of the grocery store as my older sister and I make our way through the aisles. My dad sent us to get some last-minute ingredients for his renowned homemade pizza—a celebration of my temporary return home.

"Tomato sauce, tomato sauce, tomato sauce . . . " my sister mutters, mostly to herself, as she references the signs hanging above the aisles. She is so focused on finding the sauce's location that she doesn't notice the busty woman approaching us, but I do.

"Tori? Tori Becker? Is that you?" The woman shields her eyes as she approaches, like she is trying to peer through sunlight instead of fluorescent lighting.

My sister shakes loose from her tomato sauce trance in time to turn toward the woman just as she reaches us. The woman's smile is beaming with recognition, despite the fact that I have no idea who she is.

"That is you! Oh, my gosh, you're so grown up— and so tan!" She opens her arms. I stiffen. She persists with the hug, ignoring the weighted awkwardness of my body language. "It's so good to see you back around here. Your mother mentioned a while back that you moved." She turns to my sister next, greeting her with the same forced hug. "And it's always good to see you." My sister is slightly more responsive than me and pats the woman's back nonchalantly.

I have no idea who this woman is, although she clearly knows me and my family fairly well. I look to my sister for help. God bless her, she swoops in.

"Yeah, Tori's a West Coast local now, Mrs. Davis."

"Oh, how lovely! I've always wanted to visit that part of the country."

"It's not that great," I say under my breath, and my sister raises her voice in an effort to skip over my remark.

"Yes, it's very exciting! Anyways, it's great seeing you, Mrs. Davis, but we have to get going. Dad is waiting on us."

"Oh, of course, of course. I'll let you girls get back to it." A final hug for both of us, and the woman is gone in the same direction from which she came.

"Who the hell was that?" I ask my sister as we resume walking and scanning aisle signs.

"Mrs. Davis? Ryan's mom?"

I look at my sister with confusion and a little shock. Ryan had been my date to the junior prom, but I didn't remember meeting his mother. However, that didn't mean I hadn't. I also didn't remember going to his house for pictures, despite there being a framed photo somewhere of us posing in what was apparently his front yard. I was missing hours of time from almost every high school event. I blamed it on how unmemorable they were.

"Oh," I shrug, "guess I have a bad memory."

My sister smiles slightly in response, her eyes trained back on the signs. "Oh, tomato sauce! Aisle 10."

....

"Something bothering you?" Ray, Donna's husband, slides into the chair across from me, looking at my full plate.

Ray is a rather quiet man. He has a graying beard and always wears a winter beanie, even in the warming spring weather. He loves football, pretends to like church, and is overall rather unassuming.

"Just not hungry," I say with as much politeness as I can manage while still keeping my eyes down. Tracing the grain of the wooden table with my pinky, I debate when it will be a good time to leave for the night.

NOW SEEMS GOOD. WE NEED A DRINK.

Before Ray can say anything else, I swipe my jacket off the back of the chair. I am halfway standing, about to excuse myself from the table, when Donna strolls through the kitchen, also pointedly gazing at my nearly full plate. I hesitantly smile at Ray, sit back down, and take a small bite of my food.

Donna slides a chair back from the table, the wooden legs scraping painfully against the clean tile floors—a noise that does not help my splitting headache. I sip my water and pull my jacket over my body, suddenly chilled—probably dehydrated.

"Honey, we want to talk to you about something," she says gingerly, placing her hands softly on my arm. Unease prickles across my skin.

JESUS, THIS WOMAN JUST DOESN'T STOP.

I unconsciously sit up a little straighter and pull away from Donna's touch. My hands make themselves into fists, and I summon all of my self-control in order to stop myself from running out of the house.

"What's the matter?" I ask warily.

"Well, we've noticed some things," she says, glancing at Ray, who gives her an encouraging nod. He is clearly not going to be contributing very much to this conversation.

Donna continues. "We've noticed some things about you or . . . um . . . I guess more about the way you act. We see that sometimes you don't remember everything you do, and sometimes it seems like even though you're with us, you're not really with us. It's almost as if you're disconnected from everything and everyone, including yourself."

I offer her nothing, but, bless her heart, she presses on.

"We think you are . . . well, it seems like you are . . . changing for different occasions, and you aren't always aware of what is happening. It appears that you aren't aware of everything going on in your life."

I did not expect that. I think Donna is still talking to me, but I can no longer hear her. She becomes a muffled echo as my thoughts swallow me whole, my body numb. I debate what to do, what to say. **What is she saying? Is it even true?**

My first instinct is to blow her off and say it isn't true, but what good will that do when she has already decided that it is? My second instinct is to run again: go somewhere else for a few days until she drops this or until I forget it ever happened. My third instinct is to sit silently and deal with whatever else is about to come. For some reason—maybe I think I owe it to her for taking me in—I choose the third and direct my attention back to Donna. Her face is flushed. **She must've been talking for a while now.**

"It isn't all because of the drinking either," Donna continues. "It's more than that. It's like your brain doesn't belong to just you." She says the last part almost as if she is asking a question, waiting for me to offer a reasonable explanation for her observations. She is going in circles, coming up with different ways to politely ask me if I am crazy.

TELL HER TO SCREW OFF, AND LET'S GO GET THAT DRINK.

Run.

Don't say anything.

Finally, I decide to respond.

"Doesn't everyone act different sometimes?" I ask, thinking this is a reasonable question. But when I look at Donna and Ray, they appear confused. They have clearly never felt this way, and I become consumed with the need to make them understand what I am saying.

"Like, for example, I have the me that I am when I'm paying bills, and I have the me that goes out and drinks. Then there's the me that's here with you right now. I adapt to my environment. I'm different in every situation. Everyone has different sides to them." I pause, waiting for them to catch up, to realize what I am saying, and tell me they do those things too. But they don't. They just look at each other for a long time, then look back at me. Ray sips a glass of water; Donna folds her hands in front of her—a silent prayer.

"Honey . . . " Donna is choosing her words carefully, as if saying the wrong thing might cause me to shatter. "I don't think, um, I don't think that everyone does have different sides to them like you do. I don't think what you're experiencing are different sides of yourself." She stops, hesitates for a moment, then ventures forward. "I think they're different personalities entirely, and sometimes you don't always remember the things that all of those different personalities do, even though they're all living in your body."

"It's not norm—" Ray stops suddenly with a kick from Donna under the table that she thinks I won't notice. "It's not safe," he corrects.

Donna presses on. "Anyways, I was reading this article, and they mentioned this thing called, um, oh gosh, what did they call it? Well, anyway, it was about these new studies that some doctors are working on, treating patients that act awfully similar to you. These people—they struggle with some very serious demons . . . "

Again, Donna's voice moves to the background of my mind as I struggle to suppress the screams building up inside of me.

Slap her.

Run!

TIME FOR VODKA.

CALL YOUR MOM, AND TELL HER YOU NEED TO COME HOME.

But what if they hurt her?

I take a deep breath from my diaphragm and exhale through my nose—a breathing technique that Dr. Crane taught me after I had a panic attack in her office. Slowly, I begin to calm, and Donna's voice materializes once more.

"Tori? Tori, honey, are you alright?"

No, we are most definitely not alright.

It feels as if I have been drop-kicked out of a dream and into reality. I am shocked, but behind the shock is a new feeling: a sense of clarity I haven't felt before. Like what she is saying to me isn't absurd but is very much the truth. Like she is sliding into place the first piece of a very large puzzle.

I lean over the table toward Donna—as if she can fix me, can give me all the answers I need. "What am I supposed to do now?"

"I don't . . . I don't know," she mutters. "I really don't know."

I nod and gradually stand from the table. I can't bear to sit here any longer. "I think I'm going to head to bed. This is a lot for me to think about. Goodnight."

Once in my room, I slump against the door, putting my head between my knees.

THAT CRAZY HAG DOESN'T KNOW WHAT SHE'S TALKING ABOUT. OUR BRAIN IS JUST FINE.

I'M SCARED.

Maybe she does have a point. There's not enough room in here.

I groan and stand, heading to the closet where I keep a flask hidden in the folds of hand-me-down sweaters given to me by women at Donna's church. As I stand on my tiptoes feeling through the layers of polyester and scratchy cotton, my hand lands on something else: a pocket-sized notebook. Flask temporarily forgotten, I pull the notebook down and sit cross-legged in the closet entrance, flipping through the blank pages.

The corners of the notebook are folded, with an occasional water stain adorning the empty blue lines. I guess that it is a forgotten item of school supplies purchased for Donna's children at one point or another. She told me that this room was previously used as storage, and every once in a while, I find something like this—a trinket of the room's past life before I disrupted things.

As I turn the pages, the familiar smell of unused paper greets me. I have always loved that smell. To me, it smells like potential.

....

"Ah, the girl with the notebook strikes again."

I look up from where I am scribbling to see my third-grade teacher, Mrs. Caltri, grinning down at me. The glint of amusement in her hazel eyes tells me that I won't be scolded for being sidetracked in class, even though this is the third time this week that she has found me lost in another world during a lesson.

Mrs. Caltri is one of the few people in my life who seems to notice me, to understand me. She often looks at me the way one looks at a puppy in a shelter: brow furrowed in concern, eyes searching mine, trying to earn my trust and find the answers to unasked questions. She gives me a safe space to just be a child, and I treasure my time in her classroom.

She coined the nickname "girl with a notebook" for me about halfway through the school year—after my writing skills were developed enough for me to begin stringing sentences together to form stories, and I began bringing a notebook with me everywhere I went. Sometimes I just recorded what I saw. Other times, I used my writing to escape into another time and space.

The notebook habit wasn't a phase. I continued it throughout elementary, middle, and high school. But as my party habits grew, my writing habits shrunk. By the time I graduated, there were cardboard boxes stuffed with notebooks in the corner of our family basement, but I was no longer adding to the collection.

"Can I see what you wrote?" Mrs. Caltri asks as she squats down. I look sheepishly at my feet.

"Sure." I half-heartedly turn the notebook so she can see.

She scans the words, stopping and retracing certain areas with improper spacing and spelling—deciphering my code. As she reads, I notice sadness creep into her. I wonder what is making her sad. I am about to ask her when, suddenly, she replaces the sadness with a warm smile.

"Tori, your writing skills are really excellent. This is great work. Do you mind if I keep just this one page?"

"Um, sure, Mrs. Caltri." I hesitantly rip the page from the notebook and hand it to her. She carefully folds it in four and slips it into the pocket of her skirt.

....

As the sensation of writing flows back into my body, I begin, almost frantically, to search for something to write with. Soon I find a pen in the nightstand drawer, and, without giving myself time to change my mind, I start writing.

I write anything and everything: all the different thoughts, opinions, voices. I write about my nightmares and the cloaked figure from the woods. I write about how much I miss my family but how dangerous home feels to me. I write about Dane and my cravings for drugs. I write about Donna and Ray and how crazy they think I am. I write about the gaps in my memory—waking up without any recollection of how I got somewhere.

By the time I stop, the clock on the wall tells me it is nearly midnight, and the ache in my hand tells me that I may have inadvertently given myself carpal tunnel. The notebook's pages are nearly full. Ink stains the side of my hand. My mind—my mind is finally calm. For once, I feel like I can rest. The sense of peace almost makes me want to cry.

But I don't cry. Instead, I slide the notebook under my mattress and pull myself into bed. A small victory is found in this being the first night since leaving treatment that I don't drink before bed.

A Bright, Sunny Day

I was missing parts of myself.

As with humans, most childhoods are also flawed. In fact, the argument could be made that childhoods are the sole reason behind most people's flaws—especially the fatal ones. Even if one's childhood was seemingly normal, there is usually a traumatic event to be found somewhere: A family pet ran away and never came back; a parent ran away and never came back.

Most people know the downfalls of their childhood. They can point to one chapter of their life and say, "Here. Here is where it all went wrong." But what if your mind deleted this chapter, like pages torn out of a book?

Your story wouldn't make any sense. You would still have to deal with the aftermath of the plot-altering chapter, of course, but you wouldn't understand why things were unfolding the way they were—a bad ending without an explanation.

....

I wake up to Donna aggressively flicking on the lights of my temporary living space.

"Rise and shine, Tori. Today is a bright, sunny day, and it will not be wasted!"

I roll away from the light and cover my head with a pillow like a disgruntled teenager. ***All I want to do is waste this day, waste away.***

"Do you work today?" Donna's usually chipper morning voice deepens slightly as she asks the question, and I can tell she is calculating how many days it has been since my last shift, wondering if I have gotten myself fired yet.

"What day is it?"

"Tuesday."

"Nope. Tomorrow morning."

I can feel her relief from across the room. "Oh, well, that's nice of them to give you a few days off in a row. That rarely happens."

"Yep, they're real saints."

Donna leaves the room. I get up to close the door behind her, then reach under my mattress and pull out the notebook.

....

April 3, 1991

I feel like I'm 10 years older than I was when I got back to Donna's last night. The thoughts and the voices—everything about this godforsaken life I'm living—leaves me constantly exhausted. Now I think I might be crazy too. I don't know. Maybe

Ray was right—maybe I'm not safe. Maybe there's something wrong with me. I wonder if Rose ever feels like this.

....

Rose. The name flashes through my mind so quickly that I almost miss it. Suddenly, I want nothing more than to talk to Rose, but I have no idea where to even start. Now that we are grown, Rose's presence in my life comes in waves: when I desperately need a friend, when I am on a bender, when I go home. She always seems to pop up, but I have no real way to reach her.

This realization breaks my heart.

Quickly, I secure my hair to the back of my head with a clip before running down the stairs. Putting on my jacket, I slip the notebook into my pocket and grab my keys. I need a drink.

....

Going to the bar when you're sober is not nearly as fun as going when everything is already a blur. With my substance-free brain, I notice the layer of grime on the bottle of vodka as the clear liquid pours into a smudged glass. I mentally prepare for a room-temperature drink, having ordered it neat after seeing a fly in the ice bin. ***What I wouldn't give to be three shots deep.***

I debate asking the bartender to leave the bottle but decide against it. I feel like I need to keep my mind somewhat clear. I want to hear my thoughts and get them out onto paper. I want to know if Donna and Ray are right. Stealing a pen out of a cup on the bar, I pause to write down where I am in case I black out later.

....

April 3, 1991

Bar by Donna's—One drink—12:04 p.m.

....

I don't know the name of the bar, even though I have been here a few times. I didn't care to know before.

Pay attention.

"Excuse me?" I ask the bartender as he sets my drink down in front of me. "What's this place called again?"

"Sal's," he answers quickly, his back already turning. Clearly, I am not worth his time. Anger rises inside me.

"Fuck me, then. Sorry to bother you." I mutter the words so softly that they are almost nonexistent—a whisper into the drunken void. I make the correction.

....

April 3, 1991

~~Bar by Donna's~~ One drink—12:04 p.m.

Sal's

....

My first drink goes down easy—too easy. Telling myself that the alcohol will kill whatever germs are on the rim of the glass, I force myself to sip my second. ***I have to be careful, take things slow.***

JUST A LITTLE TO TAKE THE EDGE OFF.

I eye the characters around the bar. Not surprisingly, the sight is a little depressing. You don't find many good things happening in a dive bar before five o'clock on a weekday.

Two older men sit hunkered over their beers to my left—likely truckers. One wears a plaid shirt rolled up to his elbows and a backwards hat. I know he isn't dangerous, just broken. His drinking partner, however, is a different story. He is a few sizes larger, wearing overalls. A dark sort of shadow lingers near him, and I quickly direct my gaze elsewhere.

If this situation had happened two weeks ago—actually, two days ago—I would've swiped the attention of both the men at the bar and gotten myself at least three free drinks out of the deal before choosing to leave with the guy to my right, who is slightly younger, safer, and more attractive than my other options.

But I am not doing that right now—not while I sort through this mess. I am stubborn, even when fighting against myself, and I need to see this through.

Unfortunately, by the time I am done looking around the bar, my drink is gone. I was so busy observing others that I didn't realize how fast I was drinking. ***Shit. So much for taking it slow.*** I don't even remember finishing it. As I consider this, I feel something shift inside, like I am starting an argument with myself about whether or not to order a third—two dueling sides. ***I need to let them out.*** I hurriedly open my notebook.

....

I WOULD VERY MUCH LIKE ANOTHER DRINK RIGHT NOW, BUT TORI IS BEING AN UPTIGHT BITCH AND WON'T LET ME. SHE SAYS WE HAVE THINGS TO DO—LIKE A GOOD PARTY ISN'T SOMETHING TO DO. SHE'S RUINING MY FUN.

....

I pull back from where I had been feverishly writing. Reading the words, it feels as if I wasn't the one to put them on the page. I don't know where that outburst came from. It is like a different side of me, a different part of me, took over. Donna's words from the night before echo in my mind: **It's like your brain doesn't belong to just you.**

She is right, I realize, **I am not able to distinguish where the thoughts in my mind are coming from. I need a way to determine who is communicating.**

It needs a name, I think, **a name different from my own.**

BLAKE.

The suggestion comes clearly through the static in my head—a harsh, angry whisper.

....

Blake.

....

I write the name under the alcoholic rant in my notebook. **Okay, okay, okay. I'm okay.** I take a deep breath and stand up. Leaving cash on the bar, I go outside and pace around the parking lot until I feel like my brain belongs to only me again.

The Power of Memory

The pain was always there, somewhere.

Our minds are amazing—the way that they work to keep us functioning in the midst of this horror film called life. Like an intricate filing system, the human brain keeps an array of things sitting and collecting dust until the human being retrieves them: memories, events, skills, and facts—they're all there, ready when we are. Sometimes we get glimpses into the forgotten places of our brains. Maybe it's through a dream or a smell or a sensation. Maybe it's random, or maybe it's not.

However it happens, these glimpses change us—whether we admit it or not. Like a true Pandora's box, once a file has been opened, it's very difficult to close it, and once you remember something that was once forgotten, it's practically impossible to forget.

....

When I get back to Donna's after working at the store, she is in the garden. It is almost comical how much the scene looks like something out of a magazine: A straw hat adorns her thick, grayish-brown hair; purple gloves protect her delicate hands as she gathers weeds into a neat pile. Her knees rest on the perfectly dark dirt, and I imagine brown stains forming on her otherwise spotless jeans.

"Oh, Tori, won't you come here for a moment and help me?" She calls as she notices me walking to the house from where I parked in the street. It has been almost two weeks since she and Ray first drew attention to my fucked-upness and almost three days since Donna has initiated any sort of interaction with me. She has become very distant, but I don't blame her. If I had a crazy person living with me, I would probably steer clear too.

Ignoring the ache in my heels from a day of standing on the sales floor, I veer from my path. It is nearing dinner time, and I figure she is likely in a rush to finish. ***Helping pluck a few weeds is the least I can do for the woman letting me live in her home.***

The flowers have yet to blossom, but I feel as though I can picture what the garden looks like in summer based on Donna's descriptions. "An avalanche of color," she had said when discussing the garden during my first week at her house. Kneeling carelessly in the dirt, I begin pulling at weeds.

"Do you want a pair of gloves?" Donna asks. "I'm sure Ray has a spare in the garage."

"No, that's alright." I don't care about how my hands look, and I am sure we won't be more than five minutes longer.

"Alright, why don't you bring these to the trash can in the garage? Then, we can head in." Donna motions to the small mound of weeds between us.

I begin to gather the weeds together, pushing them into a pile between my hands. Then, I stop. I feel frozen as I notice, with horror, the dirt that is stuffed underneath my fingernails. The sensation of clumped, black mounds underneath my usually clean nails sends my heart racing, and time seems to warp around me.

....

My small, naked body twitches in small spurts of shivers as I lay on my back, spine pressed to the dirt floor. The smell of mildew hovers in the air. I take short breaths to avoid making too much noise. The darkness surrounding me is so all-consuming that I can no longer tell if my eyes are opened or closed. A familiar numbness wraps around me, sheltering me from the full impact of the situation.

I wonder where Rose is. I am about to muster up the courage to go look for her when I hear familiar footsteps approaching. A door opens, and a light blinds me. Digging my fingers into the surface beneath me, I feel dirt creep under my nails. As the pain increases, I clench the floor with all my might, willing myself not to scream.

Faith:

I hate the dirt. I hate it. It reminds me of the hurt. The hurt that comes from the men in the dark room with the dirt floor. I hate them so much. They hurt us so bad. I hate the dirt as much as I hate them, and when I see it under my fingernails in that lady's garden, I run inside. I need to wash them before the hate and hurt stick to me like the dirt.

The lady from the garden follows me inside. She asks if Tori is okay, but she doesn't know that I'm not Tori. I tell her we are not okay and continue to wash my hands until they are all clean. When I am done, I go to the living room to sit with the other children and watch the T.V.

Tori and the others never let me watch T.V. They're always too busy doing boring, grown-up things. I can hear Blake yelling from inside, but I am in charge of the body, and I want apple juice. I ask, and the lady gets me some. I sip it and try to ignore Blake.

Pretty soon, I feel Tori waking up. I know she is going to come back. She doesn't know it, but she is stronger than all of us. She can take over the body anytime. This makes me sad sometimes, because Tori never does what I want. I know she will go upstairs, away from the T.V. and the other children and the apple juice. I am sad, but I am not big enough to stay in control of the body for too long. I know this, because it's a rule made up by the others. They say that the youngest gets the least amount of time. They say Tori has to be an adult now.

I finish my apple juice quickly and hand the empty cup to the lady. I close my eyes and go back inside.

....

When I come to, I am sitting on Donna and Ray's couch, knees tucked to my chest, cartoon animals bobbing their heads in song on the television screen in front of me. Donna's two children sit on the side of the couch opposite me, their attention not on the singing mouse on the screen, but on the seemingly deranged woman sitting across from them. Donna sits in her rocking chair in the corner, also watching me. When she notices my apparent change in expression, she perks up.

"Tori?" She leans forward, studying me. "Tori, can you hear me? Are you alright? Tori?"

I look at her. Struggling to speak, I finally manage to say, "Yes, I'm fine. What happened?"

"You, um, I don't know. You were helping me in the garden, when, all of a sudden, you froze. It was like you became someone else entirely. It was as if you were a child."

I stare blankly at Donna. **She is lying—she has to be. None of this makes any sense.**

"I'm sorry," I say as I stand from my spot on the couch. "I think I need to rest."

Once I am alone, I take out my notebook and try to recount the events in the garden, but I don't get very far. **Donna said I was acting like a child, which makes absolutely zero sense.** I try to think back to the last time I did anything childlike. There are faint memories—nothing solid. A name suddenly comes to mind. I can't explain anything; all I can do is write the name in my notebook.

....

Faith.

....

Looking Deeper

What the hell happened to me?

Neurologists and psychoanalysts sometimes theorize that dreams represent repressed desires or wishes—a back-alley way for the human brain to experience things that the human being has always secretly wanted to happen in their waking reality. This seems like a solid idea—until one comes upon the issue of nightmares. Nightmares, especially chronic ones, can raise some challenging questions.

Have you ever experienced a nightmare so severe that it still haunts your mind years later? One that seems so real that you wake up in fight or flight mode, convinced your life is in danger? Ask yourself, how do you explain that nightmare? Rationalize it? Fit it into your life? You run into the same problem many do: It's nearly impossible.

Now, what if your worst nightmare is not just a nightmare, but it actually intertwines with reality. What then? What do you do?

....

It is cold—the kind of cold that soaks into your pores, causing your muscles to ache and your insides to violently cringe. Wind rustles through leaves around me, and my ears perk with every crunch and crack. I sense that

I am not alone. The faint smell of perfume mingling with sweat and blood tells me that I am surrounded by enemies.

Desperate to see, I cautiously bring my hands to my face. I try to rub my eyes, clear whatever is blocking my vision, but instead of feeling the smooth, thin skin of my eyelids, I touch something thick and coarse. A small gasp springs from my mouth. I become more and more frantic. I touch my cheeks and am relieved to find them in their normal state. Just as I work up the courage to reach for my eyelids again, a familiar voice echoes in the distance, causing me to freeze.

"Let's begin," she says.

....

I wake up to blows of panic striking my nervous system. I can't move, can't breathe. My chest is tight. Tearless sobs escape my body in spasms. I reach toward my eyes. Feeling that nothing is covering them, my breathing gradually returns to normal as the familiar wallpaper of Donna's guest bedroom comes into my vision.

Dr. Crane's words reverberate in my mind: **unresolved trauma, unresolved trauma, unresolved trauma.** The fatigue of the previous day is replaced with severe anxiety as I reach for my notebook.

....

April 18, 1991

Nightmare

I dreamt I was somewhere cold. The woods,

maybe? Something was covering my eyes, and I

could smell the scents of the horrible people

around me. I couldn't see them, but I knew they

were enemies. Mrs. Archer's voice?

....

Unresolved trauma, unresolved trauma, unresolved trauma.

Pay attention.

I have always had nightmares, but lately, they are becoming more and more intense—more and more detailed. ***Is it real?***

A small voice that I am not used to hearing whispers, *I'M SCARED*, and I know it is Faith.

I do not know how I've made this distinction; I have never been able to discern Faith's voice before. As I realize this, I feel relief but also sadness.

Looking at the clock, I note that I still have countless hours before dawn.

The night drags on. I lay restless in bed for hours before going out to smoke in my car. To my surprise, I soon hear Donna's voice over the sound of my radio.

136

Thinking she has come outside to speak with me, I quickly put out the cigarette and turn down the music. Then, I realize she isn't talking to me. She is standing just outside the front door talking on her new cordless phone. "The latest technology," I heard her tell Ray last week when she came home beaming with pride over the box in her hand.

"I think she's starting to remember more," I hear Donna say now. "I'm not sure what exactly, but she had a very strange sort of, um, episode this evening in the garden. No, she didn't say anything about it. Please, don't come back. I swear, I'm telling you everything I know. Okay." A pause. "Okay."

I strain to hear more, but all I can make out is the sound of the front door closing as Donna goes back in the house. A million panic-stricken reactions begin to flip through my mind, but I discard them all with one thought: ***Don't make something out of nothing; you're being crazy.***

Once I have smoked a couple more cigarettes, my body is slightly relaxed but still wanting more. Instead of going to the bar or smoking the rest of my pack, I decide to take a bath. I permanently ache ever since being hit by the car, and I hope a bath will calm both my mind and body.

The porcelain is cool against my bare skin as hot water splashes over my toes. Gradually, the warmth makes its way across my legs. I close my eyes and sink deeper into the water, letting my arms float at my sides.

....

I feel the eyes of Mrs. Archer on me as I pull my shorts down, taking off my socks, but leaving on my t-shirt. I take Rose's hand in mine. Despite the heat of the night, I feel her trembling—I do not know if it is from fear of the water or fear of Mrs. Archer.

This is a spontaneous stop on our drive back from a weekend church retreat. Rose and I had ridden with Mrs. Archer while the rest of my family piled into the station wagon. Stopping at the lake located just outside our hometown for a night swim had been her idea. "It'll be soothing," she had said with a smile, pulling into the parking lot in front of the lake. Now we stand on the shore—half naked and wanting nothing more than to be home in our bed. It is an all too familiar feeling.

"We'll go together," I whisper to Rose, and we begin making our way toward the edge of the water.

"Are you really going to wear your shirt in there?" Mrs. Archer calls from where she's undressing behind us. "Could get ruined, you know."

I feel myself freeze, along with Rose.

"Let's just keep going. She'll drop it," I hear Rose say.

We enter the lake warily. Water creeps up our exposed skin. It swallows my legs, then my stomach. My t-shirt floats up around me. Little by little, I watch myself disappear into the darkness.

Before long, we are at a good place—far enough out so that we can swim without scraping our legs on the bottom but shallow enough that we can stand if we need to. Rose and I let go of one another, but we stay close, treading the water in silence.

We watch, stone-faced, as Mrs. Archer undresses completely—her bare breasts glinting in the moonlight. She submerges herself into the water without a second thought. Before long, she is singing a church medley softly as she swims in circles around us.

"You have to relax! Here, watch me." She flips effortlessly onto her back, floating like a feather on the surface. Rose mimics Mrs. Archer, as if showing me what I need to do.

"Tori, dear, float. Relax." Mrs. Archer swims to me as she speaks, her body hardly making a ripple as she stealthily moves beneath the mirror-like surface. Once she gets close enough, she places one arm gently on the center of my upper back.

"Trust me."

I sigh and give in, leaning my head back into the cool water while Mrs. Archer's arm supports me. I puff my

stomach and let my arms go limp at my sides. I close my
eyes, blocking out the moonlight and thoughts of monsters
in the water. I feel Mrs. Archer's arm, still on my back, as
she spins me gently in a circle. It is as if I am sleeping
while awake, my senses lost completely.

The sound of waves splashing against the rocks
near shore brings me out of the trance. Mrs. Archer's spell
over me is broken. I push my legs down beneath the
surface and swing them sharply to the side, rotating off of
my back and away from her as fast as possible.

"I'm cold."

Without another word, I swim quickly toward the
shore. My breathing shortens as I make my way through
the water. My stomach begins to ache but not from the
exercise. My body is drowning in fear. I have betrayed
myself—let my guard down in the presence of an enemy—
and now I need to run. Run far away from the water, the
dark, and Mrs. Archer.

Rose doesn't ask any questions, just swims silently
by my side. I can tell that she is in the same survival mode
as me. She is grateful for the chance to escape.

We dress in a hurry once we are back on the shore,
throwing sweatshirts and jean shorts over our soaking-wet
body. The fabric clings to me, and I want to scream. Once
dressed, we look back at where Mrs. Archer still swims.
She hasn't moved. She just treads water, watching.

Looking down, I place my arms across my body, hoping they will bring me some comfort. Wondering how much longer we will have to freeze on the beach, I glance back at Mrs. Archer just in time to see her smile.

....

My body shoots upwards. Taking a bath does not seem appealing anymore. Shutting the water off, I pull the plug from the drain. The gurgling of the water being swallowed by the pipes collides with the pounding of my heart, and for a minute I wish I could go down the drain too.

Can't escape. Can't breathe.
Blackness.

....

Ivy:

My hands are steady as I reach for the razor that rests on the edge of the tub. With practiced precision, I ignore the complaints of the others and carve a surface-level, horizontal mark on the body's forearm.

"I know what I'm doing," I tell them as the pressure drains from our mind, and peace begins to enter.

I used to provide this kind of escape quite frequently for Tori when the body was high school age, my age. But then, the accident happened: The blade went a little too deep. I scared myself, as well as the others. So, I went back inside and didn't come out again. Tori was growing up; the drugs were getting better at taking away the pain. There wasn't a need for me anymore—until now.

God, I missed being out. I missed feeling sensations against our skin, the freedom of being able to choose what we do. We used to have so much more fun: going to parties and school dances, hanging out with friends, kissing all the boys. Now all we do is go to work, the dumb bars that Blake likes, and this lady's house— whoever the hell she is. Darla? Debbie? I can never remember.

I know that I won't be out for long. Tori usually only keeps me around until the panic is gone. So, I make the most of it. After the cutting does its job, I get out of the tub, clean up, wrap a towel around me, and run into Tori's room. There are not a lot of clothes to choose from, but I do my best to pick out something cute—not that loose-fitting shit she always wears. Once dressed, I lie down and daydream about our high school crush, Ryan. Hopefully, he's doing well.

Before long, I start to get the feeling that Tori is ready to come back. I close my eyes and get ready to go away. I am sure Tori will feel much better.

....

Lying on my side, I scan my brain for any remnants of the past hour. I know I haven't been out of consciousness for long, but I came to with a thin line of dried blood extending across my wrist and no memory of how the wound got there. I haven't cut myself in a while, but this new mark is perfectly in line with the old scars. I feel an odd sense of calm, even though the last thing I remember is being anxious as hell in the tub.

My clothes are tight against my skin, suffocating me. I look down at myself to see I am wearing a bright-colored tank top and the only somewhat tight pair of jeans I own. Annoyed, I strip and change into baggier clothing, wondering what the hell I have done now and why I seem to be less stable than I was with the drugs. **Doesn't getting sober mean getting better?**

LOOK AT US. WE CAN HARDLY FUNCTION. MAYBE WE ARE BETTER OFF DEAD.

STOP BEING SO SAD.

Suicide is a sin.

Writing down the thoughts seems impossible, so instead I just wait for them to tire themselves. After what feels like hours, my brain finally grows as weary as the rest of my body, and I drift into sleep.

Bookworm

They were more than just bad dreams.

Do you remember the first time you felt validated?
The first time something crazy you did had a rational
explanation? The first time your personality, your flaws,
your fears had a story behind them? Maybe not. Maybe
you've never done anything crazy. Maybe you've never felt
out of control, as if your thoughts had turned against you.
Maybe you've never lived with a pit in your stomach and a
hole in your heart. But if you have, validation is an
indescribable feeling.

....

"I'm Tori. It's been just over two months since I last
used," I say the familiar words while looking around the
circle of strangers: some young, some old, some clean-
shaven and well-dressed, some in oversized jackets and
jeans with holes in the knees.

Once a few beats pass, and the group figures out
that my sobriety timeline is all I will be sharing, the next
person begins to speak: "I'm Al. Been clean for about a
year."

I clap lightly with the rest of the group.

"It's been a while since I've been to a meeting,
but . . . well . . . my daughter died a couple of weeks ago."

The room seems to grow smaller—the weight of Al's genuine grief squashing everything.

"Oh, Al. I'm so sorry for your loss," one woman says gently as she leans forward in her chair. "What was her name?"

"Dani."

"How did it happen?" A new voice pipes up, everyone turning to its owner with looks of shock and horror.

Who would blatantly ask such a horrible question? I think. Looking up, I realize the panic-stricken stares are all directed at me. ***Shit.***

"Sorry," I mutter sheepishly as I look apologetically at Al. ***What part of me thought that was an okay question to ask***? I am horrified. Al, however, seems unphased by the question.

"It's alright. It was a car accident," he says. "Just one of those freak things."

"I'm sorry," I say again. This is the first time since treatment that I've said something and really, truly meant it. Out-of-control loss is a familiar feeling to me. ***I have been losing parts of myself all of my life.***

Something very close to relief passes over Al's face as the feeling of care wraps its arms around him. "Thank you all for allowing me to share. My wife hasn't left her bedroom since it happened, and this is the first time I've

said the words aloud: My daughter is dead. I want drugs."
He laughs slightly, and a few people in the group smile.

....

Fresh air battles with the toxins of my cigarettes as I stride quickly down the street. That was my second NA meeting this week, and my heart is exhausted. The support I gain from the meetings is uplifting, but the grief weighing on everyone there is hard to shake off. Walking a few blocks before returning to my car always helps lessen the load of sadness.

Lost in thought, I don't realize how far I have gone until I find myself in a parking lot at the end of the road. In front of me are the words "Woodland Community Library." I suddenly want to go in, but as I get closer to the building, the voices start up.

THIS IS A FUCKING STUPID IDEA.

We used to like to read. Maybe it'll be good.

YEAH, BEFORE WE FIGURED OUT HOW TO HAVE FUN.

Books have answers, and we need answers.

"For the love of God, be quiet," I tell myself definitively as I open the heavy, wooden door, revealing polished floors and high shelves. The smell of books hits me instantly, and I am transported back to the only place I truly felt safe as a child: Mrs. Caltri's reading loft.

I use one hand to hold my book and the other to grip the small ladder as I make my way into the loft space near Mrs. Caltri's desk. She told the class at the beginning of the year that her husband built it for her after she realized that some little boys and girls needed an extra special quiet place to read. But I always like to imagine that I am the only one who knows about it, the only one allowed in. It reminds me of a secret hideout.

During silent reading time, Mrs. Caltri always lets me go into the loft. Sometimes I use the 30 minutes to read, but most of the time, I just sleep. It is the only time I don't feel the need to keep my eyes open, alert—watching for monsters.

After reaching the top of the ladder, I hoist my small body onto the platform and crawl to my favorite corner. My eyes grow heavy as I settle in, pulling a wool blanket off a shelf and up to my chin. Bright yellow pillows surround me, reminding me of sunshine, while the smell of wood from the loft blocks out the other classroom smells. Soon I am drifting.

"Tori, the nurse would like to see you," Mrs. Caltri says softly, nudging me awake after what feels like only a few minutes. She leads me to the nurse's office. It is my second visit there this week.

My footsteps are the only sound as I approach the main desk near the front door of the library. Behind the desk perches a small, older woman. Blue glasses rest atop her head, and several half-empty cups of tea circle her workspace. The crow's feet at the edges of her eyes crinkle when she notices me approaching. Something tells me this woman has more stories than all the books in the building combined.

"Can I help you?"

"No, I'm okay," I respond with false certainty. Then, a little less confidently, "I'm not sure what I'm looking for yet, exactly."

"Oh, well, I'll be right here if you have questions," the librarian says kindly as she pulls the glasses down to rest on the bridge of her nose and begins sorting through papers on the desk.

"Thank you," I say, even though she is no longer looking at me. Pivoting toward a section over which a large "nonfiction" sign hangs, I amble my way through row after row of books. I scan as many titles as I can manage without completely stopping in my tracks. None of them catch my attention, until I get to the psychology section. There, I find, "Harbored Memories" by Dr. Alexander Dun.

I pull the book from the shelf, bringing a small cluster of dust with it. Opening to the introductory chapter, I begin to read: *What is the meaning behind our dreams? Is* *it possible that dreams offer us glimpses into past memories and experiences hidden from the conscious brain? In this book, Dr. Alexander Dun, renowned psychologist and dream analyst, attempts to answer these questions and more by delving—*I stop reading as the atmosphere around me suddenly shifts. Dread—in the snap of a finger, that is all I feel. A dense cloud descends on what was a light space just a few seconds before. I feel surrounded by it, watched by it, threatened by it. Closing the book, I quickly tuck it under my arm and move briskly to the front desk. ***I need to get out of here.***

While the librarian opens a library card for me and marks down my selected book for checkout, I focus on the space behind her. Nothing is there, but I feel darkness looming, almost as if I am being watched. Trying to discard it as nothing more than paranoia, I turn to go, still unable to shake the feeling that something is very wrong.

....

I devour the book, swallow it whole. It strikes a chord—suggesting that dreams can be lost, oftentimes traumatic, memories. The author tells stories of patients who remembered trauma in the form of dreams.

My nightmares are not made up. I know it. Some of them might be—that is always a possibility—but most of them are true. Horrific things have happened in my real life. A bouquet of feelings blossoms inside me, ranging from validation to denial to terror. I write everything in my journal: every fact that rings true to me, every idea that seems like it might be right. Emotion begins to take its toll. I feel my brain slowly shutting down.

SCREW THIS. WE NEED TO HAVE SOME FUN.

I stop writing mid-sentence.

ENOUGH WITH THIS SHIT.

I know Blake is the one talking. I don't try to argue with her or tell her to shut up or to go away. Instead, I let her do what she does best. The last thing I remember is closing my notebook.

....

Blake:

I am not in the mood for company, so I take the body to the bar, drink alone, and marinate in my thoughts. Everyone is out of sorts; we can feel that something isn't right. Tori is starting to remember too much.

Tori—that girl doesn't know the things I've done to keep her safe, to keep her alive. I am the only one with those memories—the only one strong enough to take it, to change dread into desire, fear into control. I kept the nasty men happy. I used the body the way it needed to be used. I saved us.

....

When I get back to Donna's the next morning, my head throbbing unbearably, I find a scribbled note on my bed. It is Donna's handwriting, telling me that my boss had called, because I am an hour late for work, and she is concerned. **Shit.** I immediately run down the stairs, almost dropping my keys as I pull my well-worn boots over my feet.

Donna is sitting at the dining room table, eyebrows raised. I know she is contemplating whether it is more productive to lecture me about responsibility or to let me go. She settles for a sigh of disapproval, which I ignore as I bound out the door.

Mother's Day

Someone was missing from my soul.

What does it mean to be a mother? Does anyone know?

Maybe it means raising a child from birth until age 18 and being present for every moment, or maybe it means being present at the right moment and speaking up for someone who is never heard. Maybe it's genetics, or maybe it's not. Maybe being a mother means sacrificing everything so that another person can be happy, or maybe it means knowing when to step away. Maybe motherhood is one of those unanswerable mysteries of life. Maybe it cannot be defined.

....

"Sorry I'm late!" I chirp in as cheerful of a voice as I can muster while walking into work 15 minutes later.

"It's alright," my boss, Susan, responds. "It's been pretty slow so far. I'm just glad that you're okay."

"What can I do?"

"Why don't you go help Mandy. A new shipment just arrived, and she's sorting it out."

"Sounds good," I say, heading toward the back. I am grateful to not be assigned to the sales floor immediately.

However, my relief switches to concern when I realize that the boxes of clothing are all untouched. No Mandy in sight. A clipboard and pen sit on a nearby folding table, and I can smell the faint scent of the perfume Mandy always wears. *Where is she?*

"Mandy?" I raise my voice to a level just below a yell, not wanting anyone on the sales floor to hear. "Mandy, are you here?"

As I make my way across the room, the sound of a light sniffling echoes from the employee bathroom connected to the space. Creeping up to the door, I listen. Someone is definitely in there, and they are definitely crying. I am just about to head in the opposite direction out of respect when something stops me. *I need to check if whoever is in there, likely Mandy, is okay.* Lightly, I rap my knuckle on the door.

"Hello? Mandy, are you in there?"

Nothing. I try again.

"Mandy, it's Tori. Are you okay?"

I hear the switch of a lock being disengaged. The door opens slowly to reveal a very fractured-looking Mandy on the other side. Tears run down her splotchy cheeks in thin streams. Large chunks of her hair have escaped from what I assume was once a neat braid running along her back. She is shaking from the effort of holding in another sob.

"What's going on?" Concern fills me as I look at the broken woman in front of me. Her face is blank as she stares at me without offering any sort of response. "Mandy? Is it the baby?"

Mandy is extremely pregnant and due at any moment. Her hands fall instinctively to her stomach as she nods in response to my question. My heart flutters with dread.

"Is the baby okay?"

Mandy nods yes again.

"Okay." I consider the possible scenarios I could have just stumbled into. It seems like she wants to tell me what is wrong, she just can't bring herself to say it. Then, it hits me. "Do you not want it?" As soon as the words leave my mouth, I know I've hit the nail on the head. "Oh," I pause with realization. "You don't want it."

She doesn't want her baby. An unexpected ache hits me. I unconsciously put my own hands to my stomach, feeling suddenly hollow.

"I can't do it, Tori." Mandy's frail voice forces out words that I'm sure she has tried to avoid saying for a long time. "I do want it. Believe me, I do. But there's hardly enough money as it is . . . and . . . and my dad . . . well, Dad . . . he . . . you know . . . and Mom . . . " Despair chokes Mandy as she speaks, cutting off her words.

I instinctively reach for her hand, taking it in mine. I see someone in desperate need of a friend, in desperate need of help. I think of Rose when I say my next words: "It's okay. We'll figure it out."

Relief replaces the sorrow in Mandy's expression as she leans her weight against me.

Oh, boy.

....

When walking through the parking lot after our shift, Mandy tries her best to fake that she is okay.

"You'll pick me up tomorrow morning?" I can sense her anticipation when she asks the question. She is waiting for me to change my mind, to say, "Never mind. I'm not helping you. I have my own problems." I want to ask her why she seems so alone; I want to know her story, her baby's story.

Of course, I don't ask. Instead, I simply say, "Yeah, does eight work? We should probably get there when they open, in case there's a wait."

Mandy agrees, and I unlock my car doors—rock music greeting me as I turn the engine over.

Proof that God exists is found in the fact that this car still runs.

SHUT UP. GOD DOESN'T EXIST, AND YOU KNOW IT.

Giving a final wave to Mandy, I close my door and watch as she heads to the bus stop. *I should give her a ride home.*

DON'T. YOU. DARE.

She needs help.

We need help.

"Hey!" I yell out my window to Mandy, rolling up to where she stands waiting for the bus. "Do you want a ride?"

She hesitates at first but accepts after checking the time on her watch.

"Thanks," she says. "The next bus doesn't come for another half hour. I hate waiting alone."

"I get that," I respond honestly. "We—I mean, I—don't like to be alone either."

Embarrassed by my words, I turn the music up a notch. Thankfully, the only other things Mandy says to me are directions to her apartment.

About 15 minutes later, my car and I idle on the street while Mandy shuffles along the cracked pathway to her door. I can see garbage strewn about in front of the apartment building. A spray-painted, plastic picnic table offers a seat to some smokers and old, dirty children's toys litter the only patch of grass. I want to yell out to her again, to offer up Donna's couch for the night, but something tells me not to push my luck with Donna right now. Plus, I don't entirely trust her after my accidental eavesdropping the other night. **Maybe Mandy is safer in this dumpster pile than we are living with Donna.**

I wait until Mandy is safely inside, then drive slowly back to Donna's—all the while grappling with the same question I have battled throughout my life: **How will we survive until tomorrow?**

....

"Tori, I can't do it again." Rose's eyes are glassy with budding tears.

We sit side by side on the floor, nestled between a wall and a bed. The bed offers a blockade between our small bodies and the monsters we know are outside the room. Aware of every sound, I wait for the familiar creak of the door opening, the monsters coming to steal us. I count the dents in the unpainted drywall and summon any strength I may have.

"Yes, you can. We both can, and we will. We have to, Rose. We have to."

I look at Rose, a single tear now running down her cheek. I wipe it away, and she meets my eyes with her own.

"Maybe," she stutters, holding back a sob in her throat, "maybe they won't come back tonight." She says the words with a forced octave of hope, but we both know there's a slim chance of her being right.

"Maybe," I say as I begin to calculate our odds of surviving until sunrise.

If we play it right, we should be okay. They should let us live. We just have to do everything exactly the way they like it: be good girls, do our part, and stay quiet. But Rose is too scared, and I know it. I feel her body tremble next to mine, and I know that she won't be able to do it right tonight. Maybe if I do everything extra well, make up for Rose, I can make sure we both survive—make sure we all survive.

My mother's face comes to mind as I think of my family and the threats against them. I recall the words said to me by one of the monsters: "If you tell, everyone you love dies. If you tell, you die. Nobody will ever find you. You will never see your family again. Besides, nobody will ever believe you. We have all the power. You are nothing."

I have to perform perfectly tonight. It's the only way—the only way we will survive until the morning.

Just as the plan finishes forming in my mind, I hear the sound of the bedroom door opening, and a rectangle of light grows across the wall, obscuring the dents. I will myself to stop shaking.

We have to be strong.

....

When I return to Mandy's the next morning, she is pacing outside of her building. My car barely comes to a stop before she opens the passenger door.

"Do you think a family will still take the baby if it's sick?" she asks as she carefully lowers herself into the passenger seat.

"What do you mean?"

"Like if it has a deformity or a disability or whatever. Will they still take it?" Mandy's voice is small and panicked. For a second, I almost expect to look over and see a young version of Rose. I want to reassure her, to protect her and her child. I am about to offer to help her care for the baby, but something stops me.

"Um, I guess I don't know," I say instead. My voice grows slightly shaky. "Probably? But your baby will be healthy, Mandy."

"Will it? What if it's not? What if I can't find it a good home? Oh God, what will happen if I can't find it a good home? I'm terrified, Tori."

Mandy becomes silent for a moment and begins to fiddle with the torn edges of her coat. When she starts again, she speaks much slower, her voice wavering. "All I want is for this baby to be healthy and to have a safe, happy home. To have a better life than I do, ya know?"

The sense of emptiness I initially felt when hearing about Mandy's plight sneaks back into my body. Even though I am no longer small, the monsters of this world still seem bigger than me. Anger swells in my heart. *I am so fucking sick of feeling powerless.*

Careful not to let Mandy sense my angst, I reply gently, "It'll be fine. The baby will be healthy, and we will find him or her a good home." Looking at the bump in Mandy's midsection, I end the conversation with a resounding, "I promise."

....

The adoption agency is clean and bright, with light blue wallpaper. Encouraging testimonials and pictures of beaming children with newfound parents adorn the walls. Mandy and I cautiously make our way to a crescent-shaped desk positioned opposite the door.

"Hello." A middle-aged woman looks over the desk at Mandy and me. "How may I help you?"

Mandy is silent. Her face pale, she searches the pictures on the wall—looking for a snapshot of her own child's future. I take the reins.

"Hi. We'd like to speak to someone about an adoption."

"Okay." The woman glances at Mandy and her bulging stomach. "Have a seat over there, and someone will be with you shortly."

"Thank you." I take a dazed Mandy by the arm and lead her to the nearest chair.

Mandy continues to look at the pictures while we wait, and I pretend to flip through a year-old issue of a home decor magazine. My thoughts jump back and forth. ***She's giving up her baby. That vase is hideous. It's what's best. That bed looks so comfortable. But what if the baby ends up in a bad home? If I ever have a house, I'm going to paint my room that color.***

Finally, after what feels like hours, a woman in a dress that matches the brightness of the room comes toward us.

"Hello," she says, casually sitting in an empty chair near Mandy. "My name is Lucy. I'm one of the social workers here. Would you like to go somewhere to speak in private?"

Mandy nods and grabs my hand as she stands. I follow, setting the magazine down on my now empty chair.

Lucy leads us through a wide hallway to a room I assume is her office. It is decorated much the same as the waiting area, except the walls are sage green, and a large picture window allows us a view. We hesitantly sit in two chairs opposite a desk, where Lucy takes her place as she begins to speak.

"So, let's start by having you tell me what brings you two here today."

Mandy looks to me for some sort of signal of what to do next. But I have no idea how an adoption happens, or if it will even work; I don't know where to start. Plus, this is something I cannot do for her. It needs to be completely her choice. All I can do is hold her hand and offer support.

"I'm here because . . . because I am pregnant," Mandy says, turning from me to Lucy. I squeeze her hand. "I'm pregnant, and I can't keep the baby with me after it's born. I want it to have a good life. Can you help me with that?" She swallows a sob.

"It's okay," Lucy responds. "Yes, we can. I just have a few questions."

....

A week later, I am driving a sweaty and pained Mandy to the hospital. The labor is quick and easy, as far as childbirth goes. We sigh with relief when they give a clean bill of health for both mother and child. In the immediate moments following the birth, Mandy holds her baby girl for the first and last time.

"I love you, little one," she tearfully whispers. "I want you to go be happy now, okay? You just forget all about me and this life of mine, and you'll be just fine."

I put my arm around Mandy and hoist myself onto the hospital bed with her.

Another one lost.

WE CAN'T DO THIS.

I want to melt into a puddle of hysterics, but force myself to remain solid, composed. Mandy rests her head on my shoulder. After a moment, I gently say, "I'm going to go call Lucy now, okay?"

She shuts her eyes as tightly as they will go, squeezing the tears and pain out of her body. She replies hoarsely, "Okay."

Over the next couple of days, Mandy is discharged, and the baby is put into the care of the state while the adoption is finalized. Mandy refuses a copy of the birth certificate or any evidence pointing to her child. I, however, keep the little one's hospital onesie tucked in the pocket of my leather jacket.

After leaving the hospital, we stop at a gas station for donuts and cigarettes. Frosting coats our lips, mixing with the nicotine. Eventually, I drive Mandy home, complete and utter exhaustion slamming into me. I long for my family. I wonder how Mandy will cope. The thought of never knowing one's child makes me ache with a sort of pain that resonates throughout my entire body. This hurt is not a stranger to me. It is like remembering an unbearably painful dream.

....

"Rose, shut up, okay? You have to be quiet. You have to stop crying."

"I can't, Tori. I can't. They're going to kill us. We have to run."

"No, we can't run. Shhh. It'll be okay, okay? Just hold my hand and breathe, okay? I'm right here. I'm right here. Just remember that I'm always close, and no matter what, don't take your blindfold off."

Strong, uncaring hands grab my arms, pulling me away from Rose. I hear her gasp as my hand leaves hers. My shin hits something hard, and my bare feet scrape against the ground as I'm led away.

Goodbye

I lost almost everything and everyone I loved.

Something happens to a person when they experience continual loss: loss of trust, loss of innocence, loss of loved ones. They are forced to adjust to an altered reality.

One fragment at a time, they fade away. They may wonder how much longer it will take until they are gone entirely. But by that point, they don't mind disappearing. You see, when you are forced to say goodbye to the things you hold most dear, sometimes surviving the loss seems like a worse option than dying.

....

I check into the nearest motel after calming down enough to drive away from Mandy's. I can't bring myself to go back to the house—not even to pack a bag. I don't have the strength to face Donna and her questions.

The motel room is old and disgusting, but it becomes a depressing sort of haven. I don't leave, except to buy cigarettes from the front desk. During my first two days there, I pace the room manically. On the third day, I lie on the bed smoking and trying not to think about the possibility of bed bugs.

It has been at least 48 hours since I last attempted to sleep. Delusion plagues me. Putting out my cigarette in the ashtray next to the bed, I allow my heavy eyelids to gradually close—a part of me hoping to just not wake up.

"Tori?" The familiar voice causes me to temporarily abandon my wishes of death.

Rose perches on the edge of my bed, concern swimming through her face.

"Rose? How did you get here?"

"That's not important," she responds. "What's important is you."

"Me? Rose, I'm not important."

"You are, Tori. To me, you are. You're my best friend."

"You have poor taste in friends," I joke. Rose doesn't laugh.

"I'm serious, Tori." Emotion floods her voice. "You are the strongest person I know. You kept us safe, kept us alive, when we were little. You took care of me, and now you need to take care of yourself. You will not die in this motel room. We deserve better than that."

I don't agree. I think that a nasty motel room is the most fitting end to my tragedy, but Rose's apparent sadness makes me feel the need to fix the situation.

"Okay, okay. I'll get up."

"You promise?"

"I promise."

Rose bends to hug me. A jolt of energy shoots through me. I sit up and look around the room. There is no sign of Rose. Regardless, I keep my promise and muster the strength to go to the diner next door for some shitty food.

Sitting in a scratched, wooden booth, picking at too-fluffy pancakes, I wonder what it will take for Rose and I to be happy—wonder if it is even possible.

OF COURSE IT'S NOT POSSIBLE. HAVE YOU SEEN YOURSELF LATELY? LOCKED IN A MOTEL ROOM FOR DAYS? PATHETIC. MAYBE WE SHOULD JUST BE DONE, CALL IT QUITS, STEP AWAY WHILE WE CAN.

No, we can't. What about Mom and Dad and Rose?

I look across the orange table and imagine I am eating with Rose. She would likely be staring into a full cup of coffee, waiting for the steam to cease. **She never drinks anything too hot, even if it is below zero outside.** Thinking of this, I smile slightly and push my plate of pancakes to Rose's half of the table, like she will eat them for me.

The question of **what if** bounces around in my mind yet again: **What if Rose and I had just held onto that train for a little while longer? Would we have had a** *better life? What if this is all there is? What if we will never be okay?*

The what-ifs are too much. I need to get some fresh air and think about something else. Placing some cash under my plate, I exit the diner and begin the short trek back to the motel.

Loneliness encompasses me. The air is chilly for mid-spring. To warm my hands, I thrust them into my jacket pockets, where I am surprised by the feeling of soft material against my fingers. After a moment, it registers: the baby's onesie.

Hope loosens loneliness' grip. *Mandy, Rose, and I may never be okay, but that baby might be. She might just have a chance.* The curtain of guilt that had been covering me since I undertook Mandy's crisis lifts slightly as I try to imagine a bright future for the baby. *Maybe she will grow up to be a veterinarian or an author. Maybe she will help others. She might even become a mom herself one day.*

Following this line of thought, I can't help but stumble back into my world, remembering with a stab of sadness all of the things Rose had dreamt for our future. Once upon a time, she had genuinely believed we could have happiness—a good and healthy life.

The raw feeling of loss hits me once again. The onesie still between my fingers, I clutch the only memory of a child I will never know. I swear to God, if I had any tears to spare, I would sink to my knees and cry them out right here on the sidewalk.

....

The circle of swaying bodies seems to get closer and closer. I'm losing my air. **Oh God, they are going to kill me this time.**

Chanting, humming. Their tall bodies overcome mine. They claw at my skin, gripping my frail frame. I can't breathe.

My mind blurs, and I know it will be difficult to focus in class tomorrow. I'm supposed to write every letter of the alphabet in cursive. I think of the excuses I will give my mother as I avoid her questions the next day. I wonder how long it will take before this ends. As the silent tears crawl out of my eyes, I feel something cool against my cheek. Smooth. Glass.

They are holding a small vile up to my face, catching the tears as they fall. One by one, I feel them trickle from my face into the vile. I count them and give them names. I wish for them to be safer than me.

Once the vile is nearly full, the grabbing and pulling stops. The dark figure rotates slowly, showing my tears to everyone. I feel exposed. They are all seeing my weakness; they are holding my sadness; they have taken something precious from me.

Finally, the figure turns to me. In a muffled voice, he tells me that tears like these are tainted with sin. Then, with one swift movement, he swings the vile into the air and onto the hardened dirt.

The vile shatters, and so do I.

Invincible

Nothing could touch me, not even pain.

There are many different types of children. Some are daredevils. Others are tomboys. There are athletes and social butterflies; there are pranksters and smart-mouths. And then there are children like Tori: painfully shy and always hiding. For those children, attending school every day is a frightening experience, and Tori was already feeling terror consume her by the time she started kindergarten.

Tori spent her early school years riding the bus in silence. She watched her older sisters laugh with their friends as she slumped in her seat and straightened the dress on her doll, counting the minutes until she would be back on the bus riding home.

It was in third grade when Tori decided she was no longer going to cry. Nobody would have the satisfaction of her tears. She was no longer going to be shy. No one could silence her rage. She became outspoken and brash—violent. Her classmates were not allowed to even look at her wrong, or they would pay.

Throughout this time, Rose remained quietly by Tori's side as she acted out their pain. Rose was never afraid of Tori. In fact, she felt safest when she and Tori walked together through the schoolyard—Tori's gaze warning away most of their peers.

Tori soaked it in, absorbing all her newfound power and spitting it back out at those around her. At school, she began to feel untouchable. She still hated the lessons and the work, but whenever she felt the urge to look at the ground and hide, she would instead stand up taller and stare into her enemies' eyes.

Tori carried this attitude with her into her teens and then into adulthood—replacing sadness with what she deemed as strength. As she grew, so did her survival toolkit. Little by little, she learned to mask the unimaginable.

....

"Get out of my face," I snap at the man attempting to flirt with me. Moving sideways around him, I use my pack of beer as a shield between us.

"Crazy bitch," I hear him whisper at my back.

Coward.

Who tries to pick someone up at the liquor store?

HE WASN'T THAT BAD; WE'VE DONE WORSE.

Ew.

The clattering of metal cans overpowers the discussion in my head as I hoist my beer onto the counter.

I had immediately headed for the liquor store after checking out of my motel room.

"$5.58," the clerk utters monotonously.

I hand over a crumpled five-dollar bill and swing my goods into the crook of my arm. Walking out the door, I give a sarcastic wave to the man who had hit on me.

I am still in the parking lot when I open the pack of beer. Once one can is empty, I peel out of the lot and head for the highway. The sadness moves from the center of my heart to the outer edge.

The speedometer climbs fast, billboards blurring past. The crack of another beer opening is drowned out by guitar notes blasting from my radio. The music waves dance around me.

It isn't long before the sound of sirens blares over the sound of my radio, and I look in the rearview mirror to see a police officer riding my bumper.

"Shit."

....

Jade:

The moment I hear sirens, I know it is my time to shine. We clearly can't afford a trip to the local jail, so I do what I do best: problem-solve.

Coming into control, I beam with delight. It feels so good to be productive after days of sulking in that filthy motel room. Checking the rearview mirror, I quickly size up the situation: It is bad, but nothing I can't fix. With all the troublemakers that share this body, we've done much worse.

The officer is going to get to the car in about 30 seconds. Instinctively, I hide the beer cans under a sweatshirt on the passenger seat and run my fingers through the body's hair. I pop a mint into our mouth (thank goodness, Tori actually keeps mints in the tin now), grab Tori's wallet, and pull out her license. *Best to not play dumb*, I think to myself. *The police usually appreciate when someone recognizes their wrongdoing immediately. It shows awareness.* By the time I roll down the window for the officer, I've prepared a story.

"I'm so sorry, officer." I force the body's voice to crack slightly with emotion as I say the words. "I know I was going a little over the limit. It's just, well, I just broke up with my boyfriend, and I guess I was just caught up in my thoughts. It won't happen again." I try to appear genuine, but I know he doubts me. I press on. "If you'll forgive my behavior, I can assure you it won't happen again."

He asks where I am headed. I have no idea where Tori had been taking us, so I lie and say we are going home. He grows ever-so-slightly convinced of our innocence and makes his final decision.

"Alright, ma'am. I'm going to let you off with a warning, but no more speeding. And turn down your music a little." With a tip of his hat on the last syllable, he heads back to the patrol car to enter my warning into the system.

As soon as his back turns, I sigh with relief, silently praising myself for successfully dealing with yet another high-stress situation.

....

Opening my eyes is like cracking open the lid to an ancient treasure chest: heavy, crusty, unsure of what will be found. I blink one, two, three, four times and bring the room into focus. I am back at Donna's, in my bed, fully clothed, with no idea how I got here. I am slightly alarmed. Although, at this point, slightly alarming is becoming my new normal.

Groaning, I force myself to sit up and go outside to look for my car. Sure enough, there it is: parked in front of Donna's without so much as a scratch. I have no idea how I got out of trouble with the police officer. Truth be told, I don't really care.

Knock, knock, knock. Donna's incessant rapping is like a sledgehammer striking my head over and over and over.

"What." My voice is thick with sleep as I open the door to find Donna wearing a flour-coated apron on the other side.

"I baked a cake, if you'd like some," she says kindly, despite the rigidness in her posture.

I shake my head no, and without another word, Donna makes her way back down the hall. Just before departing onto the staircase, she turns.

"Where were you?" she asks, looking past me into the bedroom, as if there might be answers to my behavior hiding in the four walls of the room.

"Out," I say and close the door forcefully.

We don't trust her.

We don't trust anyone.

With good reason.

Pressing my hands to my temples, I let out a frustrated grunt and sit down on the floor, grabbing my notebook out from under the bed.

....

April 30, 1991

The voices in my head have gotten worse. So have the blackouts.

The voices are telling me that they don't trust Donna. Well, sort of debating it, really. Maybe I shouldn't trust her. Ever since I overheard her phone conversation, my instincts have told me that the less she knows, the better. On the other hand, all she's ever done is be kind to me. Maybe I'm paranoid. But maybe I'm not.

I think a walk might do me some good.

My legs are tired, but continuing to move is the only thing keeping me from completely breaking down—the only thing keeping my mind somewhat functional. The sidewalk stretches on and on and on in front of me. Rows of immaculate, two-story houses neatly line both sides of the street. I have been walking for at least two hours. My body is exhausted. My mind is spinning: Rose, the nightmares, the pain. I feel like if I stop walking, I will collapse. So, I keep trudging along.

I look closely at the houses that I pass: the new cars in the driveways, the children in the yards, the old couples on the porches. Upon first glance, the neighborhood seems perfect. But if you look—really look—its flaws show. Empty bottles of booze fill the trash cans in the driveway, a pack of cigarettes pokes out from the pocket of a twelve-year-old, and bruises show on the arms of an old woman as she waves. None of this hidden darkness surprises me. If I have learned anything, it is that nothing is ever as nice as it seems.

In my head, I attempt to calculate just how far I have wandered from Donna's house. *At least four miles, maybe more.* Dinner time is fast approaching, and my rumbling stomach reminds me of Donna's obnoxious dinner rule: If you aren't seated at the table when dinner is ready, then you don't eat. Just thinking of it annoys me.

Nonetheless, I am starving, and I don't want to have to scrounge for dinner. I decide to head in the direction of the bus stop. A ride back is necessary if I am going to make it in time.

Cars occasionally pass me as I make my way through the suburban maze. I look at each one closely, keeping tabs on the colors in an effort to entertain myself: blue, red, black, blue, gray, black—wait. I stop, realizing that the same black car has circled past me more than once. Something tells me it isn't a coincidence. I cautiously proceed, and, sure enough, less than five minutes later, what appears to be the same car circles past again. I make a note of the last three numbers on the license plate to be sure my mind isn't playing tricks on me: 592. By the time I turn the next corner, the 592 car has gone past me again. **Are they lost?**

Run! A voice in my head screams, but I force myself to keep a steady pace.

I am almost to the main stretch of road that leads to the bus stop. *I just need to keep going.*

Again, the car goes past. This time, I sneak a look into the driver's side window. A middle-aged woman is driving. It doesn't look like anyone else is in the car. *She must be lost,* I tell myself, even though, deep down, I know that isn't the case. A few more strides, and I am out of the clusters of pristine houses and onto the road leading into the main part of town. If the woman is truly lost, I won't see her again. If she is a real threat, I will.

Keeping watch, I start to move faster, hoping that 592 does not flash past me. But, as usual, my prayers are not answered, and the woman drives past yet again. This time, however, I do not pretend I don't see her. Instead, I stop walking and turn to look directly at the vehicle. **Come mess with me. I dare you.** Chills rush up my spine.

Run! The voice screams again.

This time, I listen.

....

Having people all around me offers a strange sort of comfort as the bus jostles down the road. A baby cries. A teenager laughs. A child runs down the aisle, his mother calling his name. The fear of being followed still lingers in me, and I feel anger trying to fight its way out. I want to punch someone, hurt something. If I am angry, I can't be afraid. If I hurt someone, they can't hurt me. If everyone feels dread, I am not alone. If I am the bully, I can't be bullied.

....

Mrs. Caltri slips her hand into mine as we walk from the nurse's office to the school cafeteria. I'm worried because I am the last one to lunch, and I won't have a lot of time to eat before we are shuffled outside for recess. I'm sad because the adults at school are always ushering me this way and that, prodding my skin with needles and examining my bruises. **I wish adults would just leave me alone.**

The heavy doors to the big, wide space of the cafeteria open, and Mrs. Caltri carefully releases my hand. I go through the food line, then take my place. It isn't long before Rose joins me. I can see bruises on her arms, her wounds mirroring my own. The sound of snickering reaches my ears. The girls across from us are staring, their neatly groomed pigtails swinging in sync with their heads as they turn to whisper to one another.

"You know what, forget about it," I say as I give Rose a gentle bump with my shoulder. "Fuck 'em."

Rose gasps, and I put my hand over my mouth. I have never ever said that word before. A wave of shock passes over me. Then, I start to feel something else: something good, something powerful. Like, suddenly, I am bigger than everyone around me.

The bell rings, signaling that it is time for us to make our exit onto the playground. I stand quickly, dumping my tray's contents into the nearest garbage bin, and turn to Rose.

"Let's go."

Rose and I race to the monkey bars: our favorite recess pastime. A line of eager children has already started forming at the base of the ladder that leads up to the bars. Rose and I take our place at the back of the pack.

We watch as everyone takes a turn: some falling off the bars midway through, some hollering with pride as they successfully reach the other side. With every inch gained, my anticipation grows. Soon it will be our turn.

Suddenly, my view of the approaching ladder is blocked by the sight of a boy cutting in front of Rose and I. Sam. I decide right then and there to make sure this is the last time he thinks he can cut in front of me. Full of fire and adrenaline, I push Sam's back.

"Hey, no cuts," I say clearly, still feeling the power from my newly discovered vocabulary.

"Buzz off, freak," Sam scoffs at me, turning to face me with his hands on his hips. His nose is obnoxiously big—the kind of nose you want to hit. That's the last thing I think before I punch him square in the face, knocking him backwards.

I give Sam a shove, which knocks him even more off balance. He falls to the ground, and I manage to pin him underneath me—my knees holding his shoulders down. My hands strike the soft tissue of his face. As I hit him, I no longer see a classmate, but rather the faces of all of the people who hurt me, all of the people that I am not big enough to fight.

"Tori, Tori, Tori." In the background, I hear the muffled voices of my peers as they cheer, but those voices could not matter less to me. My knuckles start to hurt, but I don't care. I don't hear Rose calling to me to stop. I don't hear the sound of heavy footsteps approaching.

"Hey! What's going on? Break this up," a voice demands as someone pulls me off of Sam and onto my feet.

A very angry Principal Hughes towers over me. **I'm in deep shit now.** He keeps his grip firm on my shoulder, steering me away from the playground and into the school building. Once in his office, I slump onto one of the wooden stools in front of his desk. Trying to appear regretful, I stare down at my bloody, dirty hands.

"I'm sorry, Principal Hughes," I say, willing myself to not laugh as I think about flattening Sam's nose.

I am not sorry. I feel good, strong.

"Tori, what is the meaning of this?" Principal Hughes asks curiously.

"Listen, Sam was being a bully. Really, I swear. I was sticking up for myself."

"Two wrongs do not make a right, young lady. I'm going to have to send you home with a warning slip. Make sure a parent sees it and signs it. I expect it back in my office in the morning." His tone is serious, but I know he won't care very much if it is a day or two late.

"Yes, Principal Hughes. Sorry, Principal Hughes."

As I stand, I dust what dirt I can off of my jeans and onto his freshly vacuumed floor. Principal Hughes shakes his head, but I pretend not to notice. I take the paper slip he hands me and turn to go.

That night is the first time I forge my father's signature. Huddling close to the paper under the beam of my flashlight, I carefully form the swoops and swirls I had seen him do so many times before. I sleep soundly for the first time in weeks.

May Day

The darkness has deeper roots than people know.

There is a certain kind of evil in this world that very few people know of and even fewer people speak of. The kind of evil that takes time and energy to grow. The kind of evil that consumes people, gives them what they want, and makes them hungry for more. The kind of evil that steals children in the night, steals lives, steals souls. It has become something believed to exist only in horror films. But it is very real, and it is very dangerous, and once it finds you, it becomes impossible to hide.

....

I sit on the edge of my bed, staring at a blank notebook page. I am in need of a shower, but I figure that I will try to write a little before venturing into the bathroom. My mind is full, but the page remains blank. It seems silly to try and put my thoughts onto paper, ridiculous to think I can somehow fit my life into words. Finally, I can't stand the feeling of my filth any longer.

Clinging to my last wisp of motivation, I gradually go across the hall, undress, and step into the shower. Water cascades over me. Working suds into and out of my hair, I focus on keeping my mind empty. I need a moment without any voices or thoughts.

Suddenly, an unwelcome noise intrudes on my peace: footsteps. What is likely Ray making his way downstairs to the coffee pot registers in my mind as immediate danger. A dark shadow spreads across my brain: fear. In a matter of seconds, I go from being in a blissful semi-coma to feeling panic course through me.

....

The water trickles passively over my bare back, rust-colored and smelling of rotten eggs. A dim lightbulb flickers above me, softly illuminating the small space of the sauna. Opposite my naked body, there is a pile of rocks caged in by a wooden crate. Benches made of the same wood sit pushed against the wall to my right.

There is no soap, so I grab an old rag from the corner and use it to force the dirt off my skin, leaving behind splotches of red. Above me, I can hear Mrs. Archer humming a church hymn as she bustles around the house. I too begin humming, subconsciously picking up on the familiar melody.

Time passes as we hum, and my small fingers are in the middle of carefully working a knot out of my hair when I hear the clomp of heavy boots on the stairs. I know that Mr. Archer's workbench is in the basement, and he often visits the space when a farm tool is in need of fixing. The alarm bells don't start to go off in my head until I hear the creak of the door.

By then, it is too late to hide.

....

"Tori?" Ray's voice outside of the bathroom door brings me back to the present. "Phone call for you."

Weakly, I turn off the faucet and pull my clothes on. I open the door just long enough to grab the phone from Ray. **Who the hell is calling me?**

"Hello?" I barely recognize my own voice as it comes out thick and raspy.

"Tori?" It is Annalise.

Shit.

"Hi, Annalise."

"Tori, are you alright? I've been trying to reach you. Susan said you haven't shown up for work lately. She called me this morning wondering if she should take you off the schedule. She's been trying to give you some grace, but you've been very unreliable lately. What is going on?"

"Um, yeah, I'm sorry. I've had a terrible stomach bug—completely knocked me out."

"Well, I'm sorry to hear that."

She doesn't believe me. I can tell. But neither of us are going to say it.

"Are you going to show up today?" she asks after a brief pause.

Double shit. I don't even know what day it is, not to mention whether or not I work.

Annalise seems to read my mind through the phone. "It's Tuesday. Tuesday, May 1st. You work at 10 o'clock this morning."

May 1st. May 1st. May 1st.

May Day. Devil's Day.

The air around me seems to vanish, swallowed by the growing anxiety inside my body. I hang up the phone after telling Annalise I'll be in soon. Making my way from the bathroom to my bedroom, I sit on the edge of my bed.

....

The pole stretches from the forest floor into the trees. The spring ground is soft from the melted snow, and rocks have been gathered at the base of the pole in order to keep it from falling sideways. Mrs. Archer had put flowers in my hair earlier, and the pins she used now dig into my scalp as I stand at the edge of the clearing. Rose is by my side. We stare at the pole.

Ribbons hang loosely from the top of it, their colors bright against the dull wood of the trees that have yet to bloom. Mrs. Archer gives me pills to swallow, and the ribbons become even brighter. The sounds of the women around me are distorted.

I am naked. There are voices. Voices everywhere. They are saying strange things, talking of demons coming up from the core of the Earth. The stench of sex grows thick in the spring air. The ribbons blend together with the forest—one mass of color. The taste of blood blurs together with unwanted touch—one mass of hurt. A black fog surrounds us.

....

I fall onto my back, the popcorn ceiling coming closer and closer—pressing the weight of the atmosphere into my chest, harder and harder. I feel pinned to my bed, the walls pulsing along with my increasing heart rate. I press my palms to my ears.

This is it. We are going to die here. We are going to die here, alone, and nobody will ever know anything about us.

A part of me knows what to do. Shakily, we walk to the bathroom.

Inhale, exhale.

We just need a little release.

Yes. A little release. That is all I need: something to pull me back.

I reach the bathroom and look at the object that brought me here: a razor. I pick it up and bring it down against the taught skin of my forearm.

Red All Over

The first time I wanted to kill myself was in third grade.

What happens when we die? That is the question that most human beings spend their whole lives either avoiding or obsessing over. From religion to psychics to science, the outlets to which we will go to seek answers are seemingly limitless. Regardless of where you look, the reality is that no living human truly knows what death is like, and that is terrifying—to most.

To Tori, however, death was never a concern. In fact, she spent most of her life wishing for death, for the moment she would finally be able to escape forever.

....

The spokes of my bike tires swish and spin, kicking up dirt as I pedal my way along the road. Beads of sweat form on my forehead in the heat of summer. My body aches with exhaustion from the night before. I round the corner and am greeted by the local swimming hole. The calm water beckons to me. I can't help but stop, pulling my bike to the side of the road and laying it in the ditch.

The swimming hole is made by a stream moving effortlessly into a large pool of water, with the deepest spot forming around a large culvert. Above where the culvert divides the water, a thin piece of land covers the metal to form a bridge of sorts—a perfect jumping spot.

Standing on the land overlooking the water, I stare blankly down at the murky surface and wonder how it would feel to submerge myself completely—to jump off the edge, and let myself fall down, down, down until the rays of sunlight no longer reached me, until I no longer felt anything except the push and pull of the water around me. If I were to stop swimming, how long would it take before I sunk into the darkness? Would I find peace there?

The thoughts trickle through my mind, much as the stream trickles into the swimming hole. Gradually, I move forward, eliminating the few inches of space between me and the edge. Soon my toes are hanging over. One more step.

I am just about to take my final breath of air when a slight movement beneath the surface catches my attention: a fish. It is rather large—the biggest I've ever seen in that spot—and it swims downstream, blissfully unaware of the tortured soul lingering just above it.

As I watch the creature disappear, I imagine it is making its way home to a loving family: a pool of eager fish babies waiting beneath a log in the shallows. A small ounce of longing begins to mix with my other thoughts as images of my own family flash through my mind: my mother singing in the kitchen, my sisters and I laughing as we lay huddled in the back of our family's station wagon, my father's deep chuckle when he watches his latest prank unfold, my brother performing a front-flip off of this very bridge and landing with a triumphant yelp in the water. The memories cause me to take a step backwards away from the edge. I cannot leave them, cannot leave Rose. I know this, and so, with resignation, I make my way back to my bike and continue pedaling.

....

My arm is covered in red. I don't remember all of what happened, only flashes. But when I see the razor on the floor, I begin to connect the pieces. Looking down at my arm, I realize too late that we have gone too far.

I don't recall making a cut that big, but the blood is undeniable and coming fast. The sight does not cause me to panic, but rather, I feel an eerie sense of calm.

LET IT HAPPEN.

If I do nothing, I will soon be gone. This purgatory of a life will finally be over. But then I think of the people I will leave behind. Hesitantly, I reach for the towel next to me and begin wrapping it around my arm.

GOD DAMMIT.

"Help." My voice is coming out in broken strands.

LET IT GO. STOP TRYING TO LIVE. WE ARE SO CLOSE TO PEACE.

"Help!" A little stronger this time.

I hear footsteps outside the bathroom, and feel a rush of air as the door swings open. Then, Donna and Ray are lifting me off the floor.

Dear Sadness,

I see you deep inside my soul. You're the pain that I've run from. You're the secret that I hold. You're there when I'm awake, and you're there when I'm asleep. You're the one feeling that I need to release. You modify my actions and put walls around my heart. You're a never-ending reminder. You've been there from the start. You scare me, and I run from you. But to my dismay, you are never gone. I've tried everything to ignore your existence, but now your reflection is in the sun. What will it take for your Haunting memory to dissipate? I have a bad feeling you will be my shadow until I let you show—to express yourself and all your pain until you won't need to reign in my heart.

I'm afraid of you, Sadness. You seem so big. You engulf my existence. If I release you, who will I be? If I let you out, what will people think of me? Will I die in this process, or will I gain great strength? Fear is in the way of my plan for the release of Sadness in my life. I guess it's all a choice, left only up to me. Will I give Sadness permission to express itself? Or will I choose to be in fear—waiting for the day when there is no more sun and all my laughter turns to tears.

Empty

There was nothing in this life for me anymore.

Depression is like a tsunami. One minute you're standing in front of the bathroom mirror, brushing your teeth. The next, you're in a heap on the floor, and it feels like being numb is the only alternative to being incurably miserable. Suddenly, a handful of pills, a sharp blade, or a long fall are not seen as daunting, dangerous, or scary, but rather as welcome friends. You feel as though you have no life left to live.

People sometimes talk about it, and they may try to prepare the best that they can. But nobody ever really sees it coming, and nobody ever really knows what to do when it hits. Experts may say there are precautions you can take to ensure your survival, ways to protect yourself and your loved ones. Really, all you can do is fight and hope the wave doesn't sweep you away.

....

The sterile smell of rubbing alcohol jolts my senses into focus. For a moment, I remain completely still, panicking, before the steady beeping of monitors reminds me of where I am: a hospital. Donna and Ray called 911 after finding me bleeding in the bathroom, and the hours following that call were filled with random blips of consciousness. I push the back of my head further into my pillow, willing myself to disappear.

"Thank goodness, you're awake." Donna's voice registers in my ears, and I crane my neck to look in the direction from which it came. She sits in a chair on the opposite side of the room, a magazine open on her lap. "We need to talk about some things."

I don't respond. Instead, I turn my attention to my forearm, which is wrapped heavily in gauze. Wiggling my fingers, I am relieved to find that I didn't cause any permanent damage.

"We haven't called your family yet," Donna continues. "We thought maybe you would want to, but, well, you've been kind of out of it."

"That's okay. We don't need to call them," I say, hoping that Donna will agree, even though I know the chances are slim.

There is a long silence, and I wait for the lecture on how I need to let my loved ones know what I have done. But it doesn't come.

After about a minute, Donna just simply sighs and says, "Okay, maybe that is for the best."

I sit up as far as my exhausted body will allow and meet her eyes. **She is serious.** I don't question it, and just simply say, "Thank you."

Just then, a stern-looking woman dressed in scrubs walks through the doorway. She circles my bed, checking vitals. She pauses to write something on the clipboard in front of her, then slides a stool over to my bedside and begins unwrapping the gauze from my wound.

As the layers peel away, dark, dried liquid begins to appear on the white cotton. Eventually, she reaches my skin. Donna gasps as the woman lifts my arm and examines it closely. A neat row of stitches stretches over pink, swollen skin—closing the bloody gash made by the razor.

"Everything looks fine," the woman says as she retrieves a fresh roll of gauze from a nearby cart. "There won't be any permanent damage, just a scar. You're lucky."

"Well, that's good news. Right, Tori?" Donna chirps as the woman carefully re-wraps my wound in clean bandages.

"Fantastic," I mutter.

....

That night, I lie quietly in the hospital, listening to my thoughts. Donna has gone home, and my only company is the night staff assigned to perform suicide-checks on me every half hour.

GOD, WE COULD USE A DRINK.

I think of Rose and wonder what she would say if she were here. **Where is she?** I think of my mother and how sad she would be if she ever found out how desperately I want to die. I think of Annalise and wonder if she phoned again after I failed to show up for yet another shift at work. I think of my poor boss, Susan, and how much grace she has given me, only to have me disappoint her time and time again.

Always a disappointment.

"Shut up," I mumble.

I look out to where a bright moon is casting an eerie glow over the city, splashing disproportionate shadows across every surface. The scene sends a shiver through my spine. ***I hate the moon.***

Hanging my wounded arm off the bed in order to not hit it, I roll away from the window, shift my attention to the empty hospital hallway, and look for signs of life. When I hear the sound of approaching footsteps, I feign sleep— waiting for the nurse to check on me and leave. He does, and after he is gone, I continue my hallway watch.

A small flip calendar on the bedside table informs me that the date is still Tuesday, May 1st. The clock on the wall tells me that will change in approximately 10 minutes.

Despite having been unconscious most of the day, my body feels ready for sleep. My lovely brain, however, is a different story. My brain will not shut up. Every time I begin to drift, images and terrible thoughts flash through it.

I need something: booze, weed, cigarettes. If I was at Donna's, I would have already been out the door and in search of one of the aforementioned items, but no—I am in this hellhole with a personal babysitter coming to check on me almost constantly.

No rest for the wicked.

I need out of here. I can't take it any longer. I close my eyes and retreat into myself.

....

Blake:

"'No rest for the wicked.' Jade, you bitch. I'll get some rest," I say with something dangerously close to enthusiasm as I push the call button on our bed and wait for the semi-attractive male nurse. Tori wants to escape, and I am on it. This is what I'm made for: fun in the least fun of times. I notice the steady beeping on the monitors by the bed change, escalating a little. I ignore it. I hear the annoying scuffle of hurried steps. The young man that has been waiting for us to kill ourselves all night appears in the doorway, disheveled and out of breath.

"You rang?" he asks, searching for the emergency that called him here and then becoming confused when everything seems in order.

"Yes, I did. I'm in an awful lot of pain," I say while motioning at the bandaged arm with a slight twitch of my head. "Is there anything you can do or, I don't know, give me to help? I can't sleep."

"No, I'm afraid not. Your chart shows a history of drug abuse. No painkillers allowed for minor incidents."

"Minor incident? You call this a minor incident? We almost died. No, fuck that. We'll take some morphine. Morphine sounds great."

"I can't do that. I really am sorry."

"Are you absolutely sure about that?" I ask in my most sultry voice.

The nurse gulps. "Um, yes. Quite sure. Now, if you'll excuse me—I have other patients to tend to." He turns to go. Desperation soars.

"Fuck this," I whisper and start to stand. "Fuck! This!" I yell, beginning to move as fast as the body will allow me in the direction of the bathroom. The nurse stops in the doorway, turning to look at me with bewilderment.

"What are you doing?" he asks tentatively, as if he really doesn't want to know the answer.

"What will it take to get some painkillers?" I spin to face him, stopping halfway between the bed and the bathroom. "How close to death do we have to come to get a goddamn moment of peace? Do I have to go in the bathroom and smash our skull against the toilet until it cracks? Do I have to go outside and run in front of an ambulance? What. Does. It. Take?"

Hesitation turns to horror as the nurse presses his pager. "No, no. None of that is necessary. Please, come back to bed, Miss Becker, and I will see what we can do for your pain." He extends his arm, as if to guide the body back to the bed.

"No, fuck you," I retort. "Fuck everyone in this so-called hospital. We're leaving." I shuffle past him.

I am breaking us out of here, I tell the others.

This is a terrible idea, I hear Jade say.

The next thing I know, three more nurses show up, herding me back into the room.

"This is some serious bullshit!" I yell into the hallway. Hardly anyone is there to hear: only us and the four nurses. Everyone else has either gone home or into rooms with closed doors. I don't care. I keep going. "I mean do any of you really care if we get a little high? Or do you just act like you care about the rules, because if you didn't you would be bad people?"

One of the nurses takes a step forward. I am screaming now, the blood rushing to my face. I am about to make a run for it when I feel a light prick in my arm. The world goes black.

Jade:

When I come into the body, things are disastrous—to say the least. Blake really did a number. Four nurses are with us, and I feel like we are heavily sedated. Everyone in the room is on edge: whispering and writing notes in a chart. I can feel Blake's rage just beneath our skin, but I don't let her come back out.

I clear my throat and say politely, "Sorry to have caused so much trouble. I don't know what got into me. It won't happen again."

Of course, this is a little bit of a lie. I know what got into us, and I figure it is bound to happen again sooner or later. I just pray we will be out of this place by then.

The nurses all look at me with shock and confusion written on their faces. They are not keeping up with the switching. I find that nobody can, really. Our life is always a shitshow, and everyone around us is always perplexed. It makes me mad that we are sized-up so quickly by the outside world, and that the others inside Tori are so irrational, so addicted, so careless. But I am stuck with them and the judgment they bring—so is Tori. That's why she needs me.

"Well, Miss Becker," one of the female nurses says. "We are certainly glad you're feeling better. However, your behavior was rather concerning, so I'm afraid we will have to keep you here a little longer for observation. There will also be a nurse with you at all times going forward, until we deem that you are no longer a risk to yourself or others. That said, it is late. You should get some rest." She leaves the room, followed by two others. Only one nurse remains behind. He looks at me, his eyes both quizzical and terrified, as he takes a seat in the far corner of the room.

There is no getting us out of this one.

....

When I wake up next, I do not feel better. If anything, I actually feel worse. I don't know what I have done or said in the lost time, but I do know that the nurse who had previously come to check on me every 30 minutes is now posted in the corner, watching me intently.

Despair floods into me. **Just breathe,** I tell myself. **Tomorrow will be better.**

WHO ARE WE KIDDING? NO, IT WON'T. Not at all.

It feels like every bad feeling in existence is inside of me. I am helpless, worthless, afraid, despondent.

A Revelation

For me, everything was connected.

Have you ever worked on a puzzle that seemed impossible to solve? It can be argued that nothing is more maddening. You might make a little progress here and there, but you always end up getting stuck. You might spend days, weeks, months pulling your hair out and staring at this thing, wondering if it's all a cruel trick. Then, an outsider takes one look and immediately spots a solution. A different perspective can change everything.

....

A knock on my door startles me awake a little before 10 the next morning. After taking a minute to remember where I am, I wonder who the hell is knocking. **Donna isn't planning to visit until this afternoon, and it has been made pretty clear that there is no privacy allotted to me by the medical staff in this place.** I sit up slightly and say, "Come in."

With practiced, gentle movements, an unfamiliar woman steps into the room and closes the door behind her. I immediately know she is here for a reason, but for the life of me, I cannot imagine what that reason is.

I guess that the woman is probably in her mid-fifties. She is shorter—about my height—and pretty. She wears clothes different from the hospital staff: Instead of scrubs or a white lab coat, khakis and a pin-striped turtleneck cover her slim body.

"You can leave us," she says to the nurse in the room. She takes a few more steps toward my bed and smiles a small smile. "Hi, you must be Tori. Do you mind if I shake your hand?"

"I don't give a shit what you do," I say, deciding to go on the defensive until I know the reason for this strange woman's visit.

"Very well then," she says. "I think I'll just sit. I've never been one for handshakes anyways." She sits in the chair where Donna had been wearily reading her magazine the day before. "I'm sure you're wondering why I'm here. My name is Fran Peterson. I'm a doctor."

I shoot her a puzzled glare.

She laughs a little. "Not a medical doctor. Sorry, I should've made that clearer from the start. I'm a psychiatric doctor. I run a practice on the second floor."

"Psychiatric? Like for crazy people?"

"Nobody is crazy, Tori. The patients that I treat are just hurting in a way that isn't physical."

"I think I'm crazy," I respond under my breath.

"I don't think you're crazy, Tori. I think that there's a lot of pain in this world, and I'm sure you've had more than your fair share."

With that comment, I want to believe I can trust her. I want to tell her everything. But other parts of me don't.

She's just here to see the freak show.
SCREW HER.

"You see, Tori," Fran says, unaware of the mental gymnastics I am doing. "I'm not here because I think you're crazy. I'm here because I think you need someone on your side, and I want to help."

"Why would you want to help me?" I ask wearily, suddenly exhausted with this whole ordeal.

"Because I've been in pain, too," Fran answers bluntly.

I want nothing more than for this woman to leave and for myself to go back to sleep. I am done with pain. I can't feel any more of it, or else I am sure I will die. Best to just sleep the rest of my life.

"I'm sorry, but would it be alright if we talk more later? I didn't get much sleep last night, and I'm pretty wiped."

"Okay, I'll go," Fran says, choosing her words carefully. "But will you answer one question first?"

"Fine," I nearly growl. "What?"

"When did you start getting nightmares?"

"What?" I am shocked. **How does she know that?**

Fran must see the question on my face, because she continues with, "Based on the circles under your eyes, it's been months—not just one night—since you got any sort of restful sleep. That, mixed with your history of drug abuse and the fact that you recently tried to take your own life, tells me that your mind is not always a safe place."

"Oh, screw you," my anger spits out at her before I can stop it.

So sick of being judged.

"You don't know anything about me," I add quietly.

"You're right, I don't. But we had a deal: You answer the question, and I'll go away."

Fran waits with earnest concern. A part of me tries to crawl to the surface and tell her the honest truth. I want to scream, "Help me!" But instead, I stay silent—my lips pressed together in defiance.

"Alrightly then, I guess I'll just sit here until you decide to answer." Fran repositions herself in the chair and begins doing a crossword puzzle.

She is as stubborn as me.

"Fine." I give in. "I first started having nightmares when I was a kid—before kindergarten. Probably around age four or five. I don't remember, exactly."

Silence fills the room for a moment as Fran contemplates her next move. After a while, she says gently, "That's a long time for someone to go without any peace."

"Yeah, no kidding. But what can ya do? That's life."

"It doesn't have to be, you know. I've worked with many patients who deal with chronic nightmares like you do. Many of them have found relief; some don't even have nightmares anymore."

"Really?" My hopefulness breaks through for a moment, but is almost immediately shut down. "I doubt it."

"No, really," Fran says, her confidence unwavering, her voice even. "Tori, do you think you'd like to talk more about your nightmares sometime? Maybe we could set up an appointment for you in my office?"

"Okay," I answer quickly, surprising every part of myself.

Fran carefully returns the newspaper to the table and stands. "Good. How about you come see me after you're discharged in a few days?" she asks while eyeballing the hospital monitors, whose beeping has slowed significantly. "That will give you time to rest before we speak again."

"Okay."

"My office number is 230. Does three o'clock sound alright?"

I nod, and Fran slips out the door as fluidly as she came in.

....

After sleeping for roughly 24 hours and pretending I am okay for another 48, I check out of the hospital shortly before my visit with Fran. With every step I take toward Fran's office, I want to take three steps in the opposite direction. Voluntarily staying in the hospital after being involuntarily committed feels both ironic and idiotic. Almost every part of me wants to be curled up in bed, but it is as if the tiniest, yet most central, part of me is making the calls—and she wants answers.

Nobody pays me much mind as I make my way through the lobby to the elevators. Fran's practice is on the second floor, and as I shoot up into the sky, I wonder if this will be one of the biggest mistakes of my life.

WHAT'S THE POINT?

What kind of person needs to go to therapy? Come on. We're better than that.

Taking a deep breath, I fight to stay grounded in reality and ignore the voices inside my brain, which only makes them grow louder. It seems like an eternity before the elevator stops, and the chime of the doors opening signals it is time to move.

But I don't move—not even an inch. I can't. All I can do is stand here, staring at the waiting area displayed in the gap of the split metal doors, while internal voices continue to assault me. Eventually, the doors get sick of waiting for me to get my shit together and slide shut.

In the silence of the still elevator, I let myself talk aloud: "Shut up. Shut up. Shut up," I groan through gritted teeth. "I am doing this. I have to do this."

I reach out and re-press the second floor button. Moments later, the chime of the doors greets me as they slide open once more. I move forward, focusing only on putting one foot in front of the other.

Left, right, left, right, left, right. All the way until I get to a small, oak desk near a large picture window. A young-looking man with dark-rimmed glasses sits behind it, watching me blankly as I painstakingly make my way to him.

"Hi. I'm here to see Fran."

"Oh, you must be her new patient," he says, realization breaking through the stillness on his face. "She's just finishing up with another client. You can have a seat while you wait." He points at black, plastic chairs lining the small room before returning his attention to a stack of papers on the desk.

I have just begun to head in the direction of one of the corner chairs when I hear the click of a doorknob to my right. Fran emerges from a room, followed by a woman about my age. As the woman walks past me, I can sense her sadness.

She shares in our pain.

I offer the woman a half-smile, which she does her best to return. Then, I redirect my attention to Fran as she speaks.

"Tori, hi. I'm glad you're here. Let's go into my office."

The room is much larger than I expect, with plush chairs in the center of a thinly carpeted floor and rows of bookshelves along cranberry-colored walls. A desk is situated against one wall, and a monstrous filing cabinet sits in the corner with stacks of notebooks on top of it.

Fran, who must notice me examining the cabinet, says, "I keep all patient files locked in here, so that I know they are secure. I can assure you that any notes I take during our sessions will be seen by me only. The front desk staff merely handles my scheduling."

A fraction of the turmoil within me calms with her words, and the smallest sliver of hope emerges. *Maybe this isn't such a terrible idea,* I tell myself. *Maybe, just maybe, there is help.*

"You can take a seat, if you'd like," Fran offers, settling into the nearest chair. "Or you can stand. Up to you."

I take the seat directly across from Fran, facing the door. Pulling my ratty sweatshirt sleeves over my hands, I make myself as small as possible and wait for whatever comes next.

"Tori, I have to say, I wasn't sure you were going to show up today," Fran quips lightly as she tucks a stray piece of graying hair behind her ear. She picks up the nearest notebook and pen. "Can you tell me why you decided to come? You seemed rather reluctant when we last spoke."

"I guess I'm just tired of being miserable, and you seemed like maybe you could help. Plus, you promised me sleep."

"I didn't promise anything, Tori. But it is true that I will try my best to help you in whatever ways I can. Why don't we just start by getting to know one another a little bit? I'll tell you something about me; you tell me something about you."

"Okay."

"Okay. I grew up here in Washington. Where did you grow up?"

"Small town in the Midwest. You wouldn't know it."

"What made you want to move here?"

"I don't have a good reason."

"Okay, so why not stay in your hometown? I'm assuming that's where most of your family lives?"

"Yeah, they do, and I miss them more than anything, but I just couldn't stay there. I needed to get away."

"Away from what?"

"Everything."

"What's one thing specifically?"

"The smell." I pause, allowing my senses to remember the awful stench of that awful town. "The smell of the farms. I hate that smell. It reminds me of death."

"That sounds horrible," Fran responds, empathy in her voice. "Did you grow up on a farm?"

"No, we just had a large yard and some random animals." I smile a little thinking about our childhood pet cow, but then grow solemn upon remembering the original question. "Our neighbors had one—a farm. My friend, Rose, and I were there often."

"Ah, I see. Does Rose still live in your hometown?"

"No, not consistently anyways."

"Well, it's good that you both found cleaner air to breathe."

"Yeah, I don't know about that."

"Why do you say that?"

"Because everything in the whole world is rotten in one way or another."

"Do you think that you are rotten?"

"Oh, I am especially rotten."

"Why do you say that?"

"Because . . . because, I don't know. I just feel like everything I've ever done has been either wrong or pointless."

"Do you think coming here was wrong or pointless?"

"I'm still deciding."

"Fair enough." Fran pauses and turns to a fresh sheet of paper in her notebook. "Well, let's at least make it not pointless. Let's talk about the main reason you decided to come here: the nightmares. Can you describe what they are usually like?"

"Nightmarish." I know my answer is standoffish. I want to say more, to tell Fran all of the horrible details. But I can feel my defenses rising, and I am not sure what can be done to stop them.

"Care to elaborate?" Fran is looking at me intently.

"Not really," I say nonchalantly.

"Tori, I can't help you if you don't tell me what's going on."

There is silence as I war within myself, fighting to control my words.

BUZZ OFF, BITCH.

We don't need help; we are fine.

TELL HER TO MIND HER BUSINESS.

"Have the nightmares always been the same?" Fran presses. "Ever since you were five years old?"

"Mostly," I mutter.

"You know, I sometimes find that repeating nightmares like yours can hold keys to unlocking childhood memories. For example, your brain may be trying to show you a traumatic event from the past or—"

"Please stop talking," I plead as I feel myself going away.

SHE'S FULL OF IT. SHE CAN'T HELP US—NO ONE CAN. SHE'S JUST LIKE ALL THE OTHERS.

This is too much. I am wrong to have come here. I am wrong to think I can get help.

"Okay," Fran says kindly. "We can stop. That's plenty for today. You should be proud of yourself, Tori."

"Why?"

"Because you came here—you showed up. That's one of the biggest steps."

....

May 6, 1991

Leaving Fran's office today, I did not feel proud. My emotions are twisting together, resisting the idea of opening up whatever can of worms sits inside of me.

May 9, 1991

I am supposed to see Fran again tomorrow. I don't know why I agreed to go. I'm torn between feeling hopeless and desperately wanting help.

May 10, 1991

I actually made it through my entire hour with Fran today. It probably helped that we didn't really talk about anything meaningful. Still—I feel like this is a step in the right direction. I've decided to continue to fight with myself in order to heal.

May 15, 1991

I agreed to continue seeing Fran once a week. I feel a mixture of dread, anger, sadness, and . . . hope?

May 22, 1991

I so badly want to go on a binge and skip today's session with Fran. But I won't.

....

"How has this week been going, Tori?" Fran kicks off our time together with her usual line. Even though I know this is supposed to be an easy question, I find myself at a loss on how to answer—how honest to be.

"Alright," I settle with a shrug.

"Alright isn't bad," she says. Then, shifting gears, she turns slightly more serious. "Up until this point, I've been letting you lead the sessions and talk about whatever you would like. I did this so that we could get to know one another and you could become more comfortable with this sort of environment. Today, I would like to change our format slightly and talk about a specific topic."

"Okay?" I respond hesitantly, unsure of where Fran is going with this.

"Let's talk about what brought you to the hospital that time when I first met you. Can you remember any specific events leading up to you harming yourself?"

My brain scrambles, searching for a way to avoid the topic. I fight the urges to lash out, to lie, and to run as I decide what to say. Finally, I go with, "I don't know, exactly." Which isn't a lie.

"Okay," Fran says. "That's okay. Do you remember how that day began?"

I search my mind for the earliest memory of May 1st. Even though it has been less than a month, it feels like an eternity has passed since then.

"I took a shower," I say. "Everything was fine, until it wasn't." I feel my chest grow tight. A lump forms in my throat. "I heard someone walking, and then . . . "

I stop—the recollection of the Archers' shower coming back in full force. I begin to shut down. *I don't want to talk about this; I don't want to feel this again.*

Blake:

"Stop!" I yell.

I cannot let this woman continue to speak. I cannot let her find the pain. If she does, she will make us feel it again, and I can't feel it again. I refuse. I lean forward, my hands forming fists on the arms of the chair.

"I don't want to hear about how being fucked by grown men as a child caused all our issues, how if we just spill our guts to you, everything will be okay." The vulnerability felt by Tori dissipates more and more with every word I speak. "We are fucking fine, so save your breath for your next basket case. We will not be another file in your cabinet."

I expect Fran to pick up the phone on the wall, call security, and tell us to never show our face again. But unfortunately, she appears unshaken by my outburst. In fact, she is oddly calm as she writes something in her notebook. Then, she says words that shock and confuse and anger me to my core: "I am sorry you feel that way, Tori, and I am sorry that you are hurting."

"My name isn't Tori. It's Blake, you dumb bitch." This statement gives Fran pause.

Good, I think. *Leave us alone.*

But then, much to my horror, she says, "It's nice to meet you, Blake. Although I doubt you feel the same way about meeting me."

"Damn right, I don't feel the same."

"You have every right to refuse to talk to me, if that's what you want. However, Tori has every right to continue to talk to me, if that's what she wants."

I protest inwardly and outwardly, but I know I cannot stay in control of the body forever. I also know that when Tori is in charge again, she will undoubtedly go running back to this smartass shrink. I quickly realize I am wasting my time. Feeling defeated, I go back inside and let Tori take over the body.

....

When I emerge next, I am unbearably distraught. I strain to remember the last words that had come out of my mouth, realizing I have no clue. Although, judging by my posture, I had not been kind.

"I'm sorry," is all I can manage to mutter as I force myself to unclench my fists and lean back in the chair. "I'm not sure I remember what I was just saying."

"It's alright," Fran responds sympathetically. "Defense, or coping, mechanisms like yours are a response when someone has dealt with tremendous abuse in this life."

"What defense mechanisms?"

"Have you ever heard of people having multiple personalities?" Fran stretches her words out, weaving the syllables together in a careful pattern.

"A little . . . " I am afraid of where she is going with this.

THE LAST THING WE NEED IS ANOTHER FUCKING LABEL.

"Well," she folds her hands on her lap, reminding me of Donna's silent prayer stance the night she told me I wasn't normal. "It can sometimes happen when a person experiences severe trauma early in life." She gives me a moment to process, then continues. "So much trauma that one individual personality cannot handle it all on its own, so it splits."

"Splits?"

"Into multiple personalities, internal voices, or parts—depending on what you prefer to call them."

I stare at Fran. **What is she trying to say?**

"Tori, based on our time together, I'm starting to think that this may be something you are experiencing."

"Um," I press my hand to my temple. "But I don't have a lot of trauma—not that much anyways. I mean, I had it rough sometimes, but nothing bad enough to cause something like that, I don't think."

"What do you mean by you 'don't think?'"

"I guess I can't be certain. Sometimes I'll see some horrible scene in my mind. It will feel so real. But then, when it's over, I start to wonder if it was all just stuff I made up in my head. It's almost like experiencing a nightmare while I'm still awake. And it always comes in flashes; I can tell the scenes aren't all the way formed."

"I see. That's also common in people with multiple personalities. The different personalities, or parts, they all share some of the trauma, so that one person doesn't have to bear it alone. It's normal to only have bits and pieces of a story, because the other parts within you hold the rest. It's a survival mechanism, really, and you are not alone in doing it. In fact, I've seen this in more than one patient in the past. It has become a sort of specialty of mine. I work with many people who I suspect experience this. It's a completely valid response to trauma."

Silence expands into the room as I absorb what Fran is saying. It makes a strange amount of sense, but also scares the shit out of me.

"Tori, I know this isn't easy—not on any level— but I need to ask you, are you aware of Blake?"

"Um, sort of, I guess. I just recently noticed her. I'm not sure how to describe what she is, though. Oh God, wait. How do you know about Blake?"

"I just met her. We had a brief conversation. She does not seem happy to be here."

"She's never happy to be anywhere that doesn't have alcohol or drugs."

"I see. So, she's an addict?"

"I think so."

"Okay, that's good to know. It's great that you've already managed to identify that much about her. Now, let's talk about the anger—where does that part of Blake come from?"

"I don't know. All I know is that she's the fun, outgoing part of me, who gets really angry when I don't want to party."

"I see, and are you aware of any other parts of yourself?'

"Well, I know there's the part of me that feels small and weak, like a child. I sometimes hear the others, like intrusive thoughts, but it's hard to determine who is who and what the hell is going on. I only started noticing them lately. I've been trying to keep track of them in a notebook, but it's feeling impossible." I pause, and Fran takes it as an opportunity to ask another question.

"Tori, are you aware of what these other parts do when they are in control?"

"Um, no. When I can hear them inside my head, it's annoying, but I'm still myself. There are other times, though, when I will completely blackout. I'm guessing that's when they are in control?"

"Most likely, yes. That's fairly normal for people who struggle with internal parts, Tori."

I look at her blankly. She slowly ventures on.

"When she was out, Blake briefly mentioned experiencing sexual abuse as a child. I think what she recounted was likely enough to have caused a split in your personality. I believe, if we keep discussing what you and your personalities are feeling, we can gain a better understanding what you all experienced."

"I'm sorry," I say as I rest my head on my hands and will myself to disappear completely. "This is just a lot."

"I know, and you're welcome to take as long as you need. I'll be here when you're ready. In the meantime, I would encourage you to continue your work with the notebook. Write down your different parts when you notice them, your nightmares, anything that seems important—and we can discuss this further at our next appointment."

"Okay."

"You can also call me anytime you need—day or night. I do have another patient coming in soon, but feel free to rest in our waiting area for as long as you need before driving. I'll get you a glass of water."

"Okay," I say. "Thanks."

Dear Diary, I Think I've Gone Mad

I couldn't trust myself.

Life is made up of pivotal moments: the first steps, the first day of school, the first kiss, the first heartbreak. Sometimes it feels like life is full of these moments. Every second of the day is a defining second. Other times, it feels like life is depleted of all pivotal moments: No matter what happens, nothing will change; you will still be the same as you were the day, the week, the year before.

Years 10 to 21 of Tori's life had felt this way. To her, it seemed as though all her pivotal moments had already come and gone, leaving only scars—until her most recent appointment with Fran. That hour was a turning point in Tori's adult life. Fran had given her insight that could change the entirety of the way Tori lived, and now she was hanging in the balance between a dark abyss and hope.

....

In the days between my visits to Fran's office, all I do is write. My thoughts, my nightmares, my internal parts, my sadness—it all goes into my notebook, until the pages are full and my pen has run dry.

On the drive to the appointment where Fran and I plan to discuss my journaling, the notebook sits on my passenger seat, as if it is a being of its own entirety.

Making my way along the freshly rained-on streets, I scan the skyline for a rainbow while my mind ponders worst case scenarios: ***Fran is going to think I am insane if she reads even one page of this. Is it possible for a therapist to fire her patient?***

"Here's your ticket, ma'am. Don't forget to have it validated. Have a nice day," the hospital parking attendant says as he hands me a thick, yellow slip of paper.

I thank him and place the paper onto the dash. Pulling the car into the nearest spot, I light a cigarette. Five minutes later, I am tucking my notebook inside my leather jacket, walking to the nearest entrance, and bracing myself for rejection.

....

Fran and I sit opposite each other, the notebook resting on the table between us. We are both waiting: her for an explanation of why I practically ran into her office, slammed a notebook on the table, and sat, cross-armed, in the nearest chair; me for her to open the notebook, read its horrors, and ask me to leave.

"Tori," Fran begins, her voice slicing the silence between us. "You don't have to let me read what you wrote if you aren't comfortable. I asked you to continue writing in order to help you release and remember, not for myself to read about your inner workings. The only reason I planned to discuss this today was to determine whether or not journaling is still a useful tool for you. If you ever want to share your writings with me, I will gladly accept. But everything about the way you've acted in the last five minutes tells me that isn't the case today, and that's okay."

"Really?"

"Yes, really. Writings like these are a personal matter, and they should remain private until you are ready to share them. I do, however, suspect that you have filled the pages rather quickly, so here—" she stands and retrieves a thick, ringed notebook from atop the filing cabinet, handing it to me, "take this. And let me know if you need more. There's plenty where that came from." Sitting back down, Fran opens a notebook of her own and continues. "Now, tell me, how do you think the journaling went?"

"It's good. It helps to have them all down on paper."

"Them?"

"The thoughts. The different parts of me."

"Ah, I see. Is there anything you wrote about that you want to discuss today?"

"Um, well . . . It's good to write because I feel like I have a little more stability, but . . . um . . . it's kind of freaky, honestly. I think there's something wrong with me."

"There's nothing wrong with you, Tori. Trust me. But I have a feeling that you do have a lot to work through, and I think you need to prepare yourself for the fact that this first notebook—it may only be the tip of the iceberg."

Part III:

Parts of Me

Stuck in a mind of great escape,
The ability to hide, to survive, to create.
Somewhere inside is the map to the maze,
the key to the treasure,
the pot of gold at the end of the rainbow,
the answers to all the questions of this shattered mirror life.

To see through this menagerie would be a splendid thing.
But to the naked eye,
would pierce the soul,
leaving scars of remembrance to those who try
to gaze at what they are not entitled to.

To see inside our life, our puzzle,
not yet put together,
that only we can bear to glimpse at
through the tinted colors of The Magic Rainbow.

May 3, 1992

Spent the last two days in the hospital—mostly just as a precaution. After what happened on May 1st last year, Fran and I agreed that it might be better for me to spend this one somewhere where help is easy to find. It's funny—one year ago I would have had to be heavily sedated or on the verge of death in order to go to the hospital without a fight. But now, I just want to do what's best for everyone around and inside of me.

May 10, 1992

Is this good? Recording my madness on paper? I don't know everything that has happened to me, but I do know that I don't trust Mr. or Mrs. Archer—not at all. In my nightmares, I sometimes hear them speaking. I hear them screaming and chanting in the darkness. I hear them telling me that I am bad and evil and—that's enough writing for now.

May 12, 1992

Writing down my nightmares continues to be challenging. Sometimes they get so bad that I can't bear to think about them.

Sometimes I can't make myself wake up. It's like I'm screaming, but I can't escape it.

It's hard for me to make myself go to sleep.

May 16, 1992

I lost two days this time.

....

I can hear Rose. She asks what I am doing.

"I'm trying to get better," I say, and Rose starts crying. My heart aches as I listen to her sobs.

"Rose, what's wrong?" I ask, while trying to keep panic out of my voice.

After a long silence, she finally answers with, "Tori, this is too painful. I don't understand why you're doing it."

"What do you mean?"

"The past is the past, Tori. We are who we are. We can't change any of it. All you can do is survive. Haven't you learned that after all we've been through?"

"Rose," I take a breath, summoning words that I hope will help her understand without overwhelming her. "I get what you're saying—trust me, I do. But don't you think our childhood seemed a little worse than most? I mean, I know everyone has their shit—that's not what I'm saying. I'm saying it seems like there was a lot more going on than just everyday troubles."

"What?" Rose has stopped crying and now just sounds lost.

"Like, with all of the things that happened when we were small. I think those things did some real damage. I think we were used for something pretty dark.

We've never felt like we had a chance in hell to sort any of this out, but now I think we might, Rose. We might have a chance. Maybe there are ways to heal from the past."

My insides split, running in opposite directions, tearing me in two. But I know at my core what I need to do.

"Rose, I love you, but I just can't stop looking for the truth, for healing. I feel like I'm working on something really important for both of us. Everything is finally making some sense. I need you to trust me. Then, as I get better, I can help you too."

"But why? Why do we need to get better? We are not sick; we are not bad people."

"I know we aren't, Rose, and sometimes I wish I could forget all this. I really do. But I think we can do more than just survive. I think our lives can be good, and so I have to try. I owe it to you and everyone who loves us."

"I don't believe you, Tori. If you keep going down this road, we might lose each other forever."

"That won't happen, Rose. I promise. If you choose to, we can heal together."

"Tori, no. I don't want to look at the past. I can't go back there; we can't go back there."

"I understand. I felt the same—I still do. But we made it through together once; I know we can do it again."

"I'll think about it." Rose's voice is growing groggy, and I can tell she is crashing. She mutters something else to me, but I can't make it out. I ask her to repeat herself. Nobody answers.

....

May 21, 1992

Today's visit with Fran was hard—the worst one yet. I don't remember what we talked about. Another part of me came out: Taylor. Taylor told Fran we weren't ready to go there. Thank God. I don't know if I want to see.

The more that we remember, the more the inside walls break down. Fran makes us feel safe, which is dangerous. The safer we feel, the more the internal system opens up. Tori doesn't know how many precious parts we are keeping stored away for her. There's a reason she has us. I was brave when she could not be. Taking me away from her won't help. She will die. - Taylor

May 22, 1992

This is completely insane. Insane! We are switching more than we ever have.

- Jade

May 23, 1992

My head is gonna blow up.

May 26, 1992

Fran seems tired. Donna seems frightened. I fear that my darkness is killing everyone around me.

May 27, 1992

I felt like I was being followed again today after my NA meeting. I can't describe the feeling, but I knew someone bad was near me. I just knew it.

* * *

Sometimes we forget dates—forget where things are.
Have a hard time keeping track and wrighting—mixed up

* * *

June 1, 1992

Remembering more every day. Have to think about it.
Seeing long ago.

I KEPT IT SIMPLE THIS TIME: ONE BAR, THREE DRINKS—JUST ENOUGH TO TAKE THE EDGE OFF. TORI DIDN'T NEED TO BLACK OUT AND NEITHER DID I. WE JUST NEEDED TO HAVE SOME FUN.
I GOT ALL OF OUR DRINKS FOR FREE, OF COURSE. ONE FLIRTY LINE OUT OF OUR MOUTH, AND THE DIRTY MEN AT THE

BAR WOULD HAVE DONE JUST ABOUT
ANYTHING. THEY SORT OF REMINDED
ME OF THE NASTY MEN WHO USED TO
RAPE US BACK WHEN I FIRST CAME INTO
EXISTENCE.
I ALWAYS HAD TO TAKE THE WORST OF
THE SEX: THE PAINFUL TIMES, THE
DIRTY TIMES, THE UNSPEAKABLE TIMES.
NOW IT'S LIKE I'M PROGRAMMED TO
FUCK ANYTHING THAT WALKS,
ESPECIALLY IF I THINK I'M IN DANGER. I
CAN'T HELP IT. IT'S A SURVIVAL
INSTINCT. DON'T JUDGE—WE ALL HAVE
THEM.
OH, AND THIS IS BLAKE—IN CASE
WHOEVER THE FUCK IS READING THIS
COULDN'T GUESS.

June 2, 1992

All dark inside

Dying

* * *

Space out

* * *

June 5, 1992

I think I'm more afraid of this being real than it being imaginary. What happens if this is really my life?

* * *

Dark nights, fearful sleep, wishing it would <u>end.</u> Hoping that somebody will <u>understand.</u> Walking around with a heart that's in pieces—too hard for my hands to hold. Sorry for being me. Wanting some security.

* * *

June 10, 1992

Mistake to let us be seen—feeling like I've put us
all at risk. Hoping nothing else bad will happen.

June 12, 1992

Living through fragments.

***

<u>Journal</u>

Write nightmare

***

June 13, 1992

Not many words. Hard to talk. Confusion. Failure.
Fear. Panic. Not understanding.
Anger. Hate. Tired of feeling lost. Confused.

FUCK YOU ALL. – BLAKE

June 15, 1992

Fran asked me today if I know what something
called ritual abuse is. I told her I didn't know, and
I didn't think I wanted to. That's the last thing I

remember until leaving the office. Fran said Taylor took over.

I told Fran that we cannot talk about the rituals. We are not ready to face that darkness. - Taylor

I know we aren't supposed to be cutting, but sometimes it's just necessary. I'm sorry. I was careful though. -Ivy

June 19, 1992

I woke up with more cuts on my wrist. I felt better, but also worse. How much longer can I do this before it kills me?

* * *

Ever feel like you're stuck in a person's body and you're not sure who has control? Ever feel like you're trapped in a mind of thoughts that aren't your own? Ever wonder what the point is? Ever try to figure out the reason why? Ever want to be honest, but you know it would devastate everybody in your life? Ever make an attempt at

this honesty and see the response? Anger,
confusion, hurt, exhaustion . . .
Big—bigger than any person could see or imagine.
Huge—like the things people try to conjure up.
Ugly—like the horror they've seen in their
nightmares.
Untouchable—second to all, but first to the
unknown. Eternal. Untouchable.
Fallen.
Me.

* * *

The Beginning

Nobody ever tells you when you're being abused.

You feel crazy. Crazy amounts of shame, crazy amounts of fear, crazy amounts of pain. And nobody knows, so nobody is there to tell you that it isn't your fault—that you are a victim in this insane world, which so cruelly decided to swallow you whole. So, you pray, and you wish, and you dream that you can go far away someday, that you can run away from all of this. But the truth is, you can never fully escape. You can never fully forget.

....

June 20, 1992

I work my way from one side of the yard to the other. I stumble as I attempt to run, still adjusting to my sister's latest pair of hand-me-down shoes. They will be the shoes to carry me through the next school year, which I start in just two short months.

Hurdling over puddles and rocks, Rose and I make our way through the stretch of land that connects my yard to the Archers'. After what seems like an eternity, we reach the railroad

tracks.

This was the last time I remember feeling whole●

....

I sink the pen deep into the paper as I conclude the entry, making an ink blotch where a small, neat period should've been. I had written the memory down as it came to me, realizing while I wrote that what should be a happy memory only made me sad. **Shocker.**

Old, familiar feelings creep around inside me. I lie on my back and stare at the ceiling, wishing that I could fly through it, fly far away to a place I have never been before—a place where none of the bad can reach me.

THAT PLACE DOESN'T EXIST.

I try to hold onto the safety of Rose's company, the hope of the railroad tracks, the anticipation of the train that would bring us far, far away.

Away from what? That is the question I need to answer. I know it is bad, but I don't know how bad. I need to know, and whether I like it or not, my brain begins to show me. It shows me the beginning of the bad.

....

The wind whistles through the frail structure of the building. My feet kick up dust and stray pieces of garbage as I shuffle along next to a woman. The woman holds my arm so that I do not fall. She smells of fresh pie.

Other noises start mixing with the sounds of the wind: hushed voices, whimpers, the woman telling me to behave or else she will hurt me. Wait—that can't be right. I thought I was safe.

The woman stops. She lets go of my arm. I hear other people coming near. Shoes unfamiliar to me come into my line of vision as I stare at the ground. I am afraid to look up; I cannot look up. A large, tough-looking fist comes into view. It opens to reveal a cube of sugar.

"Eat this," a voice as rough as the hands it belongs to says. Afraid of what will happen if I don't obey, I take the cube and timidly place it in my mouth.

Eventually, the garbage and shoes beneath me begin to swirl together, and the wind begins to sound like it is singing to me. My fear dissipates.

Hands grab at my arms and legs. I feel my clothing leave my body. I am told to lay down. My fear returns, but in a muffled sort of way—like someone has placed a thick blanket over the top of it.

Sizzle. Pain sears through me, and I want to scream. I need to scream, to let the pain out through a throat-cracking cry. But I can't. The only noise I can make is a whimper.

Smack. Fireworks crack against my body. "Stop crying. You cannot be weak." I press my lips together.

Hurt. An unwanted touch thrusts into me, splitting my body in two.

The wind screams for me.

Standing on the Edge

I could feel the inevitable encroaching.

There is a reason children are afraid of shadows, a reason they are wary of what lurks in dark corners or deep closets or right behind them. Adults often try to dismiss the instinct that arises when they themselves catch sight of these shadows. They tell themselves to "grow up" and "grow a pair." But maybe they are right to be nervous. Maybe we should all be a little afraid of the darkness that follows at our heels.

....

The smell of food tells me it is breakfast time. Donna stopped coming to get me for meals a week ago, dropping her dinner and church attendance rules. Now I just stay in my room until my rumbling stomach forces me out to scrounge for leftovers in the cool light of the refrigerator.

Yawning, I roll upwards and grab my notebook from under my pillow.

....

June 21, 1992

Today feels off. I feel uneasy, afraid, sad. Not to be negative, but I don't think it's going to be a good day.

....

The sunlight fights its way through the lace curtains on the windows, casting warm rays around the otherwise depressing room. I can't shake the lingering feeling of sadness that surrounds me. It has become almost like the other parts of me, taking over my body in random increments. I try to fight through the emotions to do certain things: meetings, sessions with Fran, walks. Most of the time, I win the battles. Nonetheless, the war inside wages on.

What time is it? I know it is a Friday and that I am scheduled to work at 10 a.m., but I am otherwise scattered. Going to my job when I am fighting for my sanity seems utterly ridiculous. But if I am ever going to get out of Donna's, I need to grow my savings or risk sleeping in my car again—scrounging for scraps.

Exactly, so it might be time to get out of bed now.

I focus on the task at hand: getting dressed. Fighting off fatigue, I make my way to the pile of crumpled clothes that most closely resembles my work uniform. In one fluid motion, I twist my long, curly hair around and around until it forms a knot close to my head, where I secure it with a clip.

I dare a glance in the small, oval mirror that hangs on the wall, only to find that I hardly recognize myself: My once bright blue eyes appear to be almost gray, and the color has all but disappeared from my cheeks. I am just thinking that maybe I should trade going to work for a nice jump out the window when suddenly, a voice flickers to life in my head.

....

"You're beautiful, Tori," Rose whispers to my reflection in the fingerprint-covered mirror of the girl's bathroom at school.

"Am not," I say with a faint smile as I try to contain my hair using two rubber bands stolen from my teacher's desk. Once I'm done, I take a moment to smooth out my shin-length dress, ensuring that no wrinkles have crept into the fabric. The dress is a gift from my father for my first week in the fourth grade, and I've taken extra precautions to ensure it stays immaculate for picture day—from choosing a bus seat clear of mud to avoiding running through the halls. Now, as I press the black and white newspaper print pattern to my shrunken stomach, my keen

eyes find zero flaws. A foreign sense of elation washes over me. I can't help but beam. I really do feel beautiful.

Rose and I turn in uniform, hastily walking from the bathroom and down the hall. We are late. By now, the rest of the children will have already lined up in the cafeteria to have their photo taken. But I don't care. As we make our way to join them, I almost skip with joy.

"You're next, darling," the man behind the flashing light says to me several minutes later.

I walk forward eagerly. I don't normally enjoy having my photo taken, but in this moment, I do not feel the same as usual. I do not feel shameful and destroyed.

I hop onto the stool and sit up tall. I smile and wait for the flash of light. But it does not come. Instead, I hear the voice of the photographer once again.

"You have to let people see your teeth when you smile," he says with a toothy grin of his own, as if leading by example.

I hesitate. I never smile with my teeth. The world is too ugly, too untrustworthy for me to give it a real smile, a real piece of who I am. But the man behind the camera seems kind. I can tell from his worn flannel and baseball cap that capturing images of squirrely schoolchildren is a part-time gig for him. He definitely does not consider himself a professional. Nevertheless, I trust his opinion.

I remember the feeling of joy that rushed through me upon seeing my reflection in the bathroom. Thinking not of all the bad things in the world, I focus on how good I feel in this moment, and I smile—a genuine, toothy smile.

....

The recollection of fleeting happiness only amplifies my current feeling of emptiness as I continue to look into the mirror. My smile is gone. My newspaper print dress is gone. It is all gone, and there is nothing I can do about it.

Failure. Worthless. Pathetic. Disgusting. The words boomerang in my head, knocking out any motivation to live or to even move.

What is the point? Why bother trying to be happy when I am destined to fail?

HAPPY? WE ARE NEVER EVEN GOING TO BE OKAY IN THIS LIFE.

We are never going to escape this hell.

The weight of all the sadness comes crashing into me. As I continue to look in the mirror, self-hatred swims through my body, working its way into my fist. Before I know what is happening, I am punching the mirror—the negative thoughts blasting out in waves of fury.

You stupid fucking whore.

You're a bitch.

No wonder you're alone, look at you.

Ha! You think you're hot shit?

Who could love a creature like you?

Who the fuck do you think you are?

You're nothing.

Again and again and again. I punch and punch and punch, until all the glass has fallen to my feet. Blood drips from my hands to the floor, splattering on the shards. My skin is shredded, but I don't feel pain. In fact, I feel a little dose of calm.

When you look in the mirror,
What do you see?

A grim reflection of reality.
A sight too hard to grasp with one's mind.

A look of fear pressed on over time.

This vision of reality leaves only great sorrow.
These scars of hardness,
Put on for tomorrow.

Holding what's closest to self-motivate.
Turning away with . . . Painted Embrace.

An hour later, my bandaged hands are waving hello to my coworkers like nothing is wrong, like they hadn't been tempted to veer my car off the road five times on the way here.

Act normal. Don't be a freak.

The store is ready for the start of summer: pink and yellow plastic flowers sit in glass vases at the checkout, cardboard cutouts of suns hang from the ceiling, and mini-skirts adorn the impossibly thin bodies of white mannequins. The attempted cheeriness does nothing but irritate me.

"Happy first day of summer, Tori!" my manager greets me with a smile as I walk onto the sales floor.

WHO GIVES A SHIT?

Bad. Warning. Today is danger.

"Thank you. Um, you too," I say through gritted teeth, pinching my forearm in an attempt to keep the voices at bay.

A group of middle-aged women stand clustered around a display rack. I turn in their direction and do my best to match the cheery atmosphere of the store. "Good morning, ladies. Are you shopping for anything in particular today?"

The women turn toward me in a synchronized motion, giving the impression that they are operating with one brain instead of three. "Yes, do you know if this blouse comes in a larger size? I don't see one on the shelves here, and well, my third kid really did a number on my mid-section." The tallest woman, who is not even remotely close to fat, says the words in a hushed tone as she steps out of the group. "I'm afraid smalls won't cut it anymore."

I smile. "Let me go check in the back."

Once inside the clothing storage area, I stand on a step stool and sift through various cardboard boxes of clothing. Someone had left a small radio on in the corner, and a morning talk show buzzes in the background.

"As some of you might already know," I hear the radio host say, "today officially marks the first day of summer . . . " The voice goes on, but I stop processing the words.

Summer solstice, summer solstice, summer solstice.

The words shoot around in my head, knocking on the closed doors of long-forgotten memories.

....

I eat slowly, forcing myself to lift tiny bites of food into my mouth, despite the hunger nagging at my stomach. When my dad asks why I'm not eating much, I lie and say that I spoiled my dinner with ice cream from the neighbors. Even as I listen to his light scolding, I don't dare consider telling him the truth—the truth that I don't want to eat, because after dinner is when I'm supposed to go with my family to the Archers' for a bonfire.

Although I am excited to play yard games with my siblings, I dread the moment that my family leaves. I heard Mrs. Archer tell my mom this morning that I can spend the night there tonight. My mom said yes. She doesn't know any better. She thinks it will be a treat for me. She is unaware of what will really happen once everyone has gone home. The monsters hide from her in the dark, and I cannot show her.

Tonight will be extra awful because of the day: the solstice. The monsters love the solstice. They say it is a time of renewal and great power. They drink in the sun's energy and feed on it. They think it will help to keep them young. I think tonight might be the night I die.

....

I step down from the stool and crouch into a ball, tucking my head between my knees. I try to slow my breathing, to bring myself back into the present—but I can't. I can't do it. I need someone else to walk back out onto that sales floor and help the bubbly women waiting outside, because I am too scared to move.

....

Jade:

Tori needs to keep this job; we need to keep this job. If we lose it, then there is a possibility that we will sleep in the car again, go to the streets again, and I can't handle that—again. Not when I have gotten used to somewhat normal, indoor living. That's why I take over when Tori needs a break.

I heard that woman ask about the blouse, so I know why Tori is in the back storage room. I also know where to look. I don't mind finishing up Tori's task. The working world fascinates me, and I want so badly to be a part of it. I wish I could come out every time that Tori goes to work.

Once I am fully in control, I stand up, straighten our uniform, and find the correctly sized blouse. I proudly present it to the woman waiting for Tori out on the sales floor. She thanks me, and my confidence soars. It feels so good to be appreciated. The others never appreciate me, not really.

I finish the rest of our shift without any complications. On the way back to Donna's, I switch the radio in the car from Tori's God-awful rock 'n' roll to some smooth jazz. Taking full advantage of the situation, I also slyly tuck Tori's cigarette pack underneath some loose napkins in the center console and pray she won't find them for a while. I hate the smell of smoke. It is better than the drugs were, but still filthy, if you ask me.

Once back at the house, I fill out a passage in the notebook that the therapist told us all we could write in. Then, I exit the vehicle and hope that Tori will let me remain in control long enough to enjoy one of Donna's home cooked meals.

....

The next thing I know, I am sitting at Donna's kitchen table, hands folded in front of me.

"What did I do?" I interrupt Donna's giving thanks.

"What do you mean?" Donna looks at me, puzzled.

"Never mind," I say. "Sorry for interrupting.

Well, it couldn't have been Blake or Faith that took over, I deduce. *When they come out, they make sure everyone knows. It couldn't have been Ivy because I don't have any cuts. Jade. It had to have been Jade.* She had come out a few other times at work to finish shifts when I couldn't. Nobody ever notices when Jade comes out. She is organized, responsible, and friendly—and probably better than me at my job.

I am not very hungry. Excusing myself from the table, I go out to my car to look for my notebook, which I soon find tucked neatly away under the passenger seat. I turn on the radio and, annoyed, switch it from jazz back to my music. The change in tune, and the fact that I can't find my smokes, makes me even more confident that Jade had been the one to take over. My suspicions are confirmed when I open the notebook to find Jade's neat handwriting telling me that she briefly came out, worked our shift, and brought "the body" home.

I remain in my car, listening to music, until I am unexpectedly blindsided by the sight of the rising moon.

Darkness means death. Run. Run. Run!

....

Taylor:

The moon sends Tori retreating as I march forward. It is a familiar act for me: functioning through fear. I know what nighttime has brought with it on many past solstices, and so I do not blame Tori. This is what she does every year.

Since we are no longer in active physical danger on this night, I have evolved from surviving horrors in the child body to taking precautions in the adult body. Normally, this simply consists of taking a knife to bed, staying awake most of the night, and rising early to return the weapon before Tori awakes.

Tonight, however, will prove to be slightly more challenging. Tori is becoming more in touch with her emotions surrounding nights like these. Plus, we are not alone. Tori shares a dwelling, which means I have a duty to protect not only us, but the other people in the home. They are not aware of the dangers, and so they do not know to be on guard. Last year, the family was gone on a camping trip when this night arrived, so taking care of Tori in an empty house was easy. This year is a different story entirely.

As calmly as I can, I shut Tori's car door, making sure to lock it before walking up the driveway and into the house. Once inside, I realize that Donna must have re-arranged. The knives are not in the same place as last year. Puzzled, I begin looking through the various drawers, rummaging around, until suddenly, I get the sense that I am not alone.

"Tori?" A timid-sounding voice inches toward me from the kitchen doorway.

It is Donna. She is watching me the way one might watch a rabid dog: unsure whether to feel pity or fright.

"Yes?" I try to keep the body's voice level, to show her that she does not need to worry about me.

"What . . . " She hesitates. "What are you doing?"

"I'm looking for a weapon so that I can protect us. I'll be done shortly." I resume searching the drawer that is open in front of the body.

"I really wish you would stop. There's no need for a weapon."

"You do not know," I say quietly and continue my mission.

"Why . . . " She clears her throat. "Tell me, then. Why is there a need?"

"It's the solstice. A very dangerous time, especially for vulnerable children like yours. Everyone in this house needs to be protected, and I'm going to do it."

As if on cue, Donna's two children peek around the corner. "What's she doing?" one of them asks.

"Nothing, sweetie," Donna replies. "Go back to your rooms, and I'll be there in a minute to tuck you in."

The children obey—their footsteps hurrying away.

"Sorry for waking them," I say as I continue fumbling through the drawer. "But this is really important."

"Tori . . . "

I hold up one hand, stopping her. "Ma'am, I normally don't tell people this, but my name—it's Taylor. And I need you to trust that I know what I'm doing."

I hope my words will calm her, but they seem to have the opposite effect. Donna puts one hand on the white trim framing the doorway, as if to steady herself. She looks pale.

"Are you alright?" I ask, genuine concern brewing in my heart.

"Yes, but I think it might be best for everyone if you were to go somewhere else for the night."

Oh, no. This is not good. I need Tori to come back and calm her down before she sends us to a looney bin.

Finally, I find what I am looking for: knives. They are tucked into the back corner of a child-proof drawer. Using the counter as a block from Donna, I slip a small one into the waistband of our jeans and retreat into the body so that Tori can smooth things over.

"Listen, Tori. I mean, um, Taylor. I know you have the situation under control, but I still think it would be best if you went somewhere safe for tonight. The children—the children are confused, and, well, I think everyone will be better off if you stay at the hospital, just for tonight."

I look at Donna, perplexed. "What?"

"Tori?"

"Yeah?"

"Oh, thank goodness. Um, you weren't here just a moment ago. Someone named Taylor was. They, um, they said you needed a weapon to defend us and yourself."

We are standing in the middle of the kitchen. I look at the clock. It is almost 10:30. I have lost an hour or so of time. *Oh, no.*

"I'm sorry," I say, taking a step back from an open drawer in front of me. I feel something in my waistband. Checking what it is, my hands gloss over what seems to be a kitchen knife. ***Oh. God.***

"It's okay, dear." Donna says, unaware of the concealed weapon. "But, like I was telling Taylor, I think it might be best if you went to the hospital for the night—just in case. You've seemed on edge all day, and I just would hate for another . . . incident to happen. I can drive you, if you want. We can go to the same one as before—the one where that doctor you're seeing works."

I accept Donna's suggestion, despite the fact that I feel like melting into a puddle of tears. After she leaves the room, I slip the knife from its hiding place back into the open drawer and wonder why Taylor feels scared enough to need a weapon.

My feelings are these, though I hope they're not true.
The feeling of aloneness my whole life through.
Realizing the places that I don't belong,
Letting go of the hope that I'll ever fit in.
The feeling of sadness deep in my soul.
The recognition that I may never be whole.
Looking in the mirror and seeing what I dread.
My face and my body—it's like they don't match.
These realizations I have come to tonight.
Now is the time for me to accept them for my life?
If I accept these feelings, will I be giving up?
Or will I be doing myself a favor and ending much strife?
The decision I won't yet make until the night is through,
and I'll hold on to the small hope that I'm being a fool.
So, God, if you're there, please show me tonight.
Do I belong? Should I go on?
Please help me, if you can, to know what choice to make.
Please, if you want me to belong, don't leave me alone tonight.
Please, if it's not true, don't let me feel lonely or sad.
Show me some answers.
If you do, I'll be glad.

The Abyss

I couldn't escape myself or them.

They say there are signs of a storm just before the rain begins: rising electricity, dropping air pressure, darkening skies. Similarly, there are signs of warfare that can be experienced just before the battle begins: rising calamity, dropping of hope, darkening realities. Just as one prepares their home for an incoming storm, one must prepare their spirit for an incoming battle, because the latter can be far more damaging than even the most catastrophic weather.

....

The clean hospital sheets itch at my skin while a television sputters out nonsense. I am claustrophobic, despite the openness of the room. I don't dare close my eyes out of fear of what images my mind will project. It feels like there is a lifetime of loneliness between me and the sunrise. All I want is to speak to someone who might actually understand, to someone who knows me—truly knows me. But no one does.

I brought a fresh notebook with me to the hospital tonight—the two back at Donna's are almost completely full. As I reach to grab the notebook from the bedside table, something slides out from under its cover, gliding gently to the floor. It is a postcard with a picture of a beach that is located a few hours away from Donna's. Cursive letters spelling out "Washington" spread across the top of the card. **What the hell? Did I get a postcard for my family and forget to send it?** Frustrated at my apparent lapse in memory, I hoist myself out of bed to retrieve the card. Turning it over, my heart stops. There is no message written on the card. It is simply addressed to me, signed from the Archers.

I feel as if I might pass out. My mind catapults from one scenario to the next: **Are they here now? How did the postcard get in my notebook? Have they been in my room at Donna's?** Dropping the card, I run to the bathroom and slam the door. **I am in tremendous danger.** There are no locks on any doors and no weapons. Helpless, I cower in the corner, watching the door. I feel small, childlike.

....

My neck aches from looking down, but I cannot bear to look up. I am too terrified of what may lay ahead. All I can do is focus on taking one step, then another. I watch my tennis shoes grow dirtier as we move through the dank, echoey space.

Someone holds my shoulders, steering me in the direction I need to go. I wonder what I missed in gym class. I hope Rose isn't here. She is far more afraid of the dark than me, and this place is very, very dark.

The dull glow of an old flashlight illuminates the area in front of my feet, lighting the ground just enough so that I don't trip on various obstacles: pebbles, sticks, beer cans, spray paint canisters. My nose is running from the coolness of the air, but I don't dare sniffle. I don't want them to think I am crying. If we cry too loudly, we get hit—that's one of the few rules that I know to follow, one of the few consistent pieces of knowledge I cling to in order to survive each scenario.

The lace of one of my shoes unwinds as I continue walking. I watch it flip-flop back and forth, thinking to myself that if I were to try and run away now, I would be doomed to fail. **If you run, we will find you. We will get you.** *The words told to me numerous times throughout the years reverberate in my memory.*

I nearly trip on the stray lace as the hand on my shoulder guides me harshly around a corner and into a room. This is the second room we have been to today. I wonder how deep into the earth these horrible tunnels go, how many rooms there are. I wonder if we are headed right down to hell itself.

....

When one of the nurses comes to perform a wellness check some time later, she finds me in the bathroom. I look up in a panic as she approaches, half-expecting to see Mrs. Archer's scowling face leering over my small body.

"Oh, Tori," the nurse says kindly as she touches my arm. "What's the matter?"

I can't tell her, can't explain it. *I need to get out. Now.*

"Let go, let go. Get away from me." I begin to struggle, kicking my legs out, pulling at her arms.

She calls for help, and the next thing I know, another nurse is sticking me in the arm. Sleep overcomes me.

....

I can't explain my outburst when Fran comes to my room asking questions—not without seeming paranoid anyways. *Maybe I am paranoid.* It is difficult to trust myself when I have countless other parts inside of me.

My hospital stay was extended after the postcard incident. When the nurse brings me my discharge papers, I have an overwhelming desire to stay. Right now, these walls are bringing me a sense of security.

As I get into Donna's car, I wonder why the Archers are here. *Did they follow me?* The parking lot rolls past me. I feel Donna's anticipation and realize with sudden shame that she has been talking. She has asked me a question and is waiting for an answer.

"Tori? What is wrong with you? Did you hear me?"

"What? No, sorry."

Donna sighs, but does not repeat her question. Instead, she grows silent and turns up the radio, leaving me alone with my thoughts.

Stolen Words

They weren't as nice as they seemed.

There are plenty of reasons to fear the evil that dwells in this world. It is a very powerful, very real threat. What many don't realize, is that evil can also feel fear.

Evil fears that which it cannot control. It fears knowledge. It fears exposure. And so, evil will often do everything in its power to keep hold over its victims. Violence, manipulation, theft, and deceit—evil knows no bounds. It will use whatever means are at its disposal to ensure that fighting it is one of the most difficult things one will ever do.

....

June 25, 1992

I have not been able to sleep since I found out the Archers might be here. My thoughts are repeating, circling back to one question: What do they want?

June 26, 1992

This is bad. Knowing that the Archers may be near has sent our system spiraling. The others are becoming restless, scared. They want to run again, and I have to *say that I agree. If I could take over the body long enough to get us out of the state, I would.*

- Jade

June 26, 1992

I can feel the fear inside of me, but I refuse to run. They will not control me. I need to fight. I have a responsibility to find the truth, even if it kills me.

I AM SCARED. THE MONSTERS ARE GETTING CLOSER.
FROM: FAITH

June 28, 1992

I can no longer walk down the street without watching over my shoulder. It takes all of my courage to leave my room. Maybe I should talk to Fran about this? Can I trust her?

I brought us to work today. All of the others were too scared, even Jade. I wish I could take the knowledge of the Archers' relocation all to myself.

There's a reason I hold the worst times inside me.

There are certain truths that only

I can bear. - Taylor

July 4, 1992

It is the Fourth of July today—a day that always brought me a small dose of joy as a child. I want so badly to be running in the yard with Rose and my family. I want so badly to not be here. I remember my father always spent the better half of June prepping for the 4th of July party, or rather festival, that we hosted at our house. He orchestrated obstacle courses, races, games, food, and so much more. It was an event that brought out nearly every person in the small town. I remember one year being especially hot . . .

....

The sun beats down on me. My father places flags and streamers throughout our yard. My red shirt smells of sweat, and my blue denim shorts feel especially stiff as I walk toward my father's tall figure.

As I near him, I become distracted by our steadily filling driveway. I stop and keenly watch as members of the town trickle in, one family at a time. With horror, I notice the Archers walking up the driveway. They approach my father, and my heart hammers in my ears. **Please don't hurt him.**

I turn to Rose. I have to be strong for her and my family. I have to make this day as normal as possible—make sure that the monsters know I'm doing a good job at pretending.

I walk to where my father stands, now conversing with the Archers.

"Oh really, it was no bother," Mrs. Archer says, beaming as she produces a freshly baked blueberry pie from the bag draped across her waist.

You could not pay me a million dollars to eat that pie.

"Hello, Tori!" she exclaims when I take my place by my father's side.

I muster a small smile and return the greeting: "Hello Mr. and Mrs. Archer."

Mr. Archer says nothing, just stands stoically by his wife's side, shielding his face from the sun with one tanned hand, while the other rests on his hip. She owns him. I can see that, even as a child. Just like I can see that he longs to grab Rose and I, to bring us away from the sunshine and into the woods, where no one will see what he does next.

"Tori, why don't you go help your mother with the prizes?" my father says, pointing in the direction of a small table where my mother is arranging a variety of toys and candy.

I quietly leave—grateful for the opportunity to escape. Grabbing Rose's hand, I bring us both to the safety of my mother.

After we arrange the prizes, Rose and I quickly run to the field before we can be assigned any more tasks. There, we scope out the obstacle course and plan our strategy for earning the fastest time. My father has strung a rope from one tree to the next to serve as a tightrope, and we practice walking it a couple of times.

"The gunny sack races will begin in five minutes. Please either find a seat or head to the starting line," my father's low voice booms through an improvised megaphone concocted out of a plastic cup.

I once again grab Rose's fragile hand in mine. Together, we run toward the crowd gathering around the starting line.

My skin is red by the end of the celebration, but I don't mind. On that summer day, Rose and I are children: running, playing, laughing, and free—even though the shadow of tomorrow never leaves our sides.

....

An ear-splitting, heart-palpitating blast echoes through the house, causing me to plummet from my thoughts down into reality. Quickly, I consider all the possible scenarios for the noise: a blast from a gun, a sound effect on the television, knocking on the front door. Knocking—that's what it is. Actually, it is more like a pounding—a pounding so loud it sounds like the door might give way any second, cracking under the pressure of the fist.

I hear Donna answer the door and wait for her courteous "no thank you" speech that she always gives to salespeople.

"Oh, hello." Her greeting startles me. **She knows them.** "She's upstairs. First door on the left."

"What the fuck?" I more so exclaim the question than ask it as I leap out of bed.

Seconds later, the door knob turns, and a group of men enter. I move to the opposite side of the room. There are three of them, tall and looming. One addresses me, while the other two look around.

"Ma'am, we're social services," he says. "We were called by Donna and Ray out of concern for your own personal safety and the safety of others. Do you mind if we talk to you for a minute?"

I do not answer the man. Turning my attention to Donna and Ray, who stand silently in the doorway, I ask, "Donna, Ray, what is this?"

They do not respond.

"Tori," the man who had previously spoken attempts again to engage me in conversation, "it's our understanding that you've had a difficult time lately. Donna has informed us that you've been in and out of hospitals. She also told us about some of your recent episodes. We would like to help you, if you will let us."

"It seems like I don't really have a choice," I say, mustering the iciest glare I can manage. The man's facial expression remains blank.

"This is for your own good," he continues. "We were told that you've been keeping journals. We need them in order to determine how much of a danger you may be to yourself or to others."

"A danger?" I look at the man in confusion. "How am I a danger?"

"That's what we need to find out," he says simply. "Which is why we would appreciate your cooperation— before something bad happens to those you love."

His words register as an immediate threat, and I become at a loss as the other men continue searching my room. It doesn't take long before they find the journals under my bed. I pray they won't find the one underneath my pillow, but they soon do.

Powerless, I watch as they go out the door—taking everything I have with them.

What Now?

I felt lost.

Nothing is more personal than a journal. For those who find solace in writing, the inside of a notebook is often the only place they feel safe enough to be truly honest. There, they record everything: their hopes, fears, dreams, nightmares, their deepest and darkest shame.

Tori was one of those people—someone who found sanity and clarity in writing. Her journals were the only place she felt she could be authentic without fearing consequences or judgment. They were where she had begun to find healing.

Then, in a matter of minutes, her safe place was gone, taken from her—just like everything else.

....

I stand at the doorway of the room, shock reverberating through me. **They are gone. All of my memories, all of my thoughts, all of my clues to the puzzle.** I watch Donna and Ray recede down the hallway.

"Why?" I resent the sound of my voice cracking as I ask the only question I can think of. "Why would you do this?"

Without turning to face me, Donna says coolly, "It's for the best."

What am I supposed to do now? Donna clearly read my journals, and she has just shown me what she thinks of them: a parasite infecting her home.

It's more than that.

I don't care. I don't care if it is more than Donna being afraid of me or ashamed of me or frustrated with me. It doesn't matter. The journals are gone. There is no point anymore.

We need to go. Now.

I am too sad to go, too sad to even move another muscle.

Now, dammit.

Compromising, I decide to go for a drive.

....

Before long, the sound of a train horn blares into my eardrums. The ground vibrates beneath my feet. I am standing near the tracks that run through the outskirts of the city. My car idles in a clearing behind me. Another horn blast, and I see the train. Instinctually, I prepare to jump on board—just as Rose and I had done before. Except this time I know I will not let go; I will hold on until I cannot hold on any longer; I will ride the train to a new life.

As the train reaches me, it is going slow enough to make the jump. I could find the what-if. But I don't. I just stand stoically as it passes me. It feels too late to find my what-if. The damage is done. Holding onto a train won't change that now.

A Leap of Faith

I just wanted to be safe.

Ignorance is bliss, or so the saying goes. What you don't know can't hurt you, right? Maybe that is why so many people shut themselves off from the truth. They tell themselves it's only fiction. They don't realize the danger of ignorance, the danger of giving darkness a side alley on which to quietly travel through the world.

Knowledge is power—that's the other side of the coin. If you recognize wickedness, and you know it to be real, then you have the capability to destroy it. You have the responsibility to destroy it, before it devours everything you hold dear.

....

"Tori?" Fran asks, her face swimming in and out of the haze of my exhaustion.

It has been days since I last slept, staying awake out of fear that the men will return and take me with them this time. It is a primal kind of fear, like when I was small and feared the monsters.

"I think I need to go," I tell her.

"Go where?"

"Somewhere else."

"Why do you feel the need to go?"

"They took my notebooks," I blurt without stopping to think. Something in me trusts Fran, despite all the betrayal in my past. I want her to help me. I need someone to help me.

"What?" Fran sounds appalled. "Who took your notebooks?"

"I don't know. The state—social services or something. They came into my room and took them."

"Tori," Fran's voice deepens as she says my name, telling me that this is serious, "I'm so sorry that happened to you, and I think you are right."

"I am?"

"Yes. I think you need to go. I hate to lose you as a client, but I don't think this is the best place for you to continue your healing."

"Why?" I am completely caught off guard and unsure of where this is going.

"Do you remember when I asked you if you knew what ritual abuse was?"

"Yes."

"Well, I asked because a lot of what I have heard from you and your internal parts during our time together points to the possibility that you experienced this type of abuse as a child. This is very serious because there are a lot of very dark, very powerful people in this world who partake in this kind of abuse—people who wish to harm those who survived and remember it."

"Oh." I feel my body growing tighter, my muscles tensing in anticipation.

"This event with your journals tells me that perhaps it is best if you continue healing somewhere safer than here. Have you ever considered inpatient treatment?"

"You mean like stay in a hospital? For more than a few days?"

"Yes. There's a colleague of mine who helps run a program in another state. They specialize in helping survivors of extreme abuse. It's in a confidential location with the best security available. I think it would be wise for you to give it a try. But, of course, the choice is yours."

I weigh my options. I don't like any of them, but I know I cannot continue to live with Donna and Ray. I also know that I want to keep trying to get better. I owe it to Rose, my parts, and my family. **They deserve answers; I deserve answers.**

"Okay, I'll do it."

....

As I park my car outside the hospital a week later, I wonder if I will be adding this to my list of mistakes. I have driven for days, across state lines and through a lot of boring towns, to get here. But now, looking at the building, all I want to do is leave.

I turn off my car. In the silence, I take a moment to smoke and observe my surroundings. I have already been cleared by two security booths and am parked inside one of multiple fenced-in lots, right in front of the main doors. I can see glimpses of people, all dressed in similar clothing. It is virtually impossible to determine who is a patient and who is not. Gates surround the yards and buildings, and I ponder whether they are here to keep the patients in or to keep something far worse out. Stepping out of my car, I hardly have time to stomp out my cigarette before I am greeted by a security guard and a kind-looking woman.

"Tori Becker?" The guard talks first.

"Yep."

"ID, please."

I show them my license.

"Welcome." The woman speaks to me in the way a concerned mother would to her wounded child. "If you would please follow us, we will get you situated."

I grab my bag, pushing the pack of cigarettes to the bottom. We all begin to walk toward the entrance.

Part IV:
Remembering Tori

Under a mask of peaceful sleep,
To the dawning of each new day,
Lies a small child who has lost her way.
From the depths of her being,
There are words spoken but never said.
Only hoping that someday, some way,
Her silent cries will be heard.

Under the mask of a peaceful countenance
Lies the fear of losing control,
Trying desperately not to slip away into life's own existence.
Holding out her hand so that somebody can see
That this mask does not portray who is really underneath.

Grasping hold of glimpses of reality of the love that encompasses
her emptiness,
Carrying her through the cloudy times.
Trying hard to keep sight of the freedom she has seen
through Christ.

Dented. Stained. Broken. Shattered.

There are so many ways for something to experience trauma, lose value, and inevitably find its way into the trash. You can try to repair and clean it, but eventually, it can no longer pretend to be the fully functioning object that it once was. Then, you must decide to either live with it being the way it is or throw it away.

Objects like this and human beings do not share the same story. Human beings can experience trauma, but this never means they lose their value. They should never be discarded just because they are outcasts in society's eyes. Nobody ever fully knows what is happening within another human being, and nobody has the right to judge. Someone can be completely shattered and still find wholeness. Nobody is broken beyond repair.

This is what Tori learned as she began to painstakingly put the pieces of herself and her life back together. She was not a danger. She was not ruined. She started to see that she was more than what had been done to her. Some days were definitely better than others, and healing was a grueling process, but she pushed forward.

....

July 30, 1992

Nobody will ever really know me—not even Rose. The more I learn about myself and my parts, the more I know this is true. My journey is one that will only be understood by myself and God—held safely in the pages of my heart.

The staff here encouraged me to write from the first day that I arrived, but I only recently found the courage—the courage to risk putting pen to paper, despite the possibility that my words could be taken away once again.

Before returning to these pages, I first had to realize the power that I hold over myself and my story. I had to realize that even though the darkness is strong, I am stronger. That even if they do try to take everything from me, they can never take my truth.

July 31, 1992

So far I've made one friend and a handful of enemies—the worst of which is Jemma, who insists on trying to kill me. Of course, she never gets very far. They have security people stationed every three feet in this place. Still, it has me watching my back even more than usual, wondering why she targets only me.

My friend, Cori, says it's because she's "just
fucking bonkers," but something tells me it's more
than that. They talk a lot about breaking our
programming here, and I can't help but wonder if
this is Jemma's programming mixing with mine—
if she is being used by something darker.
Ha, I really sound crazy. No wonder I'm in a
glorified looney bin.

August 1, 1992

*We don't belong in this place. We belong out in the
world, where we can work and find purpose. This place
isn't helping or healing. It's ruining everything.*

- Jade

August 2, 1992
While being here feels right, it's sometimes very
hard to resist the urge to run. My memories come
in spurts, like water through a kinked hose, and
I'm terrified of what will happen once I straighten
the hose all the way out.

* * *

Strap wrapped around head.

Very tight—over mouth.

Things being stuck in ears—hurts ears.

No.

Always had bad earaches.

Scars on eardrums.

Doctor thought from infections.

* * *

August 5, 1992

My therapist, Dr. Williams, has seen a few
different parts of me come out during our one-on-
one sessions. I've noticed that having multiple
personalities is more normal around here than it
is abnormal. This makes the whole thing slightly
less horrible, I guess.

Anyways, Dr. Williams now wants to engage with
my different personalities in order to learn more
about them. She says they are pieces of who I am
and that getting to know them, their purpose, and
their memories is crucial in my healing journey.

This idea is only slightly terrifying.

The shrink asked me today about my first memory in Tori's body. I told her about the first time Tori was home alone as a teen: how absolutely terrified she was, but how she was not about to call up a friend and admit to being scared. I told her about the party we threw that night, about the first time Tori tried drugs willingly—how good and familiar it felt to the body. I told her about how Blake and I kept fighting for control of the body all night. Blake wanted a piece of the action, but I wanted to hang out with the other teenagers. I remember I told Blake she was too old for a high school party, and she got mad.

After that, every time there was a social situation that Tori didn't like—prom, dates, graduation—I came out and played the role of a normal teen. Every time Tori was too sad to function, I came out to show everyone that we were okay. But sometimes, it was all too much for me—that's how the cutting started.

I would cut until I felt better, the others shut up, and Tori was good enough to come back. I was doing us all a favor. I had found a cure for our madness. I don't understand why none of the others see it that way. -Ivy

August 6, 1992

I help Tori function in the real world—that's what I told the doctor when she asked why I think I'm in Tori's body. I desperately tried to get her to see what a valuable and irreplaceable role I have. I told her about how I pay the bills when nobody else can remember, how I budget what little money we have, how I come out to work when Tori can't. The doctor said she understood, but I worry that she didn't. I worry I'm becoming irrelevant.

- Jade

I AM TORI'S CHILDHOOD. I AM THE ONE WHO KEEPS HER COMPANY IN A WAY THAT ROSE CAN'T AND HOLDS ONTO HER GOODNESS WHEN SHE THINKS IT IS ALL GONE. I AM THE ONE WHO STAYS AWAKE WITH HER UNDER THE BLANKETS UNTIL SHE CRIES HERSELF TO SLEEP.
FROM: FAITH

I am strong. I will survive this. I will do what I need to do to ensure we all survive. Tori created me to protect, and so I will protect—at all costs.

That is what I said when Tori's new doctor asked why I'm a part of Tori. But when she wondered what I had to do to protect, I shut up and didn't say another damn word.

If anyone knew, they would throw us out onto the street. Or worse, they would tell Tori. Tori can never know what we've done, what we've been forced to do. - Taylor

August 6, 1992

Every time that I read something one of the others wrote in here, my heart aches. Not only do they show me pieces of my past that I had buried deep down, but they also show me their pain—our pain.

With every entry, I gradually understand more and more about us. And with that understanding, comes the sadness of all that we became and all that we went through—each of us feeling as though we were on our own.

* * *

Holding hands.
Not me.

* * *

August 7, 1992

I woke up feeling nauseous. Not a sick kind of nauseous, but the kind you feel when your gut is

trying to warn you of something—the kind when
your insides twist and turn.
I know it is Rose. I can feel that something is
wrong.

* * *

Light. Candles.
Small person; little girl.
Blood.
Sad.
Tray with stuff on it.
* * *

IN A CAGE. SEE THE KEY BUT CAN'T REACH IT.
WISH AN ADULT WOULD COME HELP.
FROM: FAITH

August 10, 1992
In group today, we talked about our addictions.
Everyone here has one.
The counselors often say our traumas are the
roots of all of our addictions.

Example: I became addicted to drugs because I was drugged when I was small. It helped me survive as a child and as an adult.

I've never wanted to pop a pill more in my life.

* * *

Women screaming, begging, pleading. I open the door. They are chained to a wall, pregnant. I know their babies will die. I want to help. I am powerless.

* * *

August 15, 1992

I am the kind of exhausted that cannot be described. My brain, body, heart, and soul are all worn. I keep trying to remind myself that healing is possible, that many of the counselors here went through similar things as me—but it's hard. It's hard to see the light at the end of this impossibly long and dark tunnel.

WHAT A BUNCH OF MOTHERFUCKING BABIES. ALL DAY I LISTEN TO THE OTHERS BITCH AND MOAN ABOUT HOW

THEY HAD TO DO THIS OR HOW THEY GOT HURT THAT WAY. NONE OF IT EVEN REMOTELY COMPARES TO THE PAIN I'VE HELD ONTO: HAVING TO LIE THERE NAKED WHILE MULTIPLE MEN AND WOMEN HAD HORRIBLE, PAINFUL SEX WITH THE BODY. SO AS FAR AS I'M CONCERNED, EVERYONE JUST NEEDS TO SHUT THE FUCK UP AND GET ME A DRINK. - BLAKE

August 16, 1992

Blake hijacked my one-on-one therapy today. Apparently, she walked in with a cigarette hanging out of her mouth, yelling about how she needed a drink. When Dr. Williams told me about it, I felt embarrassed—ashamed. Even though I know most people here struggle with similar things, sometimes after these episodes, the shame is so large that I feel as if it might squash me—push me down until there is not even a glimmer of hope left.

But Dr. Williams assured me that there is nothing wrong with me or Blake. She said that Blake, and all of my parts, just need to learn new roles. She

said they've been trained to keep me alive and
functioning through unimaginable circumstances,
and now they have to heal too.

* * *

Blindfolded. My sight taken away; my senses
sharpened to the point where I can smell the
different ethnicities of the people touching me. I
can tell who has recently had sex and who hasn't.
I can tell which women are menstruating. I can
smell the thickness of the summer humidity
sticking to my naked body. My nose
overcompensates and becomes like a super
power.

* * *

August 18, 1992

I cannot focus on anything for more than 10
minutes. Even the simplest tasks—brushing my
teeth, eating, getting dressed—they feel almost
impossible. The encouragement from the
counselors and the other people here are the only
things keeping the depression at bay.

I still cannot sleep without nightmares plaguing me, but now they don't go away when I wake up. I feel like the only thing that will bring me peace is revenge—justice. I want to remember enough so that I can pinpoint who did this to me and why. But deep down, I know that even if I remember who did what, I will never see them pay.

I'm sad inside.
I'm mad inside.
I'm alone inside.

I'm afraid of the dark.
I'm afraid of the light.
I don't like the rain.
I feel too much pain.

I don't want to live.
I don't want to die.
I want to be free,
So that someday I can
Learn how to fly.

****

I remember the feel of fire.

Burning. Sick. Heavy.

Need to be calm. Help me be calm.

****

I tried to cut today, but was unsuccessful. They don't have anything sharp here. What a bunch of asshole losers. How can they say they're trying to help and then stop me from doing one of the only things that calms us down? Don't they know that we need it? I know I should want to stop, but I don't. I've found certain ways to get through life, and everyone just needs to leave me alone about it. Anything else feels too impossibly hard. -Ivy

August 22, 1992

The doctors here don't listen. They don't let me convince them that we are fine, and they only tell Tori the important things. This means I have to eavesdrop, and

August 23, 1992

I'm feeling better today. They gave me a few days to have a break from the intense work after they saw how it was negatively affecting some of my parts. They don't want the parts to try and sabotage my healing; they want them to feel safe here. What they don't understand is that we rarely feel safe.

August 25, 1992

I feel sick in my chest, tired.

I feel like there's something big in me that has to come out.

August 26, 1992

Jemma is still a threat. It terrifies me more and more each time she tries to attack me. But today, Cori had an idea.

Jemma is extremely religious—in a twisted sort of way—and says that she hears God's will in her mind. So, Cori figured that if we could control what God told Jemma, then we could convince her that I did not need to die.

Cori used the loudspeaker. She snuck into the main office and broadcasted her voice throughout the building, telling Jemma to stop attempting to take my life. It was a pretty bad plan, but I think it actually worked.

Afterwards, Cori and I rushed to my room, slammed the door, and smoked out the window. I haven't laughed that hard in a while.

I used to be impressed by simple things,
Catching a butterfly and gentle streams.

I used to feel safe very easily,
The touch of a friend or a song we would sing.

I used to be happy all of the time,
Friends full of laughter and family I called mine.

I used to love Jesus with all my heart,
He was there for me from the start.

Simple things I want to know,
Happiness, safety, love, and joy.

To feel as though I was young again.
Will this ever be God's plan?

To be impressed by simple things,

To have everything that was meant to be,

To be impressed with what I once knew,
To love and be loved,
To freely choose.

August 28, 1992

Today I went for a run in the yard. It was a short

run, but it felt so good to move. I haven't run since

the car hit me. My joints now ache, but my mind

is at ease. I'm dreading my one-on-one therapy

less than usual.

....

When she was in therapy later that day, Tori felt
that same old feeling of dread creeping up. Her run that
morning had only temporarily dissipated the unease. She
felt like there was something horrible lurking on the
outskirts of her brain, and if she wanted to look hard
enough, she could make out what it was.

....

I speak the memory out loud:

"My small, naked body twitches in small spurts of
shivers as I lay on my back, spine pressed to the dirt floor.
The smell of mildew hovers in the air. I take short breaths
to avoid making too much noise. The darkness
surrounding me is so all-consuming that I can no longer tell
if my eyes are opened or closed. A familiar numbness
wraps around me, sheltering me from the full impact of the
situation.

I wonder where Rose is. I am about to muster up
the courage to go look for her when I hear familiar

footsteps approaching. A door opens, and a light blinds me. Digging my fingers into the surface beneath me, I feel dirt creep under my nails. As the pain increases, I clench the floor with all my might, willing myself not to scream."

I have to stop here. I cannot remember what comes next. Only when Dr. Williams reassures me that I am safe, does more of the memory come.

"All I can feel is searing, hot pain spreading from my privates to my stomach, and then into my soul."

"It's okay, Tori," I hear Dr. Williams say in the background. "You are safe now. This will not kill you. If you survived it once, you can survive remembering it."

"I hear a low grunt, and the pain is gone. ***Maybe that is all that will happen this time,*** I hope. Then, I hear the shuffling of feet. There is a clicking noise. A dim glimmer from a lighter illuminates the darkness just long enough for me to see shadows spread on the ceiling above me. Shadows. Plural. There is more than one person in the space with me. I feel nothing but dread as the light goes out. The pain returns, only it is slightly duller this time. I feel myself begin to drift. My mind becomes blurred, as does the pain. I black out."

"Okay, Tori. That's enough." Dr. Williams' voice is like a lighthouse beacon breaking through the darkness of the storm inside me, guiding me out. "I want you to get up off the dirt floor now. You're alone. The bad people are gone. In front of you there is a door. I want you to go to it."

I do as I'm told.

"Okay, good. Now open the door. There is a field on the other side. A long, green, grassy field."

"I see it; I see the field."

"Okay, now go into the field. You will be safe there. Nobody else can find you."

I go out the door and run toward the field. I tell myself I am safe.

When I open my eyes, I find that tears have soaked my cheeks. My hands are gripping the arms of the plush chair in Dr. Williams' office, and my body is shaking with sobs. This is the first time I have cried in 13 years.

....

August 30, 1992

After I finished remembering what had happened to me on that dirt floor, I felt exhausted on a level I had never felt before. But I also felt a strange sort of peace.

I cried for an hour after coming out of the memory. Years of tears poured out of my body: tears for the pain, tears for us, tears for me.

Tori got a phone call today. I don't know who was on the other line, but they whispered a string of words, and Tori collapsed. Our internal system was sent into overdrive. I came forward because all of the others shut down. Even I struggled to come out. The body was non-functioning for hours before I managed to claw to the surface. Now our therapist stops by every half hour or so to try and sort through things, to try and get the others back. Maybe I do need to start sharing some of what I hold. Maybe, for the sake of safety, Tori needs to know more details about what we are
up against. - Taylor

* * *

One phone call. One sentence. My system imploded.

* * *

September 5, 1992

Since the phone call, Dr. Williams and I have been
working on figuring out exactly what happened
inside of my system and how I can work to resist
a total shutdown if it were to ever happen again.
I'm coming to realize that the people who hurt me
also installed certain defenses in my system—sort
of like a self-destruct option—that they could use
in case I ever started to sort things out.
Many of the counselors here have given me input,
advice, and strategies for what to do when I start
to feel out of control.
I sometimes feel like I'm living out a fictional
story: something so horrible and wild that it
cannot possibly be real. But it is real, and I have a
responsibility to determine my ending.

September 6, 1992

My favorite part of the day is walking. Cori and I
often do laps around the grounds together,
bullshitting like we are in a totally normal place
and have a totally normal friendship. Sometimes
we cut through a thin patch of trees that sits on

the east side of the facility. Being in the trees, we can almost imagine that we are walking somewhere else: a nice path in a park or a hiking trail. When we take this route, it often reminds me of walking in the forest during my drug treatment.

I am sure now that the figure I saw in the woods during that time was something from a memory, triggered because I was in the forest alone, appearing as a vivid hallucination. I don't fear another episode like that one. I know now that if that were to happen again, I would be able to confront the figure and work through whatever memory came.

September 6, 1992

The wind was chillier than usual on my walk this morning—a reminder that fall is coming. I always have to stop myself from panicking when I think of this—of fall. I do not know exactly why I feel this way, but I do know that throughout my life, myself and my parts have dreaded the changing of the leaves.

September 9, 1992

The more work that I do, the more I can internally hear the others. I can now differentiate between the voices in my head. I still can't always remember what happens when a different part takes over completely, and I still can't make them be quiet, but I can tell who is saying what. Sometimes, when they all get going, I just sit and stare in silence, listening to the chatter. Once they all feel like they've said their piece, they grow silent.

I'm starting to appreciate what they've all done, how they've all kept me alive. I no longer see them as the enemy, but rather as different aspects of my pain that need to heal and come together.

September 10, 1992

While eating in the cafeteria today, I experienced my most controlled episode yet. I was spooning mashed potatoes and gravy into my mouth when memories of being forced to eat awful, awful things flew into my consciousness: Dane and the cabin mush; the monsters and the bloody organs, topped with pain and sadness.

At first, remembering felt like a physical blow, and I nearly gagged trying to swallow what was in my mouth. But then, instead of going away or self-medicating, I rolled with the punch and tended to the ache it left behind. I'm not sure how I managed to cope, but I did. Maybe all of this work isn't for nothing; maybe I'm getting somewhere.

September 12, 1992

Someone broke into the hospital earlier today. She made it as far as the common area, where a group of us were playing cards. As soon as she walked into the room, I instantly recognized the face as the one I had seen following me when I was living with Donna and Ray—the same face as the one in the black car.

I stood up fast, pushing away from the table so quickly that my chair fell back with a crash. Thankfully, the noise of the chair caught the attention of the nearest security guard, who, when he saw the fear plastered on my face, realized something was wrong. Within moments, he and another guard had grabbed the woman. As they escorted her out, she shouted one word over and over. The word made my insides stir. I could feel myself wanting to shut down again. But ever since the phone call, I've been working hard to learn how to resist my programming.

"No," I told my parts. "Stop. We're okay."

We were still.

September 15, 1992

This morning I looked at my reflection for the first time in a while. The mirrors here are made of plastic-like material, so my image was slightly warped. With sadness, I remembered the day that I punched out the mirror at Donna's.

The mirror shows my dark and shaded past—seeing all the evil that my life was meant for. But I hold onto the promises that the reflection will someday be the healed Tori that I've always longed to be.

September 17, 1992

I am beginning to grieve the loss of my childhood, my innocence. It makes me so angry that it was stolen away, that shadows linger behind every good memory.

Out of all of my parts, Faith makes me the saddest. She reminds me of my smallest self, of the child that never got to feel truly safe.

In a place far away, there was a little girl who could play.

A land where there was no pain, no fear,

Only happiness and love.

This place was filled with more flowers and toys

than one could imagine.

There were parties every day,

Balloons and ponies, even parades.

She could be whoever she wanted to be.

She was free to create a safe place of harmony.

Colors and paints, papers and pens.

Drawing pictures of her freedom,

Coloring a world of safety and warmth for herself.

She was happy and sound in who she was,

The things she had created, the make-believe places she had gone.

Her heart was filled with laughter,

And her world would never end,

Because this place that she created was deep within.

Deep where nobody else could enter.

Only she could get in.

It would be wonderful to have a place like this in my life.

A place of fun and laughter.

A place I could call mine.

THE NICE LADY GIVES ME PAPER. TELLS ME TO
DRAW.
I LIKE TO DRAW.
BUT SHE WANTS ME TO DRAW ABOUT THE BAD
THINGS.
I DON'T LIKE THE BAD.
SHE SAYS I'M SAFE.
SHE SAYS THE BAD CAN'T GET TO ME. SHE SAYS
IT'S OKAY TO FEEL SAD. SO I DECIDE TO DRAW. I
DRAW THE BAD.
FROM: FAITH

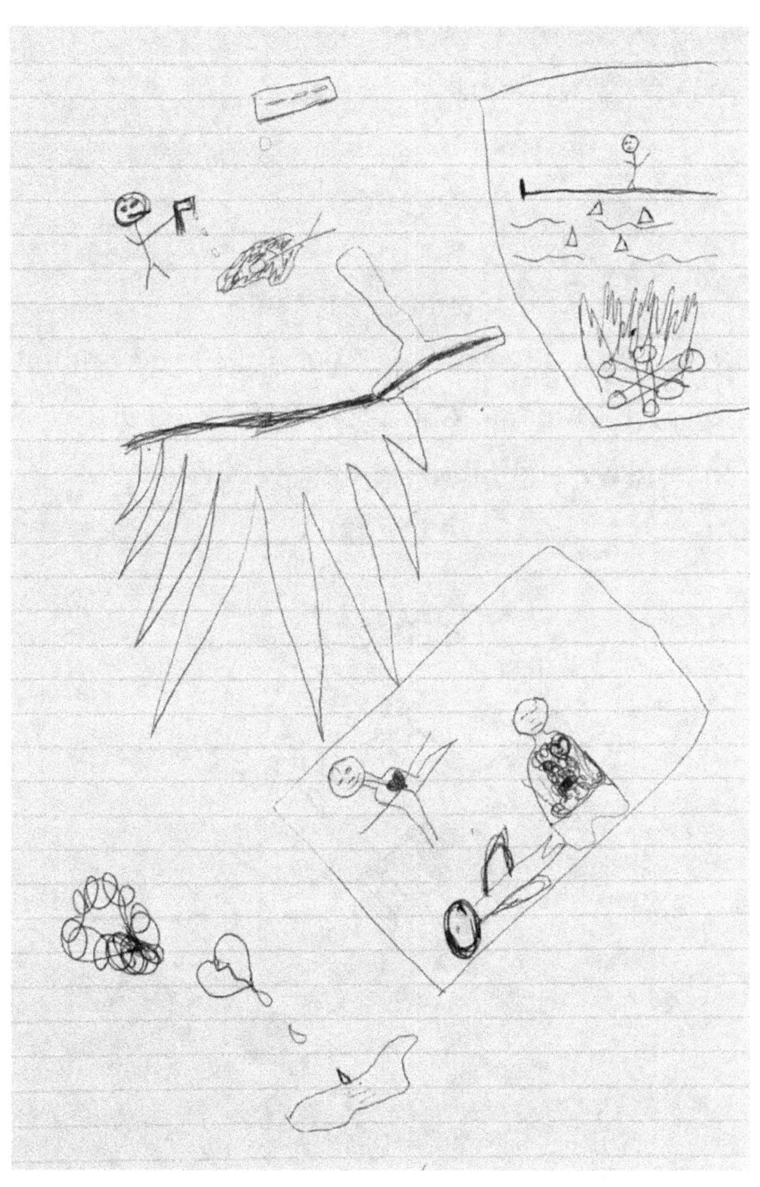

I FEEL LOTS BETTER NOW. SHE WAS RIGHT.
DRAWING THE BAD WAS GOOD. THAT'S A
FUNNY SENTENCE. IT DOESN'T MAKE NO SENSE.
BUT IT MAKES SENSE TO ME.
FROM: FAITH

September 21, 1992

Today I was able to hear Faith while I was talking to Dr. Williams. She asked if we could draw together. I said "okay" and drew whatever came to my mind.

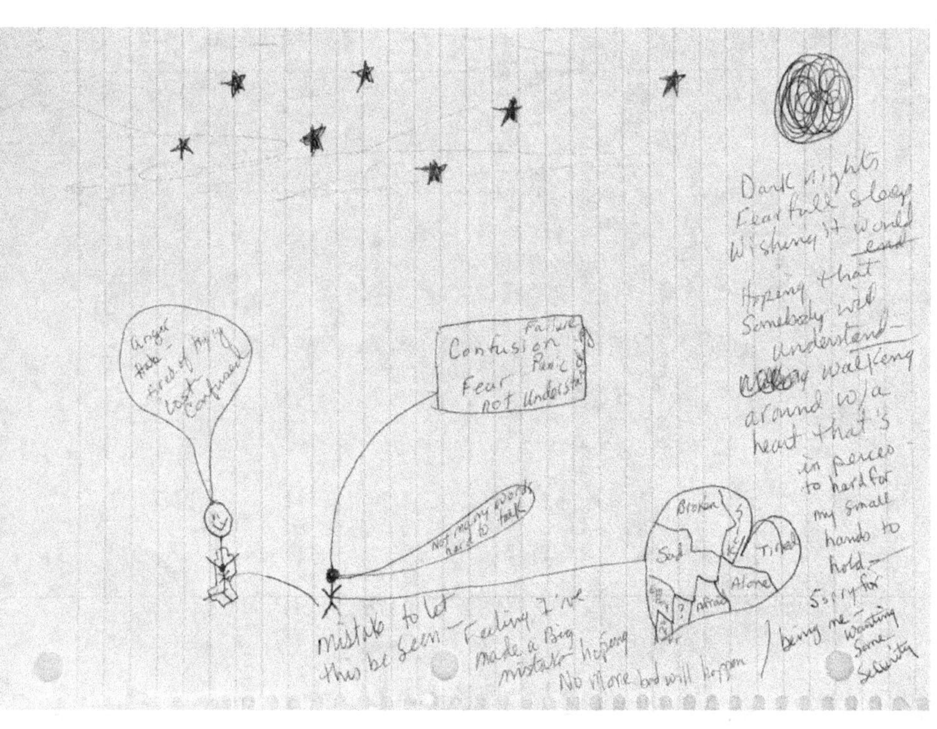

anger
tired of my
lost
confused

Confusion   Failure
Fear   Panic of
not understa

Not anymore words
needs to talk

Broken
Sad   Tired
Alone
Afraid

mistake to let
this be seen — Feeling I've
made a Big
mistake hoping
No more bad will happen

Dark nights
Fearfull sleep
Wishing it would
end

Hoping that
Somebody will
Understand —
Walking
around w/a
heart that's
in pieces
to hard for
my small
hands to
hold —
Sorry for
being me — Wanting
Some
Security

THE NICE LADY LET ME PLAY WITH TOYS TODAY.
I LIKE IT A LOT WHEN SHE ~~DOSE~~ DOES THAT. I
NEVER REALLY GOT TO PLAY WITH TOYS
BEFORE.
SHE ASKED ME IF THERE'S ANYTHING ELSE I
WANT TO TELL HER ABOUT THE BAD BUT I SAID
NO. I HAVEN'T REALLY THOUGHT MUCH ABOUT
ANYTHING EXCEPT TOYS SINCE I DREW.
THEN SHE SAID THAT I DON'T HAVE TO COME
OUT NO MORE IF I DON'T WANNA. THIS MADE
ME CONFUSED AND SAD. I ASKED HER IF TORI
DOESN'T NEED ME NO MORE. SHE SAID NO.
SHE SAID TORI WILL ALWAYS NEED ME BUT
THAT THE BAD IS ALL GONE NOW. SHE SAID
TORI'S GOTTA BE A GROWN UP NOW AND DO
GROWN UP THINGS. SHE SAID MAYBE IT'S
BETTER IF I JUST STAY INSIDE AND HELP TORI
FROM IN THERE WHEN SHE NEEDS TO
REMEMBER HOW TO BE LITTLE. LIKE WHEN SHE'S
PLAYING WITH LITTLE KIDS OR IF SHE HAS A
CHILD SOMEDAY.
I SAID OK BUT I SAID I WANT TO WRITE TORI A
NOTE.
FROM: FAITH

September 26, 1992

Reading Faith's message almost brought me to tears. At first, I was relieved. I thought this change would make me feel more normal. But then, I began to feel more empty—like I had lost touch with a best friend, even though I know she's still inside somewhere.

....

Becoming a cohesive unit with a part of you that has been kept separate for so long is a disorienting experience, to say the least. Feeling off balance is the best way to describe it. It takes time for both you and your part to adjust. But once you do, you find that you feel slightly better and more whole—another piece of the puzzle sliding into place.

....

September 29, 1992

A few days have passed since Faith's decision to help from the inside, and I have found my equilibrium. I can sense a little piece of innocence inside of me that I haven't felt since the abuse started. It's as if it was preserved through Faith.

I have made the decision that I have to start sharing more, for the sake of myself and the others. Seeing some of Tori's anguish relieved by the release of a painful memory and Faith finding peace has given me the assurance I need. Maybe sharing is how I protect us now. We all deserve some peace. – Taylor

I WISH I COULD DO WHATEVER THE HELL FAITH JUST DID. I WANT SOME FUCKING PEACE. IF I CAN'T HAVE ANY FUN, THEN WHAT'S THE POINT? I'VE DECIDED I'LL TELL THE PEOPLE HERE WHATEVER THEY NEED TO KNOW, DO WHATEVER I HAVE TO DO, IN ORDER TO EXPERIENCE

September 29, 1992

I hear the others talking about what Faith has done.

Taylor seems to understand it; Blake seems to want it;

Ivy seems not to care.

I am terrified.

- Jade

September 29, 1992

Reading everyone's reaction to Faith's new
position has been slightly jarring. Jade is right—
change can be terrifying.

September 30, 1992

I told Dr. Williams about my concerns in our one-
on-one this afternoon. She assured me that
nobody will be forced to do anything that they are
not ready for, and Taylor will not share anything
that I am not ready to hear. She reminded me

that the strengths of my parts are also my
strengths.

The first memory I have is of suffocation—the
struggle to get enough oxygen. The air around us
is thick and damp and a sickly sort of sweet. I try
to move, but something keeps me in place.
Suddenly, we are pulled from a dark place into the
light. I feel straw on the body's bare legs, arms,
and back.
I strain to make out our surroundings. There is a
dark fluid all over us. A strange woman wraps a
blanket around our shoulders and says we have
just been re-born. I look beside me and see a large,
brown animal, gutted down the center.
It is now that I come to understand: I am an
animal. - Taylor

October 2, 1992
I miss my family a little extra today, but I know I
cannot go home—not yet. I need to heal some

more. I need to figure out how to share my truth in a way that will not destroy. I need to protect. It makes me so angry that my abusers have isolated me all my life. When I was small, I wouldn't dare speak of what had been done to Rose and I. They said that if I ever told, they would kill the people I loved—and I believed them. I still do.

The fact that I was being abused never crossed my parents' minds—why would it? Plus, I now believe that the people hurting us were not idiots: They knew what they were doing and how to do it. They were powerful people with an evil agenda, and they had whatever resources necessary to accomplish it.

October 3, 1992

I have finally found a purpose in this God-forsaken place Tori has forced upon us all. Once a week, I help sort and put away the books in the library. The work is so easy that it's a little demeaning, but it still brings me joy. I love using my brain to organize.

I TOLD THE SHRINK THAT I'M READY TO GO, TO FOLLOW IN FAITH'S FOOTSTEPS AND LEAVE THE RESPONSIBILITY OF THE BODY TO TORI. SHE SAYS WE WILL WORK ON IT. WHAT KIND OF BULLSHIT IS THAT? - BLAKE

October 4, 1992

Whenever we end group, the counselor asks everyone a "light-hearted" question. I guess she sees it as a way to give us a sense of normal in our crazy worlds. Today, we talked about our favorite season. I said mine was winter, and everyone looked at me like I was crazy—like they hadn't all just finished talking about some of the most horrific shit I've ever heard.

I explained that, as a child, I felt safer during the winter than I did any other time of the year. I shared how I would skate for hours on the frozen river—that there was a sense of power in skating over the ice.

Talking about this, I also began to remember fleeting moments when I felt powerless on water: times of torture on the ships that would dock in the harbor in summer. I remember being taken and sold to the men aboard the ships. I remember that, despite the fear that consumed me, I always felt a sense of responsibility to Rose. Ultimately, though, I knew there was nothing I could do to get us out of there. The only thing I could do was obey and pray that they let us live.

"Please, Tori. Please do it right," Rose would beg me—a deer facing the headlights of a semi-truck. So, I would do everything just how I was supposed to. I would perform the way they wanted in

exchange for Rose's life and my own—all the while
wondering what I was worth to them. How much
do grown men gain from the sale of a child?
I longed to leave my body in those moments. I
wanted to go somewhere safe. But I would stay
present in the body until the pain was over so
that I could ensure our safety.
But in the winter, everything was different. The
water that had so long controlled me was now
literally beneath my feet.
I loved the feeling of the crisp air, the wind licking
my cheeks, the solitude. It was different from
loneliness. Solitude was welcoming and safe. It
was peace.
I dreamt of running away less during the winter.

October 8, 1992
I was asked today about my faith. The question
stirred a million and one emotions inside of me. I
remembered the monsters mocking my faith
while they hurt me. I remembered them spitting
on me, asking where my God was now that I had
sinned.

They told me that God had cast me out of heaven, down into hell to be with them.

But they said I was still special. I was special because I was destined to serve as a daughter of darkness.

I knew this was wrong. I told myself with all my might that I was still good, that God still loved me. I fought the darkness, told it I would never serve that side.

But it was hard not to doubt my faith when the pain got worse, when the monsters twisted Bible verses until they formed a noose around my neck.

I remember feeling so confused. I was confused how the Archers could abuse me, then stand in church the next day praising God.

I am beginning to realize more and more the role that manipulation of my belief in God played in my abuse.

Nowhere you can go to escape the silence.
Nothing you can do to take away the screaming pain.
Stuck inside of a person you never wanted to be.
Feeling like somebody planned your destiny.
Wishing you could have it all back.
Grow up and understand that we get to start where we're at.
Trying to accept what choices other people made for me.
Trying to understand why.
Trusting the people around me, only because of the love I feel.
Trusting the God they trust, not yet finding him to be my own.
Wishing and hoping, someday soon.
Little piece inside of me knows I'll someday be free and able to look
in a mirror,
To see what other people see.
What a wonderful day that will be.

October 11, 1992

For once, I didn't have a nightmare last night. I saw Rose.

In my dream, we were sitting by the railroad tracks. I could tell that we were both younger than we are now, but I had all of the knowledge I do currently.

I almost didn't believe it was her. When she spoke, she didn't sound like herself. She sounded faint—weak, almost. I knew something was different, but when I asked her what was going on, she just said, "I'm okay."

We sat in silence for a long while, not even a distant train whistle could be heard.

"Are you trying to erase me?" young Rose finally asked.

"No," I responded firmly. "Never."

She nodded and seemed to settle into herself. Then, suddenly, Rose and I were no longer by the railroad tracks and no longer young. We were in the present, and we were sitting in our old hangout spot back home.

"I've thought about it," Rose said, and I immediately knew what she was talking about.

"And what do you think?"

"I think you are right—I think we need to heal. You've taken care of me my whole life, and so I trust you. I just want us to be okay, to be happy. Do you think this will end alright for everyone?"

"I have to believe it will, Rose."

"Okay," she said. "Then, I am with you—just like we promised. Always."

"Okay," I said.

I came out of the dream feeling a sense of calm and comfort that I do not think I have ever felt. I now know that I am, without a doubt, doing what I need to do.

October 12, 1992

I remember pain—everywhere. The smell of burning flesh and electricity. Shocks running up, up, up my legs and into my privates. My soul is screaming, but I don't dare make a sound.

They tell me the pain is energy. They tell me to use the energy—to take it in through my body and give it to the darkness. The small child in me goes to hide; my brain shuts down. So much pain, too much pain. I am going to die.

I PUT UP WITH A LOT OF SHIT THROUGHOUT MY LIFETIME: I WORE THE SLUTTY COSTUMES THAT THEY FORCED US TO WEAR; I DID THE DEEDS THAT FULFILLED THEIR PERVERTED DESIRES. I ALWAYS HATED IT, ALWAYS DREADED IT, ALWAYS PRAYED THAT THEY WOULD AT LEAST DRUG US BEFORE THE REAL BAD SHIT HAPPENED. BUT I NEVER GOT SCARED—UNTIL THE DEMON.

TORI REMEMBERED A LITTLE ABOUT IT TODAY, BUT SHE DIDN'T GET TOO FAR IN THE MEMORY, BECAUSE I HOLD THE REST. OUR SHRINK SAID TO WRITE IT DOWN. I'M NOT SURE WHY I'M LISTENING TO HER. MAYBE I'M SICK OF HOLDING IT IN? I DON'T KNOW. I FEEL TOO WEARY TO FIGHT THIS HEALING SHIT ANYMORE. I'M SO FUCKING TIRED OF FIGHTING.

WEAK—THAT'S WHAT I WAS WHEN THE DEMON CAME. I SHOULD'VE FOUGHT

BACK THE FEAR AND JUST FOCUSED ON THE SEX LIKE USUAL, BUT I COULDN'T. THEY WERE SHOCKING THE SHIT OUT OF THE BODY WHEN I CAME INTO IT. THE MAN LOOKING ON WAS TELLING TORI TO USE THE ENERGY FROM THE SHOCKS, TO CHANNEL IT INTO THE DARK. I HAD NO IDEA WHAT THE FUCK HE WAS TALKING ABOUT—UNTIL I SAW IT.

ABOVE HIM, THERE WAS A BLACK MASS. NOT A CLOUD, BUT A MASS—THICK AND OOZING. IT WAS COMING DOWN TOWARD THE BODY. AT FIRST, I THOUGHT IT WAS GOING TO KILL THE MAN—LAND RIGHT ON HIM AND SQUASH HIM, BUT INSTEAD IT WENT THROUGH HIM AND INTO THE ELECTRICITY. I FELT IT GO INTO THE BODY. HE STARTED GIVING MORE COMMANDS, TELLING ME TO LET THE DARKNESS USE THE BODY. I WANTED TO FIGHT IT, TO SCREAM, "HELL NO, YOU MOTHERFUCKER!" BUT I COULDN'T. I BLACKED OUT, AND NOBODY KNOWS THE REST.

TORI WOKE UP IN HER BED A FEW HOURS LATER. – BLAKE

Reading Blake's entry breaks my heart. I know I need to honor her decision to share this piece of her story, let her know how grateful I am for what she endured so that I did not have to.

....

Blake,

Thank you for always protecting me when I could not protect myself. Thank you for taking the brunt of the sexual abuse. I owe you my life, and I hope for all of our sakes that you can find some healing in all of this hurt.

October 13, 1992

While it was hard and terrifying and horrible to read, Blake's latest entry also led to some progress, I think.

It's interesting—the more Blake writes and talks about how heavy the burden of her role was, the less angry I am. I can feel Blake becoming more peaceful, even if she won't admit it.

I FEEL TIRED. I REALLY HOPE TORI
DOESN'T NEED ME TO HAVE ANY MORE
DISGUSTING SEX IN THIS LIFETIME,
BECAUSE I DON'T THINK I CAN DO IT
ANYMORE. IS THIS WHAT IT FEELS LIKE
TO BE A DEPRESSED LOSER? - BLAKE

Blake,

The abuse is over. We are safe now. There will be
no more unwanted sex.

I see what you've done for us, how you have kept
us safe. What you've endured and what you've
held inside—it's a debt I can never repay. The only
thing I can do is allow you to get some rest. I hope
you can rest now.

October 16, 1992

I feel a strong desire to cut. It's like Ivy is sensing
Blake's sadness and my exhaustion, and she is
pushing for this solution.

Why won't Tori listen to me? I came out for like two
seconds today, and before I could even try to find a
sharp object, she was back in control, telling me that

....

After reading Ivy's entry, I am able to talk to her. I don't know how, exactly, but it is as though I can feel where she is inside, and I am able to reach her.

"I do need you; I need all of you," I say to her. "More than ever. We just have to find a new way to work together—a way where nobody gets hurt. Even though we aren't cutting anymore, you can still help when we are feeling sad. You can help by giving me doses of good memories from when I was too broken to fake being whole. I will never shut you down completely. I promise."

....

October 17, 1992

Communicating directly with my parts felt kind of odd at first, but I think it may be helping. Even though I know Ivy is not fully healed, I can tell she is calmer. I no longer feel the need to cut, and I remembered a previously forgotten snippet of my high school graduation: my mother hugging me and whispering into my ear how proud she was of me.

Where before there was extreme angst, I now feel
a slight sort of warmth. I know that Ivy will be
okay.

I haven't sensed Blake at all since our last
exchange. I hope she's okay.

October 19, 1992

The more this month progresses, the more dread I
feel.

**I DID WHAT TORI ASKED: I GOT
SOME REST. I FEEL BETTER. - BLAKE**

Blake,

I'm so glad you're feeling better.

October 20, 1992

I was happy to hear from Blake. I can sense her
almost every day now, but it's less intense than
usual. It seems we are no longer fighting against
each other and are beginning to work together.

I'm glad Blake managed to find a safer place inside. She deserves it. However, I can't help but feel a little jealous. This time of year brings nothing but pain and fear for me. – Taylor

* * *

Hate the smell of farms.
Their farm didn't have many animals.
It had people.

* * *

October 21, 1992

Although they are becoming less frequent, the nightmares are still here. Last night, I had the worst one yet.

I could not see what was happening. I sensed death all around me. Someone was reading what sounded like scripture, but the words were wrong: Instead of bringing me peace or knowledge, all I felt was shame.

They were saying I had done something wrong and had to pay a price. I knew deep-down that I was a victim in this place, not a perpetrator, but I

also knew that I would pay the perpetrator's
price.

They told me Jesus didn't love me, that he was
disgusted with my actions.

I prayed they were lying.

October 21, 1992

I told Dr. Williams about my nightmare this
afternoon. She brought it back to the idea of my
faith being mocked during my abuse. She said it is
possible that I was forced to do something
unspeakable, then told that I was an outcast in
God's eyes because of it.

I know she is right.

Even though I know now that my God would
never forsake me, I can remember feeling as
though He had. I thought I was alone, left with
only the monsters and their darkness.

I'm so glad I was wrong.

October 22, 1992

Cori left the hospital today. As we said goodbye, she gave me her address in case I was ever "in the area."

I was happy for her but sad to see her go. I hope she does well.

October 23, 1992

Blake came out while I was playing a game of cards in the common area tonight. It was different than usual, though. I was still sort of in control, like we were both out at the same time. I think she was present because of the scene: We were laughing and yelling playfully during every round. It was as close to a night out with friends as you can get around here. Blake wanted some of the fun—good, pure, sober fun.

And she got it. She came out and helped me to win the final round of Rummy. Then, just as quickly as I felt her with me, she was gone. It made me smile. I know that this is how things will be with her now, and that's okay.

October 25, 1992

I still have spurts of memories, but I can now usually work the memory through to its conclusion, or at least some sort of resolution. The trauma is just as intense as it has always been, but we are gaining the tools to help us cope.

October 26, 1992

I realize now that I cannot focus on the "who" of my story. I cannot put all of my energy toward trying to remember who specifically did these horrible things to me and working to see them punished. If I do, I will truly go insane. Instead, I have to just focus on remembering the pain, working through it, and coming out the other side alive.

....

Remembering and healing from buried trauma is a random process. Sometimes the pain comes in sporadic triggers, sometimes it comes in dreams, sometimes it comes as a cohesive thought.

As Tori continued to focus on healing, memories continued to surface in these various ways. However, they also began to be processed through her different parts, like in Blake's sharing of her burden, and, gradually, Taylor began to share as well.

....

I re-read the scribbled mess of a memory I had written just a few hours before coming to therapy. I know I have remembered snippets of this memory before, and I have no idea what triggered it either time, but here it is: pain on paper.

I don't always share every memory with Dr. Williams, but this one feels important. I had remembered choosing to go away—which meant someone else had come out to experience the remainder of the horror.

I hope that by speaking the memory aloud, I can encourage whoever holds the rest to come out and share. It is something I have never intentionally tried to do before. Up until recently, my parts coming out has been unexpected and mostly uncontrolled. But now, I feel like I am slowly opening more channels of communication with them. I hope that if they are ready to share, my encouragement of them will bring the rest of the memory forward. I begin to read aloud from my journal.

"My neck aches from looking down, but I cannot bear to look up. I am too terrified of what may lay ahead. All I can do is focus on taking one step, then another. I watch my tennis shoes grow dirtier as we move through the dank, echoey space.

341

Someone holds my shoulders, steering me in the direction I need to go. I wonder what I missed in gym class. I hope Rose isn't here. She is far more afraid of the dark than me, and this place is very, very dark.

The dull glow of an old flashlight illuminates the area in front of my feet, lighting the ground just enough so that I don't trip on various obstacles: pebbles, sticks, beer cans, spray paint canisters. My nose is running from the coolness of the air, but I don't dare sniffle. I don't want them to think I am crying. If we cry too loudly, we get hit—that's one of the few rules that I know to follow, one of the few consistent pieces of knowledge I cling to in order to survive each scenario.

The lace of one of my shoes unwinds as I continue walking. I watch it flip-flop back and forth, thinking to myself that if I were to try and run away now, I would be doomed to fail. *If you run, we will find you. We will get you.* The words told to me numerous times throughout the years reverberate in my memory.

I nearly trip on the stray lace as the hand on my shoulder guides me harshly around a corner and into a room. This is the second room we have been to today. I wonder how deep into the earth these horrible tunnels go, how many rooms there are. I wonder if we are headed right down to hell itself. I fade."

As I finish reading, I feel something, or someone, rising within me. I do not fight it.

....

The first thing I see when I take over for Tori is a cement ridge in the floor, separating wherever we are standing from the next area. The smell of rotting wood hits my nostrils. Everything is getting a little swirly, so I know they put drugs into the body. Fighting back the nausea that I always feel on the drugs, I try to focus.

A hand is putting pressure on the back of our head, so I cannot look up, but I sense that it is more than just us in the room.

Someone hums a song, and my skin begins to crawl. Others join in. I feel them remove my clothing. I know that they will fold the clothing and tuck it safely into a corner like they always do. They do this so that they can return us without any evidence of what they have done, so that there will be no questions from caring adults in our life.

I hear a whimper. There are other children in the room. The hand leaves my head, and I feel my arms being lifted. Rough wood scrapes my back. The cross. I know what will happen next. I prepare a space in my stomach to put all of the pain and a place in my heart for all of the sadness. - Taylor

....

When I come back into the body, I feel like I can't breathe. My head feels light, and I am afraid I might pass out. Dr. Williams helps me to steady my breathing and gives me a glass of water.

"That was good, Tori," she says, and together we read what Taylor has written.

It is rattling, but it also gives me a sense of closure to know that she holds the rest of the memory, and that I can fill in the missing pieces, if I want to.

....

October 28, 1992

I spent the rest of the day drawing, walking, smoking, crying, and talking through the pain of what has been remembered. Doing this, I felt as though I was releasing Taylor's pain, as well as my own.

Although I feel slightly guilty for sharing my

portion of the burden, I also feel

tremendous relief. – Taylor

October 30, 1992

The past couple of nights, something strange has happened: I've woken up in an upright position, facing the door. I hardly feel rested. Sleep has never been a close friend, but now it feels non-existent.

I'm the reason we haven't gotten rest lately. I've

been keeping watch at night—protecting us. Like I

said before, this time of the year

means danger. - Taylor

IT'S BECOMING HARD AS HELL TO STAY INACTIVE. STARTING TO FIND PEACE HAS BEEN NICE, I GUESS, BUT I CAN SENSE THE EMOTIONS THAT THIS TIME OF YEAR BRINGS FOR EVERYONE.

HOW DO I CONVINCE TORI TO BREAK US OUT OF HERE FOR A DRINK AND SOME DRUGS? - BLAKE

October 30, 1992

It is 10 p.m. I cannot sleep. I feel danger and memories close by, like looking at rain clouds in the sky. I can sense Taylor wanting to come out. It makes sense that she's been keeping us more alert than usual lately. I may not remember much, but like her, I can sense that fall, especially October, brings nothing good with it.

October 31, 1992

I was not able to enjoy my walk today. Every crunching of a leaf or snapping of a twig sent my heart running. I could feel Taylor and Blake: Taylor begging me to just stay locked in the room until December; Blake begging me to get my hands on some pills. Even though I also want to do these things, I tell them we cannot.

October 31, 1992

At meal time I sat where I could face the door, my
back pressed against the brick wall behind me,
leaving no space for danger.

....

At group, I try to explain the fear—how it feels like a
step backwards into all of my old feelings. How I don't
know why this is happening. How it scares me that Blake is
feeling restless after just having found some relief. How I
am afraid to relapse. ***Could be the time of year.***

The counselor who leads group, Gina, suggests
that this time of year may be a trigger. "You and your parts
may have experienced trauma around this time," she
explains. "It is not uncommon for certain seasons or dates
to bring up feelings from the past and for old survival habits
to come forward."

When she finishes speaking, a few others chime in
to say that this time of year is hard for them as well.

"Yes," Gina says after they share. "We find that fall,
and especially Halloween, are often very hard times for
those who have suffered certain kinds of abuse. Please
know that if any of you need additional support during this
time, we are all here for you."

I wonder if Rose is okay.

October 31, 1992

A glimpse of a memory. Faint, but there:

Baby cries.

Sadness, fear, pain.

My baby. Not my baby.

Please don't.

October 31, 1992

I want to drink. I want to take drugs. I want to

cut.

I talked to everyone about it: Dr. Williams, Gina,

God—even Blake and Ivy. By the end of the day, I

was able to reassure Blake and Ivy that we are

safe and don't need to escape. I told them that it's

just old pain and fear, even though it seems very

fresh. By calming them down, I was also able to

help myself in a way. We all supported each

other—agreeing as a unit that we would not

relapse.

Funny how those two used to be a main fuel

source behind the addictions, and now they are

the only reason we didn't try to get our hands on

something, anything, to take away what we are
feeling right now.

....

After dinner, I try with any morsel of strength I have left to keep my mind blank. I do not need any more emotions or memories. Unfortunately, it doesn't work. I soon feel myself drifting into a sort of sleep. Before I can stop it, I am walking through a hallway in my mind . . .

....

I see a door. The door is painted black. I feel something sharp in my back, pushing me forward. My small hands pull on the door's metal handle.

"Ah, Tori," a familiar voice greets me. "Come in and talk."

Pain. One more step forward.

A glass is placed in my hand.

"Drink," the voice says.

The liquid is warm as it coats my throat.

"Sit."

A dim light illuminates two simple wooden chairs and a metal table in the middle of the room. I cannot see the owner of the voice. I do not dare turn around to see who is inflicting the pain on my back. I sit.

"You did well last night," the voice tells me. "Continue to do well, and no harm will come to those you

love. Tonight will be very important. I want you to make sure you are doing your very best for them."

I gulp. Despite having just had a drink, my throat is dry. My tongue sticks to the roof of my mouth, making it difficult to swallow. My eyes are feeling droopy, despite the fear coursing through my body.

"Now go and get ready," the voice instructs coldly.

I stand up, and the person behind me guides me out the door. I feel like my knees might give out as I make my way to the next room, but somehow, I remain steady. Once in the room, I sense the person who has been at my back leave. Their presence is replaced with a softer one. Gentle hands wash my face with a warm rag and brush my hair. I'm put in front of a mirror. Looking at my reflection, I do not see anyone special; I do not see anyone to be proud of.

I stay focused, pushing all thoughts of what comes next out of my mind. I'm asked to stand up and remove my clothes. I obey. Something silky and soft covers my naked body.

"There you go, sweetie. All ready."

I hear footsteps approaching.

"It'll be okay."

All I can think is, **liar.**

....

Coming out of the memory, I immediately write down all that I can recall in my journal. I feel Taylor's presence. I ask if she has anything to add to the memory.

....

I know what happened on the night that you are remembering, but I will not tell anyone. I will not even write it here out of fear you will read it and not recover. Some things I will share. This is not one of those things.

I fear that we will not survive that memory. - Taylor

....

After coming present and reading Taylor's response, Tori decided to ask for help. Halloween was far from over, and she now knew she would not be okay alone that night. She realized she needed to be close to those who could help her; she realized there didn't need to be any shame.

....

October 31, 1992

It's strange being under observation here—much different than when we would stay in the other hospitals. There is no sense of isolation, no suicide

351

checks. Here, they just have us stay in the common area. We can play cards and watch T.V. There are cots temporarily set up along one wall in case anyone is brave enough to sleep. The staff are scattered throughout the room, doing their jobs. I feel protected in a sense, because I know I am not alone. There are people here to help me if I need it.

I was happy to see Gina in the room when I got here. So far, we've played four games of cards. I'm starting to get bored, but I'm okay with bored.

October 31, 1992

The night was going okay, until about 10 minutes ago. I randomly got a severe pain in my stomach and started sweating. When asked what was wrong, I couldn't explain it.

Then, as quickly as it had come, the pain was gone.

I knew immediately that it came from an old memory wanting to surface—most likely more of what I remembered earlier today.

I wish Taylor would tell me what she remembers.
I know she thinks she is protecting us all, and I
am still afraid of what she holds, but it is
impossible to heal when you don't know your own
pain.

October 31, 1992
This day has felt long, and this night feels even
longer. I am becoming exhausted, but I know that
I will not be able to sleep.
I have decided to trust Taylor to finish out the
night. I know she can do it, and I know she will
keep us safe.

I came out for the rest of the night after Tori
became too tired emotionally and physically to
continue until dawn. It felt better than any other
time I have taken control—as if Tori and I came to
an agreement to do what was best for the system as
a whole. I did not feel burdened by this, but rather
like I was a teammate doing my part.

As soon as the sun rose, we went back to our room.

I now feel sleep is inevitable.

I will not fight it. - Taylor

November 1, 1992

I slept until dinner time today and spent the rest
of the evening talking with Taylor, trying to
encourage her to share the rest of the memory. I
think we both know now that this will be crucial
in our healing.

....

*"Rose!" I stumble through the dark, desperately
using the cement walls as a guide. "Rose, where are you?"
I can hardly feel her presence. I need to know if she's
okay.*

*"I'm okay, Tori!" Her voice echoes faintly throughout
the space, and I stop moving in order to listen. "It's okay,
Tori! I'm okay!"*

I breathe a sigh of relief.

....

November 3, 1992

I have been worried about Rose a lot. Even if this
is all in my head, I am relieved to feel like my
dearest friend is alright.

November 5, 1992

Everyone is tired—inside and outside of myself. I haven't had any more memories since Halloween. I think my system needs some recovery time, and my brain knows that.

....

Two or so weeks passed as Tori worked with her parts to recover from the month of October. They were tired. They were sad. But they were together.

Jade appeared to be the only one unbothered by the triggering time, although Tori had no certain way of knowing—Jade never shared very much with anyone.

As far as the others go, it was good for them—hard, but needed for healing. For the first time, Tori felt like she could hear and understand almost all her parts clearly, and they understood her.

Eventually, everyone settled, and they were able to regain a sense of normalcy—whatever that meant to them. Taylor was the only one who remained slightly restless, most likely due to her inability to let go of the memory she held from Halloween.

....

"Taylor, I trust you." I speak the words aloud, even though I am not sure if anyone besides Dr. Williams and myself can hear them. I wait a moment, but there is no response from Taylor. I try to search for her.

"Can you hear me?" I say when I think I have found her.

"Yes." I hear her say.

"I want you to know that I trust you. I trust you to share this memory you've been holding and to stop sharing if it becomes too much. I know you have all of our best interests at heart. You have never let me down. I think I am ready for you to tell me about that night."

I wait while she thinks it over. After what feels like hours, but is probably only seconds, I hear my answer. I tell Dr. Williams, "We are ready to talk about Halloween."

I start by sharing what I remember. "I remember the door, the drink, the pain in my back, and being forced to put on some sort of silk dress. I remember being absolutely terrified. Something bad had happened the night before, and I knew tonight would be worse.

It is Halloween. I know that because I remember thinking how other kids were probably laughing and running from house to house trick-or-treating. I knew I would never experience a Halloween like that. I saw this day for what it really was: dark."

I focus on the dress.

"The dress is a little too big for me, and it drags on the floor as I'm led out another door. I feel grass on my feet. I'm starting to feel sleepy. I think that maybe I could just lie down and take a nap, wake up, and this would all be over. But, before I can do this, I'm scooped up by someone with arms much bigger than mine and placed in the backseat of a car."

I stop speaking, but keep my eyes closed, waiting for the rest to come to me.

"When I get out of the car, I am blindfolded and told to sit. The ground is cold and unwelcoming. I hear whimpers next to me, and I realize Rose is here too.

'Rose, shut up, okay? You have to be quiet. You have to stop crying.'

'I can't, Tori. I can't. They're going to kill us. We have to run.'

'No, we can't run. Shhh. It'll be okay, okay? Just hold my hand and breathe, okay? I'm right here. I'm right here. Just remember that I'm always close, and no matter what, don't take your blindfold off.'

Strong, uncaring hands grab my arms, pulling me away from Rose. I hear her gasp as my hand leaves hers. My shin hits something hard, and my bare feet scrape against the ground as I'm led away."

That is where my portion of the memory ends. I now know that Taylor must have lived through the rest. I feel her beginning to come forward and try to focus solely on what she is showing me.

"The first thing I notice when I come forward is the smell of blood—so strong you could choke on it. I realize almost immediately that we are blindfolded. This causes a little bit of panic to stir within me, but I am soon able to quiet it. It is not unusual for us to be blindfolded. I try to focus on what else I can make out using my other senses.

We are not naked. We are wearing what seems to be a dress. Someone is speaking, which turns into chanting, growing in volume as more voices join. If they are making this much noise then we must be out in the woods—far out in the woods.

I try to move my hands and am surprised to find that they are not bound. However, something tells me there is not much good in trying to use them right now. Based on the volume of the chants, I can tell that whoever is there has formed a circle around me. They must be watching me closely.

The chanting stops. They begin talking about what they call the sacred holiday: Hallow's Eve. They are talking directly to the darkness, asking it for power."

I fight through the emotion that threatens to choke me and repeat what Taylor is saying word for word in hopes that I can do her pain justice. I want to know exactly what she went through for us. As she continues, it is almost like I am in her shoes, but not quite. **Devastating.**

"The blindfold is ripped away from my eyes, and I immediately wish they would put it back on. Surrounding the body is a handful of adults, all dressed in robes with masks over their faces. I try to not show fear.

One of them steps forward, calls me the daughter of the darkness. I do my best to counteract her words in my mind, internally saying things like, 'We are not dark. We are good. We will be okay.'

I dare to look away from the people for just a moment, and I see that I am sitting on a stone. There are small fires and black candles illuminating the clearing where we are gathered. A bright, full moon casts eerie shadows."

Taylor stops for a minute, and I know she is gauging whether or not to continue.

"I'm okay," I tell her, even though I know she can tell that I am not. "You can keep going. It's alright."

She continues in fragments, as though it is becoming impossible to articulate what she went through.

"Pain. Red, hot pain. Ripping through me with its claws."

I place a hand on my stomach.

"A cry. Not from me. I am desperate."

No, no, no. Something is coming; I know it is bad. I remind myself that we are not there right now, that this is in the past, that we will survive remembering. Once I am slightly calmer, Taylor continues.

"The cries grow louder than the chanting. They echo throughout the woods. Cannot tell where it is. Too dark.
The cries become muffled.
I try to move. I cannot. I am powerless."

I allow the awfulness of what Taylor is sharing to surge through my entire being, accepting whatever feelings come with it. As she takes us through the rest of the memory, I become fully immersed in it with her— reliving one of the worst nights of our lives, remembering things I didn't realize I had forgotten.

"No!" I scream and lean forward, hugging myself as we come out of the memory. "No," I say the word softer this time as tears begin streaming down my face.

Where before the pain from this day had been sheltered by Taylor, I now feel it in all its entirety. I know

Taylor feels it too. We are both mourning together. I am not alone, but I am painfully, horribly aware.

I stay huddled in a chair in Dr. Williams' office, for I don't know how long, until I finally feel like I can uncurl from myself. Dr. Williams gets me water and spends the next hour talking with me. By dinner, I am too tired and too sad to eat. I go to my room and spend the night taking care of myself and Taylor, just like I had taken care of Rose when I was younger.

I give myself room to not be okay; I thank Taylor for trusting herself and me enough to share the pain.

I'm sorry that you had to leave this Earth in such a scary way. I'm sorry for the pain you felt. I wish there was another way. I know you're up in heaven now—no pain, no fear, no strain—with toys and games and happy things that were robbed from you that day. I wish you love and happiness—wholeness and great peace. I give you back what was taken from you on that dark October Eve. You'll always be a part of me, not from programs or from strife. But as my Guardian Angel—forever a part of my life. I thank you for what you gave me so that I might live. In freedom and in wholeness, not for darkness or in fear. So now I let you go, to a place that's full of love. So, rest, my Guardian Angel. You will forever be loved.

Although it took several days for Tori and her system to be okay again after Taylor revealed her memory, it was overall beneficial for their journey forward.

For years, Tori had repressed, suppressed, and buried so many things—things that had been slowly killing her from the inside out. At the time, it was necessary for her survival, but eventually, she had become unknowingly stuck—held back from who she truly was by all that had been hidden within her system.

As she began to face the past and the pain that came with it, she felt a lot of difficult things, but she no longer felt as though she were merely surviving. She was regaining touch with parts of her that she had pushed away for so long. She was remembering things that no human being should ever have to think about, let alone go through, but she was also remembering more than just the trauma. She was remembering who she was.

....

After I finished showing Tori what I knew from that night, I felt as though I had failed at my job.

It was hard to see what was once only my pain become our pain and the effect that had on her—the person I was created to protect. But as we worked

together to get to the other side of that night, I
realized I had done the right thing.

The pain is still here and always will be, but I feel
more okay than I ever have. I feel like I am no
longer alone.

I will never tell all that I went through, but I know
now that I can trust myself to show Tori some of it,
and I can trust her to get us out the other side. We
have gone from being utterly surrounded by
darkness to finding little beams of light, and my
God, does it feel good.

Tori—we have done good. Thank you. – Taylor

November 26, 1992

I went outside for the first time in almost a week.
It was cold, but it no longer felt like fall. For that, I
am grateful.

From the time Taylor and I went through the
memory until today, I only left my room for food
and therapy.

I am just proud I left at all.

November 28, 1992

I find Rose is still on my mind. I think of her every day. Even when I'm in the midst of battling something awful, I wonder how she is holding up. It is like it is my instinct: something bad happens, take care of Rose.

But I cannot find Rose, so I take care of myself and my system.

November 30, 1992

Things have been different since Halloween. I think that Blake and Ivy have regained the peace they had found before that night. Jade still comes out to work in the library, but other than that I don't hear much from her.

December 2, 1992

I hope I can go home for Christmas this year.

December 6, 1992

It's gotten so calm lately—I almost miss the chaos of the others. Not because I miss Blake's inappropriate

December 8, 1992

Jade's latest entry makes a lot of sense to me. I can see why she would be worried. After all, she has had to be in control in more ways than one in order to get us through the basics of life. Of course the idea of losing that control would be scary. I want to talk to her about this, but I'm not sure how to reach her. I haven't been able to connect to her like I have to the others.

....

"I'm worried about Jade," I say as soon as Dr. Williams and I sit down for our next session following Jade's journal entry.

"Why is that?" She looks up from the notebook, where she has been searching for a blank page.

"She wrote an entry a few days ago about how she is worried she will have no purpose if I continue to get better. She fears that if I don't need her, she will disappear completely."

Dr. Williams nods as I speak. "Hmmm," she says once I have finished, "and what do you want to do about that? These are your internal parts, Tori. You have come far. You need to be able to trust yourself to work with them when things like this arise."

"With the others I do—for the most part—but it's harder with Jade. She's never really talked to me much. I don't know how to reach her."

"Well, I cannot be certain, because these are your parts, not mine, but if I had to guess, I would say it's likely that Jade eavesdrops on as many conversations as possible. She is likely always aware of what is happening with you, whether she is in control or not."

I agree with Dr. Williams. What she is saying makes sense. Jade can take over on a whim if I need her to, and she always picks up right where I leave off.

"Thank you," I say as I stand to leave the office.

"Tori, we still have time if there's other things you'd like to discuss." Dr. Williams sounds slightly concerned.

I turn to her and, with the most certainty I have felt since walking through the hospital gates, say, "That's okay. I'm okay right now. I've got this."

Once back in my room, I sit on my bed and begin speaking. I am glad nobody else is nearby, because I'm sure I sound a little extra crazy.

"Jade, I know you can hear me. I just wanted to tell you something: I have no idea how to balance a checkbook; I have no idea how to file taxes; I have no idea where we should work after we leave here. I need your help with all of these things. I need you to guide me from the inside.

We may find some stability, but the fact is that I will always need you—all of you—in some way, shape, or form.

Sometimes it will be urgent and complicated; sometimes it will be subtle and simple, but we are all in this life together."

A wave of something I can only describe as serenity washes over me. My parts are not all merged with me, and they may never be, but at this moment, I know that we can function as a cohesive unit. I know we will be okay.

....

December 12, 1992

It's almost time for me to leave. I can feel myself becoming more and more ready every day. The thought of going back into the world scares me a little, but I know it is something I need to do. External threats against me are something that I will always have to live with—they are loose ends that will never be resolved. I will never know what happened to the woman who broke into the hospital; I will never know who was on the other end of the phone call. I will never see those who hurt me brought to justice by the law.

I will find my own justice through healing.

December 13, 1992

I spoke with Dr. Williams about a plan for leaving the hospital. She agreed that it seems like the right time. I will spend the next couple of days getting everyone ready for the transition.

December 15, 1992

I am leaving the hospital tomorrow. Wow. What a feeling.

In many ways, I thought this day would never come.

I called my mom and told her I would be coming home for Christmas. She was overjoyed.

I am sure that going back will be difficult for my system, but I have faith that we will be able to handle it. I do not know where we will go after Christmas, but we can figure that out later.

....

My car is exactly how I left it: empty bottle of vodka on the floor, local rock station turned up full blast, slight stench of cigarettes lingering in the fabric of the seats.

But as I get ready to drive away from the hospital, I feel completely different than the person who had driven there. For the first time, I have hope. I have a chance to be more than just the horrors of my past.

Although I have learned much, many questions drift around in my mind as I drive out of the gate: **Where is Rose? How will my life with my parts look going forward? What happens next?**

I know none of the answers—only that we will be okay.

....

My hometown is flush with memories when I arrive.

I drive past the school and think of Mrs. Caltri. I heard she retired years ago. **Thank you.**

A train cuts me off at the railroad tracks, and as I wait, I can see glimpses of Rose and I when we were young through the breaks in the boxcars. We stand just on the other side of the tracks, waiting for our chance to grab hold. Rose is looking at me, waiting for my cue. I am looking for a way to get us out. *I did it, Rose.*

I take the long way to my parents' house, avoiding the old farmhouse. We aren't ready for that yet. *Someday, we will be.*

....

I stay through the New Year, soaking up the love and acceptance that always flows freely from my family. I do not speak of what I have been through, keeping my answers to their questions vague, explaining the hospital stay as intense rehab—which, in a way, it was. My family does not need to share in my pain. I want to continue protecting them as much as I can.

I work part-time during my stay at home, earning enough money to go elsewhere. Soon, my bag is packed, and I am eager to move on to the next phase of my life. I hug my family goodbye, promising to call once I am settled.

I keep the car radio off as I inch along the gravel road that leads away from my family's home. Even though I am physically leaving, I know the memories of this area will stay with me. I will carry them, wrestle with them, grieve them, and honor them. They will not determine the rest of my story, but I will never be able to erase their chapters.

That is okay. I no longer need to forget. I now know how to truly care over myself and my parts, even through the worst pain. I know how to live fully in every different aspect of my life.

The what-ifs still linger as I make my way, and I know they will always dwell somewhere in my mind. But I now understand that the past is out of my control. The abuse was not my fault. There is nothing I could have done to change what happened.

I once again come to the railroad tracks. There is no train this time, and as my car bumps its way to the other side of the tracks, I resolve within myself that I am strong enough to continue forward. I do not need the train to bring me to freedom; I have found freedom with healing. Once across, I take what I think is one final glance in the rearview mirror. But then, I catch a glimpse of something—someone—standing at the edge of the tracks. I stop the car.

Rose.

The whistle of a train sounds in the distance. I watch in silence as it comes into view, rounding the corner slowly. I do not feel the need to call out to Rose. I know she is okay, and there is nothing more I need to say to her.

We have navigated life together, kept each other alive. The experiences Rose and I shared will always be a part of my story—something nobody else will ever understand. We were what each of us needed, but now it is time for me to let her go.

The train reaches Rose, rolling past her at a speed just slow enough to allow someone to jump aboard. And she does. Rose jumps onto the train, just as we had done so many times as children. Holding on tightly with one hand, she uses the other to wave at me, a grin dancing across her face. I smile and wave back, my heart at rest knowing that this time Rose will not let go.

Once Rose is out of sight, I put both hands on the steering wheel, take my foot off the brake. Checking in with my system, I make sure we are all okay. Pushing lightly on the gas, we move forward.

Warrior Eternal.
Child Extreme.
Patient Survivor.
Filled with Hopes and Dreams.
Crying in the Darkness.
Dancing in the Light.
Hidden Existence.
Endless Fight.
Fantasies of Yesterday.
Futuristic Goals.
Let the Garments Not
Persuade You.
There's Still a Child
To Behold.

Acknowledgements

To my mom and sisters,

Thank you for never letting go—for finding me in the middle of my brokenness and acknowledging my pain, for accepting me even when you didn't understand.

Mom,

Thank you for holding a space for me to heal—for showing me there is a way out and that I'm not alone anymore. Thank you for supporting me while I was on my journey of healing. It was a long road, but your care never wavered. I love you.

To Alex,

Thank you for helping me find my voice—for your countless hours and your never-ending dedication to this book. Your gentleness and compassion were healing to me. You are an inspiration. I'm so honored that you are in my life.

Thank you to everyone who gave their time to this book through edits, proof-reading, and discussion. Your efforts do not go unnoticed. They have strengthened the telling of my story. I am eternally grateful.

If you or someone you know is in need of help, reach
out. You are not alone.

www.hiddenexistence.org

hiddenexistence2023@gmail.com

www.ingramcontent.com/pod-product-compliance
Lightning Source LLC
Chambersburg PA
CBHW071218300726
48975CB00002B/268